WOLF SPRINGS CHRONICLES
SAVAGE

ALSO BY
NANCY HOLDER & DEBBIE VIGUIÉ

THE WICKED SERIES

Witch & Curse

Legacy & Spellbound

Resurrection

THE CRUSADE SERIES

Crusade

Damned

Vanquished

THE RULES - Coming June 2015

WOLF SPRINGS CHRONICLES

SAVAGE

Nancy Holder & Debbie Viguié

REYNOLDS & JONES

This edition published 2015

ISBN-13: 978-0988734616

This is a work of fiction. Names, characters, places, and
incidents either are the product of the author's imagination or
are used fictitiously. Any resemblance to actual persons, living
or dead, is purely coincidental.

REYNOLDS & JONES

To my number one pack mate, Debbie Viguié. We hunted down another book! Thank you so much for the great run.
—Nancy

Nancy Holder, a dear friend and fantastic co-author. I'd run with you any day.
—Debbie

Who do you run to?

"I am tied to the stake, and I must stand the course."

- KING LEAR, 3.7.55

The Werewolves of Wolf Springs
Our Laws

We are the descendants of Fenris, Wolf-God. He gave us this creed to keep our pack strong and free. Follow it, or die for the good of the pack.

Loyalty is the highest virtue.

Stay in your place until you have another.

Obey the Four Commandments:

> Never hunt humans.
>
> Never hunt alone.
>
> Never tell anyone about the existence of werewolves; it is a secret that must be kept.
>
> Always obey your alpha, and be submissive to higher-ranking wolves, male and female, within your pack.

And if you misbehave, beware . . . the Hellhound will hunt you down!

1

The Hellhound. The stuff of nightmares, a rampaging destroyer. It was real. It was here. And it was going to tear Katelyn McBride to pieces, unless the flames got to both of them first.

The Bayou of Wolves was a blazing inferno; against a wall of fire, the enormous monster shot to its full height, towering over Katelyn in orange and scarlet flashes of fangs and claws. Smoke poured from its glowing red eyes as she staggered backwards in shock. Terror paralyzed her for one heart-stopping moment.

She screamed as it leapt forward. Instinctively she tucked herself into a ball and rolled to the side. It landed beside her with a huge thump that made her teeth rattle. She tumbled into the underbrush and dug her heels into the earth to push herself up through the lacework of branches. Twigs and rough bark tore at her skin and ripped at the ends of her blond hair. The bushes swayed as the Hellhound charged again. She fought down panic and stretched her arms high over her head, trying to grab a vine or a branch. Anything.

The Hellhound didn't utter a sound; its silence was one of its weapons. The closer it got to you, the less noise it made. Its hot, moist breath sprayed against the back of her neck and she poured on more speed. Her fingertips grazed the scratchy bulk of a piece of Spanish moss. She grabbed it with one hand, then bounced on the balls of her feet and clutched it with the other. Years of gymnastics paid off as she vaulted herself up and yanked her knees above her waist, fighting to put as much space between the Hellhound and herself as she possibly could.

Its breath grazed the small of her back. She grunted and swung her legs down and backwards, smacking it in the face with her boots. Her heels hit something hard. *Teeth!* Denying the reflex to pull away, she kicked as fast and as violently as she could.

She had feared it for so long. It had whispered to her in the forest, stalked her in nightmares. It was real. It was here.

And it wanted to kill her.

"No!" she yelled. "I didn't do anything! I don't deserve this! Go away!"

SAVAGE

The clump of Spanish moss jerked hard and she dropped down a couple of feet. She flailed wildly and let go, falling back down hard into the bracken . Then she took a breath and braced herself for the pain of being ripped to shreds—

—but the bushes quivered in a path moving *away* from her. The Hellhound was leaving.

~

Trees exploded like bombs on either side as she got to her feet and began to run. She was barely outpacing the flames. The Louisiana oak forest glowed with bursts of white and orange as her werewolf senses shot into overdrive and she saw through the eyes of her inner wolf. Her all-too-human feet stumbled over smoking roots and dodged fiery branches as they slammed against the ground, sending up showers of sparks. Every rapid pant out of her searing lungs was a word: *Escape, escape.*

She had fought in a war today, and her side had lost. The treacherous Gaudin werewolf pack had dumped silver, fatal to all werewolves, into the swamp and then set the dry Spanish moss and the cypress trees on fire. The enemies of the Gaudins, the Fenners of Wolf Springs, had howled in agony as silver steam and silver smoke scorched their lungs and destroyed their bodies, and the pack fell one by one..

Katelyn had been forced to join the Fenners in battle or get her throat ripped out. They'd bullied and threatened her, but no more. After months of pack life as the lowest of the low, she had the upper hand.

Katelyn was the only werewolf anywhere who was immune to silver. The metal in the bayou had done nothing to harm her.

But she was still running for her life, fighting to put as much distance as she could between herself and the Hellhound, and the Fenner survivors who even now were piling into trucks and cars and hitting the road back to their territory in Wolf Springs. They would all be on full alert and looking for her. After she had been attacked and bitten, she'd been viewed as a mistake and a threat to pack security, and she'd feared every day would be her last. But now she had the potential to be the Fenner pack's secret weapon, and everyone wanted to claim her and her power for their own.

But she wouldn't be their pawn, or their hostage, or their prisoner. She was done. Finally free—if she could outrun the Hellhound, who should have no reason to hurt her. The Fenners had told her the creature was a myth invented to keep children and the superstitious in line. That it killed werewolves who broke pack laws.

She had broken no laws, but here it was anyway

"Kat!" a voice cried. It was Cordelia.

"Cordelia, run! The Hellhound is here!" Katelyn yelled at the top of her lungs, and then she heard the roar of a werewolf in wolf form. Loud, fearless, angry.

SAVAGE

She whirled around to see a jumble of silhouettes in a moonlit clearing a few yards distant. Facing away from her, the Hellhound loomed at least eight feet over a snarling werewolf crouched in front of it; from behind the werewolf, Cordelia ran toward Katelyn, leaving herself open to attack. Cordelia had something in her hand that was catching on the bushes and branches, slowing her down. The Hellhound swiped its forepaw and the crouching werewolf leaped at the monster. The Hellhound batted the werewolf, sending it flying with a yelp.

"Hurry!" Katelyn yelled at Cordelia, running toward the Hellhound and Cordelia both. Foolhardy, yes, but then Cordelia fell into her arms, safe. Katelyn wheeled her friend behind herself and faced the Hellhound straight on.

"Leave us alone!" Katelyn shouted.

To her amazement, the Hellhound sat back on its haunches, giving her a better look at it—and she wished it hadn't. None of the drawings she'd seen did justice to how ugly it was. It looked as if it had been stitched together from pieces of dogs, wolves, and hyenas. Its red eyes were slanted, its mouth bristling with fangs. It had a flat snout with flaring nostrils and as it panted, billows of smoky breath made a veil between Katelyn, Cordelia, and it. Coarse hair cascaded down its ropy neck and grew around the base like a stand-up collar. Its front legs were malformed and knobby, as if the bones themselves were bumpy, and ended in massive curved claws.

Rows of drool-coated teeth shone in the moonlight. It cocked its head and watched Katelyn as she planted herself in front of her friend.

"Cordelia, run," she said quietly.

"Oh, God," Cordelia whispered. She grabbed Katelyn's hand and squeezed tight. "Oh, my God."

The Hellhound kept staring at Katelyn. She scanned her surroundings for an escape route and took a deep breath. The fire was sweeping through the trees mere yards away.

As if oblivious to the imminent danger, the beast growled, low and almost jubilant, as if savoring the kill to come.

Katelyn's face tingled. The hair on the back of her neck stood up and she held her breath as Cordelia squeezed her hand even tighter. It was watching her. She was afraid to so much as twitch. Why was it sizing her up? It was bigger than she was. Surely it knew it could take her out in a heartbeat.

"Kat," Cordelia whispered, and Katelyn shushed her as quietly as she could.

The thing blinked.

And then a light came on in her brain:

What if it's someone I know?

She licked her lips. "Hello?" she said.

"What are you doing?" Cordelia whispered fiercely, and Kat shushed her again.

Then the Hellhound moved slowly forward , and Katelyn lurched back, stumbling into Cordelia. Cordelia darted from behind Katelyn and stood at her side. The other girl was shaking, but she lifted her chin, staring the creature down. Shoulder to shoulder, they stood, daring the Hellhound to take them on.

This is it, Katelyn thought.

Then in a flash the Hellhound turned and bounded away and, in near silence, it disappeared into the shadows.

A horrible howl shook the treetops and made Katelyn's bones vibrate. The two girls stood stock-still for a second, and then Katelyn let out her breath.

"God," Cordelia said. "I…just *God*." The thing in her hand was a gasmask. "Here, Kat," she said urgently, raising it over Katelyn's head. "There's silver in the air. Jean-Luc dumped it in the swamp—"

Katelyn stopped her. "Keep it," she said. "You use it."

"No," Cordelia argued, and Katelyn grabbed Cordelia's hand again and started to run. Poisonous smoke drifted across the papery face of the moon as they reached the shelter of a stand of trees and stopped, panting. Katelyn tried to make Cordelia put the mask on. Cordelia shook her head. Then Katelyn froze, remembering the werewolf who had defended Cordelia. He —or she—might still be alive.

"Who attacked the Hellhound for you?" she asked "We have to find him."

Cordelia's blue eyes widened and she gave her head a firm shake.

"He only did it because of the loyalty instinct," she replied. "He didn't exactly *want* to save my life. But I'm mated to his alpha." Seeing that Katelyn still didn't get it, she added, "So he *had* to try to help me. He couldn't stop himself."

Katelyn hadn't seen anything like that in the Fenner pack, it had been mostly bickering and threatening. Pack members were always plotting and casting suspicion on each other to get ahead. Their alpha, Lee Fenner, had been losing his mind, and the entire pack was in disarray. She could almost feel Quentin Lloyd's warm blood spraying against her face again. Lee Fenner had killed him when the younger werewolf had posed a challenge to his dominance—a death Katelyn had engineered to save her own life. There had been no loyalty instinct there.

Cordelia was peering through the trees, shifting her weight and making breathy, whining noises of distress. Katelyn winced as she realized that Cordelia didn't yet know what had happened to Lee Fenner — her father. Cordelia had left the Fenner pack for the Gaudins when her father had banished her for speaking to Katelyn about werewolves after Katelyn had been bitten, for keeping it secret from him. Keeping the pack a secret from non-werewolves was a golden rule in all packs, and Cordelia had broken the rule. And paid the price. Now, at seventeen, she was married to the alpha of the Gaudins, Dom.

"Kat." Cordelia frowned up at the moon. "We have to get out of here. The fire's moving fast and I'm sure Dom's got more Gaudins looking for me. That Gaudin werewolf is your sworn enemy. You're a member of the Fenner pack, and—"

"We don't know that," Katelyn broke in. "We don't know who bit me."

"The Fenners took you in."

"And threw you out. And they have been threatening to kill me every single day of my life since then."

"Then why didn't you leave me with me when I asked you to?" A world of hurt flashed across Cordelia's features. "And don't start in about having to stay to protect your grandfather. He forced you to move here. You hadn't seen him in years!"

And I think Grandpa killed my father because he was a werewolf. And I think my mom knew. Or knew some of it.

She must have looked ill. Cordelia impatiently thrust the gas mask at her.

"Damn it, Kat. You've been exposed to silver. Take this!"

Katelyn didn't need it, but that was something else Cordelia didn't know. Unaware of Katelyn's immunity to silver, Cordelia was putting her own safety on the line by offering the mask to Katelyn. She wondered if she could trust Cordelia not to share the secret of her power with Dom Gaudin, Cordelia's new husband, because of the so-called loyalty instinct. If Cordelia had to choose, who would win, Katelyn or Dom? Katelyn knew she would do almost anything she could to help Cordelia. But she hadn't left Wolf Springs with her.

And she wouldn't leave the Gaudin werewolf to die.

"You can stay here," Katelyn whispered, "but I'm going to look for him."

Then before Cordelia could stop her—before she could stop herself—she crouched down and glided from their hiding place. Her werewolf senses had not kicked back in and as she surveyed the hundreds of trees and bushes, she realized what a hopeless task she faced. And she could smell the smoke drifting toward their hiding place. She prayed that Cordelia would put on the mask.

She sniffed the air, trying to track the werewolf. She scented earth and vegetation and smoke.

And something dead.

That didn't mean it was the Gaudin. The forest was burning and many animals could have died already.

She turned left and crept through the bushes, moving., aware that her thigh muscles weren't cramping. Another plus for having become a werewolf. She reached out a hand and touched a wet, sticky face.

She moved her fingers beneath his nostrils. No air. She jerked her hand away, then took a deep breath and felt for his neck. She placed her fingers over his carotid artery. It instantly reminded her of the man she and Trick had found in the forest. Horribly mauled, pieces missing, blood everywhere—

No pulse.

SAVAGE

A twig cracked. The low, menacing growl of the Hellhound rumbled in Katelyn's gut.

It's still there.

2

Katelyn got back to Cordelia as fast as she could. They raced deep into the forest. Katelyn kept up easily; a side effect of becoming a werewolf was an increase in strength and stamina. Katelyn's insides lurched and she followed so closely that her fingertips kept grazing Cordelia's arm. The smoke was thickening and Cordelia began to slip the gasmask on—giving up on forcing Katelyn to wear it. Then it tumbled from her hands into the dense foliage. Katelyn wheeled to retrieve it but Cordelia yanked on her hand.

"Leave it. We have to keep going!"

They ran together for what seemed like an hour. Then a cave loomed ahead, and Katelyn slowed—the Hellhound was said to live in the Madre Vena mine, which was also a cave—and then she told herself that if the Hellhound was still nearby, it was more likely somewhere behind them.

She darted inside with Cordelia. The cave was pitch dark. Katelyn's enhanced werewolf vision did not kick in. As she was a new werewolf, her powers of sight, hearing, and smell intensified to wolf levels, then declined back to human strength, at unpredictable times. With time they would stabilize, so she had been told. But for now, she was never sure when they would kick in, and for how long.

Cordelia found Katelyn's wrist and urged her forward.

"We don't want to go too far in," Katelyn said. "We don't want to get trapped in here."

"Good thinking." Cordelia stopped and Katelyn bumped into her. "You're not seeing like a wolf, are you," Cordelia said.

"No. It comes and goes. Right now I can't see anything."

"Got it," Cordelia said. Then she took another deep breath. "I'd like to kill Luc Gaudin myself. Dom did not authorize dumping silver into the swamp, Kat. When you see my daddy, you make sure he knows that."

Katelyn shut her eyes tight. It was time to tell Cordelia the awful truth. Why was that more frightening than facing down the Hellhound?

"Cor, I-I have to tell you something."

"Tell me Luc's dead, and I'll throw confetti," Cordelia said, clearly not hearing the urgency in Katelyn's voice—which, given that she was a werewolf and therefore acutely focused on body language and intonation, was not what Katelyn had expected. It would have been so much easier if Cordelia had realized that bad news was on the way.

"Luc is dead," Katelyn said. "I saw him die. Justin killed him." She didn't fill in that Justin had fatally shot him with a gun containing silver bullets. As far as she knew, the Gaudins still didn't know the Fenners had such a weapon.

"Did he suffer?" Cordelia asked, and Katelyn couldn't gauge her tone of voice. Did Cordelia hope he'd suffered?

"I don't know," she replied. "Justin shot him while they were both in human form. Justin can't change at will yet," she added, nerves making her complicate the story when she didn't need to say anything more. But she did suppose that he had suffered. Silver was poison to werewolves. So being shot with a silver bullet would be like having silver injected into your body, wouldn't it?

Is that what it was like for my father?

"If he was here right now, I'd make sure he suffered," Cordelia said bitterly. "He would beg to die."

Katelyn shivered. Cordelia sounded like a different person—bloodthirsty and cruel—but Katelyn reminded herself that what they'd both been through had been horrific. Fenners had died today. And if what Cordelia said was true, Luc had betrayed them all.

"I'm glad it was Justin who shot him," Cordelia added. "He tried to get my father to listen to Dom and accept the terms for peace. Forgiving me," she said in a hushed voice. "Daddy wouldn't forgive me." She exhaled slowly, then piped up. "Oh, I almost forgot. I found your phone in the swamp. Here." Katelyn felt Cordelia press the phone into her hand. "Someone called you during the fracas. I didn't have time to see who it was."

And then Katelyn realized that Cordelia knew that there *was* bad news. She was doing everything she could to avoid it.

Katelyn took a deep breath. Cordelia's relationship with her father had been so complicated. She had loved, hated, and feared him in equal measure. She should be glad that he was dead. And yet...

"I'm sorry. But you have to listen..."

"No," Cordelia whispered. "No." She let out a hard, heavy sob. "Don't. Don't say it."

"Your father loved you," Katelyn said. "He did. He and I had a deal. If I found the mine, then he would bring you home."

Cordelia made a low, keening noise, one that Katelyn had heard before—in the heavy rain when her grandfather had driven her from the airport to the tiny, cursed town of Wolf Springs. A howl so mournful, and in such pain...

A werewolf died the day I came here, she thought. *And he—or she—was mourned. Who died? Who did I hear howling that night?*

And then she put her arms around her friend, and held her as she sobbed.. But she couldn't help but tense at every sound, every smell.

The Hellhound was still out there. It could be stalking them even at that moment.

Katelyn...can you feel me. I'm getting closer. And then—

She gasped. The voice she heard in her dreams was echoing around in her head now—when she was awake.

"No!" she shouted.

Cordelia jerked back with a startled cry.

"What, Kat?"

"I-I think the Hellhound spoke to me. I heard him," she said. "In my mind."

Cordelia went silent for a few beats. "I can *smell* him," she whispered.

The hair on Katelyn's arms lifted and a shiver ran up her spine.

Cordelia grabbed Katelyn's hand and together the two crept cautiously out of the cave, then ran.

Maybe it was fear that supercharged her senses. Now she smelled fear rippling off Cordelia and it only made her own terror worse. Cordelia yanked down on her arm and the two dropped to the ground, sliding underneath a massive fallen log that was partially decayed. They lay still for a minute, struggling to control their breathing. Katelyn strained her ears, listening for any sound, hoping she wouldn't hear his voice again in her mind.

A minute passed. Another.

Somewhere far off a twig snapped. A minute later she could swear she heard growling.

Cordelia began to slide backwards, using the fallen log as a shield. Katelyn did the same. She sniffed the air but could only smell sweat—hers and Cordelia's, mingled. She wondered if they were upwind or down from the creature.

"Can you still smell it?" she whispered to Cordelia.

"Yes," Cordelia whispered back. "Can you see?"

Katelyn was startled. She could see—not the strange infrared luminescence that occasionally filled her vision, but a brightness as if someone had turned on a flashlight. Cordelia's tear-streaked face bobbed in front of Katelyn like a white balloon.

"Yes, I can see."

Cordelia crawled over the ground, occasionally scuttling sideways like a crab, keeping to the denser growth. Katelyn marveled at how silently her friend moved. She was right next to Cordelia and she couldn't even hear the faintest whisper of sound.

She, on the other hand, was not managing nearly as well. Crouched down on her haunches, she stepped on a twig, which cracked as loud as thunder, or so it seemed. Then her foot slid on a rock and it rolled into another. She bit her lip to keep from swearing in her terror. She couldn't help but wish that she'd tried harder, paid more attention, as Justin was trying to teach her how to survive in the woods. But she had never in a million years dreamed that she would be slinking through the wilds of Louisiana bayou country trying to hide from a monster.

She heard a shout from a ways off. Had the Hellhound found other prey? She exchanged a fearful glance with Cordelia.

The other girl had risen up to a half-standing position and swiveled her head, her eyes squinted and her nose visibly twitching. Katelyn waited. Finally Cordelia shook her head.

Katelyn allowed herself one moment of relief, but they were far from safe. Feuding werewolves were still at war, and neither side would appreciate catching her and Cordelia together. And the Hellhound could reappear at any time.

We need a place to hide. A place where we can see without being seen.

She glanced up. The trees around them were tall. The nearest branches were incredibly thick and about fifteen feet off the ground. She could jump that high, but she didn't know if the Hellhound or the other werewolves could.

Or even Cordelia, for that matter.

She stood slowly and Cordelia joined her after a moment. Katelyn gestured up to the branch above them. Cordelia's eyes widened and she shook her head.

Cordelia didn't think she would be able to jump that high. *She could with my help.*

Katelyn widened her stance and cupped her hands. Cordelia, a former cheerleader, instantly understood. She bounced up and down on the balls of her feet for a moment, the muscles in her legs cording, and then she stepped into Katelyn's hand, hopped once, and jumped as Katelyn lifted upward with all her might.

Cordelia went flying into the air and she caught the branch. She hoisted herself up with ease and then looked down at Katelyn, quick victory fading to worry as she seemed to process that now Katelyn was stuck.

Katelyn just smiled back at her. This was her world, after all, and it was time Cordelia saw exactly what she could do. Katelyn bent her knees, felt her muscles tense, and then she launched herself upward. She grabbed the branch with both hands and swung herself up and onto it in a single, fluid motion.

Cordelia's eyes widened and Katelyn grinned proudly. Then she looked down and realized she could see farther than she had anticipated. She wanted to be able to see farther, though. She climbed up a couple of more branches and Cordelia reluctantly followed her until they were perched high above the ground with a panoramic view of the fiery night sky. Now they were up higher than the Hellhound could reach, and they could search for him. But the fire still raged and it was closer. They must have traveled in a circle instead of straight away from the fighting as she had thought.

Cordelia gripped her hand and Katelyn reached out and hugged her.

She's an orphan now. Just like me. Just like Justin.

It seemed there were a lot of orphans in Wolf Springs, Trick being a notable exception.

But then again, Trick was an exception to everything. She had to find a way out of this, make her way back home so she could see him again. She had to tell him how she felt about him, even if it was the last thing she did.

Cordelia pressed her fingertips against the bridge of her nose, clearly trying to pull herself together. Katelyn knew from experience every emotion her friend was going through as she tried to grasp the terrible truth that her father was dead. Grief, pain, anger, guilt. They were all mixed up in an insane bundle that gnawed at you. It would take Cordelia days, weeks, to sort out all the emotions and to feel like she wasn't moving through some kind of hazy nightmare.

But they didn't have days or weeks. Katelyn needed Cordelia to be on her game right now so that they had a hope of surviving the next few minutes.

"Do you think we lost him?" she finally whispered.

"I don't know. I hope so," Cordelia whispered back, caution in her voice. "We have to get out of here."

Something warm covered in fur fell on top of Katelyn and she let out a shriek. Panic rocketed through her, followed by blinding pain.

She could hear Cordelia calling her name, but she couldn't answer, not with her teeth lengthening and her face elongating. Her vision seemed to telescope and her other senses went into overdrive.

I'm changing, I'm turning into a wolf.

Her nails scrabbled for a hold on the bark, gouging trenches as the bones in her thumb broke and her hands began to reshape themselves into paws.

Paws that could rip into the hide of a deer and dismember it. Paws that could churn up the earth as they carried her along. Paws that were absolutely useless to her up in a tree.

She started to tumble sideways but caught herself with a yelp. She was slipping, falling.

And then she finally heard what Cordelia was saying.

"—raccoon! We're safe. It was just a raccoon. Please, don't change, just calm down, deep breaths."

A raccoon. What had fallen on top of her wasn't a wolf or a Hellhound. And with that knowledge planted firmly in her brain she felt herself regaining control. Her thumbs rebroke and she yowled with agony but gratefully got a firm grip on the branch once again.

And then her vision returned to normal and she was staring at an angry Cordelia.

"You can change without the full moon and you didn't even tell me?"

"I-I can't. It starts to happen sometimes when I get freaked out, but I can't control it," Katelyn said.

Cordelia frowned, skeptical. "How is this even possible? You're way too young, both as a wolf and as a person, to be able to change without the moon."

"You're asking the *wrong* person. If I knew, I'd tell you," Katelyn insisted. "It's just one more thing I have to try and guard against."

Cordelia's face was white. "Did my father know? Is that why he brought you here?"

"No one knows. Except you."

An irrational desire to beg Cordelia not to be mad at her caught hold, but she held her tongue as she thought about how Cordelia had constantly apologized for things that weren't her fault and how it irritated Katelyn. It was a wolf's desire to be submissive, to want its place in the pack to be secure.

But Katelyn was more than a wolf and she didn't have to do as she was told. Not with Cordelia.

Not with anyone, she corrected herself. And with Lee Fenner dead, she realized that there was no one left in the Fenner pack whom she truly feared.

Cordelia turned her head and Katelyn twisted to follow her gaze through the smoke. The night sky was a corona of orange embers and scarlet flares.

"Look. A truck," Cordelia muttered.

She was right. It was Justin's Ford, barreling through the woods, heading, presumably, for the road out of the swamp.

But there was something wrong. Now, above the steadily increasing whine of the motor, Katelyn could hear screaming.

"What is *that*?" she asked Cordelia.

Cordelia gasped. "It's *him*!"

A split second later Katelyn saw it, too. It was a black shape that was darker than the darkest night, large and grotesque. The Hellhound.

And it was bearing down on the truck.

"No!" Katelyn said, jumping to her feet.

The branch vibrated beneath her and Cordelia wrapped her arms around it to keep from falling.

The Hellhound reared up; it was as large as the Ford. And then it slammed into the side of the vehicle.

The truck flipped and rolled a couple of times. Katelyn stared in disbelief, unable to look away. *Not Justin. Don't hurt Justin.*

But the creature had disappeared again.

She swung down to the lower branches and dropped to the ground, then took off running toward the truck. Cordelia hit the ground behind her.

The Hellhound might kill me. Maybe it's waiting to lure me out, using Justin for bait.

She couldn't care about that now.

Wood crackled and popped. A few people had been in the bed of the truck and had been thrown free. She dodged around one body, not even stopping to see if the woman was alive or dead.

As she reached the truck, Cordelia trailed behind her, hanging back out of sight of the Fenner packmates. It had to be agony for her, Katelyn realized, even as she swept the cab, searching for Justin.

Cordelia's brother-in-law Al was behind the wheel, stirring slightly and groaning. He was alive. His wife, Arial, was also inside, blood on her blonde hair. Usually so glamorous, she was disheveled as she groaned and began to stir.

Sudden growling in the bushes just behind the bumper caused Katelyn to jump back several steps. Cordelia grabbed her arm and they quickly retreated back toward the trees they had been hiding in a minute before, just as Justin burst into the clearing right next to the truck.

"I wonder where he's been," Cordelia whispered very softly.

Katelyn could only nod as she saw him checking the people who had been thrown clear of the bed of the truck.

"We can't be spotted together," Cordelia whispered again.

They moved quickly but silently away from the accident scene. Katelyn kept thinking at any moment one of the Gaudin pack was going to find them, or Justin would bound up behind them.

What she didn't want to think about was where the Hellhound had gone.

"Now what do we do?" she asked Cordelia.

Cordelia looked tired and pale. She kept scanning the firestorm, searching for the Hellhound. And…maybe someone else. It was hard to tell.

"I don't know," she admitted.

"I'll tell you exactly what you're going to do," a male voice boomed close at hand.

Katelyn gasped and whirled toward the sound. She wasn't sure who she wanted to see least, a Gaudin or a Fenner.

The bushes a few feet away parted and the speaker appeared. He wore a brown robe like a monk with a hood that draped his face in shadow, though his eyes seemed to be glowing a brilliant, electric green.

Beside Katelyn, Cordelia stiffened. Katelyn's own muscles quivered. There was a buzzing in her ears. Cordelia bared her teeth, her muscles coiled, and Katelyn knew she was about to spring.

The man lowered his hood.

He was older than they, probably by five or six years. His scalp was completely clean-shaven, and his skull was tattooed with numerous crosses and at least one snarling wolf's head. There was something completely and utterly disturbing about him and Katelyn couldn't say why, but she didn't want to look directly at him. It was as though facing him squarely somehow *hurt*.

Cordelia whined deep in her throat and Katelyn wondered if he was having the same effect on her.

"You're a Hound of God," Cordelia said.

Katelyn remembered hearing about the Hounds of God, a religious werewolf order that had sounded completely insane. They believed their ancestors had been changed into werewolves through rituals so that they could descend into hell to fight demons for God.

He inclined his head with an air of satisfaction, as though he was pleased to be recognized.

"I'm Magus, follower of Daniel Latgale, alpha of the Hounds of God. We are God's chosen knights, and we do His bidding in all things."

His voice was husky as if he were hoarse from shouting. There were tattoos on his neck, and Katelyn wondered if something had happened to his vocal chords.

Smoke swirled around the three of them, and Katelyn was about to tell him that whatever he had to say, he'd better tell them on the run. Then he spoke.

"I'm here with a message." His eyes narrowed, and he jutted out his jaw. Then he pointed at them both. "If you don't end this now," he said, "there will be hell to pay."

3

Katelyn looked from Magus to Cordelia and crossed her arms over her chest.

"'Hell to pay' means what, exactly?" she asked.

He shrugged as if his meaning was obvious. "No less than this: If you two don't find a way to end this destructive conflict and unite your packs, the Hounds of God will rain fire down upon you all and wipe you from this earth."

"Fire is already raining down on us," Katelyn said. "And if we don't get out of here—"

"You're not listening to me," he interrupted her. "We will destroy you all."

Cordelia made a low, growling sound.

"Are you honestly warning us that if we don't end this war then there's going to be another war with *another* pack? A third pack?"

"Not a war, a purging, cleansing," Magus corrected. "We won't fight you. We'll just end you."

Fingers of ice played along Katelyn's backbone. "You're Hellhounds," Katelyn said.

"No. We fear the beast as much as you do."

"Then you know he's real," Cordelia said, sounding the tiniest bit vindicated. Most of her family had scoffed when she had insisted that she had seen the Hellhound outside her bedroom. Katelyn couldn't help but think that none of them would ever laugh at her again.

Magus slipped his hands into the sleeves of his brown robe and squared his shoulders, as if he were posing, posturing. Katelyn told herself that he was just a guy in a costume.

"Of course we know he exists. He is the devil's servant, given free rein to walk among us and kill those whom he wills, those who have been unfaithful, who have strayed," he said.

"Oh, my God, who writes your lines?" Katelyn blurted, but the quaver in her voice threatened to give her away. She was afraid of him.

"Don't mock me." He looked at Cordelia. "You know I wouldn't be here if we weren't serious."

She paled and gave Katelyn a quick nod. "The Hounds of God are…intense."

Katelyn frowned at Magus. "Why us?" Did he know about her immunity to silver?

"Why not us? I'm pack royalty," Cordelia interjected swiftly. "We were already vying for pack leadership when this war broke out."

I wasn't. But as Katelyn looked from him to Cordelia, she wondered if she should be. But those were questions for another time. They had to leave the blazing forest.

"Kat!" a voice called. "Kat, are you here?"

It was Justin. He couldn't find her and Cordelia together. And until she could figure this all out she didn't want him seeing Magus either.

"We need to go," she said to Cordelia. *"Now."* As if to underscore her sense of urgency, a burning tree limb detached and swung back and forth a few yards to their right, sending showers of sparks and chips of burning wood into the sky.

"I'll drive you home, Katelyn McBride. You and I have a lot more to discuss," Magus declared.

"Like what? What do you have to say to her that you can't say in front of me?" Glowering, Cordelia took Katelyn's hand. "We'll get out of here *together*," she said. "And if you want to talk to *us* later, you can leave a message."

"That's not your decision," Magus said, removing a clenched fist from his robe.

There was something in it. He raised a brow as he regarded Katelyn. Something he wanted to show only to her, she translated. She ticked a glance toward Cordelia, whose head was turned as she scanned the forest. Justin was still calling for her, but his voice was fading; he was moving away from them.

The heat from the fire buffeted her. They were risking their lives by sticking around to talk and Magus was scaring her. She began to walk away from him and he reached out, not quite touching her arm. But there was such a sense of presence about him that she felt as if he had made contact.

"Katelyn," Magus urged.

"No one calls her that," Cordelia snapped, glaring at him.

"Someone does," he replied, and her hair stood on end. Trick called her that.

The voice in her head did, too.

There was no way Katelyn wanted to be alone with Magus, not even for a second.

"Cordelia! Cher!" someone called.

Cordelia started and her eyes widened. "Oh, my God. It's Dom. I have to go. He can't catch us together, either."

There was the barest flush on her cheeks—eagerness to be gone, or to be with Dom? Cordelia's relationship with Dom Gaudin was equally as complicated as her relationship with her father had been. So much for the ruthless simplicity of pack dynamics that Justin was always going on about.

"Wait." Katelyn took Cordelia by the arm, and led her to an untouched pair of trees. She planted herself in front of Cordelia so Magus wouldn't be able to read their lips.

Werewolves had excellent hearing, but their eyesight was keener. She had to risk some blunt talk. If they were supposed to avert a catastrophe, they shouldn't be on the opposing sides of the current war.

"Cordelia, come home with me. Come back to Wolf Springs, and the pack."

Cordelia pulled her arm free and hugged herself. "Are you crazy?"

"They're your pack. Things…have changed," Katelyn insisted. It was as close to referring to Lee Fenner's death as she was willing to go with Magus so close by. It was obvious that he was trying to eavesdrop rather impatiently while at the same time keeping an eye on the fire.

Cordelia's brow furrowed and she looked back into the forest as if her answer lay there. "My sisters haven't changed."

"Katelyn, we have to leave," Magus called.

"Their status has," Katelyn countered. "Did either one of them accompany your father when he met with you and Dom at the bayou? No. Justin did. Your father made it clear that he trusted Justin most of anyone in the pack."

"Or else my daddy just wanted Dom to squirm a little. Justin's a great fighter. You *have* to know he's taken other wolves down in challenges."

Katelyn felt a shiver of excitement mixed in with her horror, her disgust. That had never dawned on her, but of course it had to be true. He was a very high-ranking werewolf in the pack. She'd conveniently forgotten that being the nephew of the alpha didn't guarantee him a free ride.

"Well, Justin's been put in charge of me," she informed Cordelia.

Cordelia wrinkled her nose. "Training a bit-in? An omega like you? Whatever else you might think about him, Kat, that definitely lowers his status," Cordelia said edgily. "And I'm the one who hid you. Protected you. So what does that do to *my* status? Also lowers it."

Katelyn had to think fast. That was no longer true, because the Fenners had big plans for her immunity to silver. They were also confident that she was going to find the Madre Vena mine, where it was said there were more guns that shot silver bullets as well as hundreds of silver bullets themselves. Having an in with Katelyn had become a status symbol. The werewolves who had been closest to her in the pack the longest would benefit from their relationships with her. It was like owning a piece of treasure.

But she still didn't want to risk telling Cordelia that. That was vital, private information that the Gaudins could use against the Fenners. From the way Cordelia impatiently shifted her weight as she inhaled the scents of the forest, it was obvious that Cordelia wanted Dom to find her. When she and Katelyn had first met, she'd shyly confided that she had a crush on "an older guy" who didn't live in town. It had been Dom, of course. A crush was one thing; did she actually love him—even though he had forced her into marriage? Love him enough to betray the pack she'd been born into?

You could love and mistrust someone at the same time.

That was how Katelyn felt about her grandfather.

"Katelyn!" Magus insisted. She heard him walking toward them.

"After your father kicked you out, Justin kept looking for you," Katelyn said in a rush. "He promised me he would never stop."

The look Cordelia gave her could have made a magnolia tree wither. She stood stiffly and clenched her jaw as if she were trying very hard not to say the first thing that came to her.

"Promised *you*. So you're still seeing him behind Lucy's back."

"Not at all," Katelyn said, feeling the color rise in her own cheeks.

Lucy — Justin's fiancée — had challenged her to a fight to the death over Justin when they'd come back from the forest and Katelyn had his scent all over him. Katelyn had thrown herself into his arms to thank him for sparing the life of Babette, a spy for the Gaudin pack. Cordelia's father had ordered Katelyn to kill her, and for Justin to serve as a witness. But Katelyn had managed to persuade Justin to let Babette go free if the spy promised to leave Fenner territory forever.

And Katelyn *had* kissed Justin twice in the bayou when they both thought they were facing death. But even when she'd been kissing Justin, she'd been thinking about Trick.

That wasn't the point. The point was, Justin hadn't turned his back on Cordelia.

"Oh, Kat, let's don't do this," Cordelia said, as Katelyn reminded herself that the voice in her head had warned her about Justin. She was suddenly, massively unsure that Cordelia would be all right if she returned to Wolf Springs.

Something must have shown on her face, because Cordelia turned around and studied the forest again.

"Just a *minute*," she snapped at Magus.

"The fire is spreading too fast," Magus retorted.

"Dom forced you to marry him," Katelyn said in her ear.

"Because he loves me," Cordelia said faintly. "He wanted the best for me. I had to declare my loyalty or leave."

"What kind of choice was that?"

"A werewolf's choice." Her voice softened as she studied Katelyn's face. She reached out a hand and touched Katelyn's cheek. "It's an alpha's job to keep his pack in harmony. What was he going to do with an unattached Fenner female in exile?"

"You're defending him," Katelyn said, stunned. "What he did was wrong."

"What he did was smart, darlin'," Cordelia said. "And I have to admire that in an alpha. My daddy…" She bit her lip and visibly worked to keep in control. "My daddy was going to lose control of the pack sooner rather than later."

Justin had been planning to challenge Lee Fenner to the death. The massacre at the bayou had removed the necessity for him.

"We must go *now.*"

Magus was walking toward them again. Katelyn's heart seized at the thought of moving on and Cordelia blew the rest of the air out of her cheeks.

"When I asked you to come with me, you said you'd try to help me by finding the mine," Cordelia said in an undervoice. "I'll try to help *you* by going back with Dom. I'll find out what the Gaudins are planning. I'll get word to you, Kat, *if* you swear that you won't tell anyone else in the pack. We'll do what that weirdo over there wants us to. We'll find a way to make peace. Just you and me."

Katelyn couldn't help a little bubble of hysterical laughter. Magus *was* a weirdo, with his robe and his bald head, tattoos, and creepy eyes.

And his threats? Were they all talk, or was there something to them?

"I'll get in contact when I have something to tell you," Cordelia promised.

"Same," Katelyn said, although she wasn't sure how she was going to manage it.

"Cordelia!" Dom bellowed. He was definitely closer. A whispery smile flashed across Cordelia's mouth, so quickly Katelyn was not quite certain she'd really seen it.

"*Now*," Magus said again, striding over to them, breaking up their conversation.

Cordelia gave Katelyn a hug. "I'm sorry I was so mean to you when you wouldn't come with me," she whispered into her ear. "I've never had a friend like you, Kat. Somebody who just liked *me*. Both parts of me. At school, I was one of those popular girls. A cheerleader, pretty.. And in the pack world, I was the daughter of an alpha. Now I'm the wife of an alpha. People'll be kissing up to me until the day Dom dies."

"Longer," Katelyn promised. "Your father chose you to be the alpha of the Fenner pack. Maybe we could make that happen."

"You're a good friend," Cordelia said.

"I'm really not," Katelyn replied. Then she kissed Cordelia on the cheek—what pack members did to acknowledge their kinship. Cordelia did the same, then whispered, "Put a flower on my daddy's grave for me," and darted into the forest. She didn't look back.

Magus cleared his throat again.

"We're leaving."

"Yes, imperious leader," Katelyn sniped. She didn't like him. She *really* didn't want to go with him. Her thoughts drifted back to Justin, who was looking for her right now.

As by mutual agreement, they both darted in the opposite direction of Justin. Her sense of smell kicked in; odors wafted around her like incense. Magus was wearing aftershave and that seemed so incongruous with the rest of his appearance that she had to stifle a guffaw.

She must not have been entirely successful because he hissed at her like a snake. Then he said, "What is wrong with you? This isn't funny. This is life and death."

About twenty yards to her left, something groaned. She smelled blood and remembered the dead Gaudin werewolf she'd tried to save. This had to be another one. Maybe a Fenner.

Justin's face bloomed in her imagination and she put on a burst of speed, surprising Magus, who grunted in frustration and quickly caught up to her. Then he passed her and raced on ahead. Their movements sounded like the surf as they raced each other.

Magus got there first. As brambles and thorns caught at Katelyn, her vision sharpened and she watched him grind to a halt. He was looking down into the brush, but she couldn't see who was lying on the ground. He reached into his robe and withdrew a long, sharp knife.

He raised it above his head.

"No!" she cried, loudly, without any thought for the consequences.

His hand jerked. Then he swooped down, out of sight, and she heard a second moan, and then a gasp.

Then gurgling.

"Oh, my God," she said, "oh, God, what did you do?" She ran over to him and looked down at a young man she didn't recognize, who stared straight back up at her. Blood was gushing from his neck. His eyebrows rose, and then his eyes went glassy.

"You didn't have to do that!" she cried, falling to her knees beside the dead man.

"I did. He might have heard us."

"So what?" She stared up at him, but he wasn't looking at her. She followed his line of sight: Bushes shook; trees swayed.

"Hellhound," Magus said.

She got to her feet. She could do nothing for the man Magus had just murdered. Together they ran back the way they had come; then he signaled to go to the left. He was fast. She could keep up.

"Can you change?" he said to her.

"Not sure," she replied, and he laid on another burst of speed as something crashed behind them.

She had never run faster in her life. Dodging branches, leaping over large, gnarled roots. Squirrels burst from the underbrush and skittered around her feet, nearly tripping her.

Her eyes and nose were running and she hacked on smoke as it curled around the two of them like a shroud. Directly overhead, the treetops waved as if in a storm. She flew behind Magus like a kite, her feet skimming the ground as he hustled her out of the forest and into a meadow where a shiny black truck was parked.

The doors were unlocked. There was a crash behind her and another evil-sounding roar; then she they was almost magically in a truck and Magus was behind the wheel, peeling out of there.

She wheeled around and peered through the small rear window in the cab. A black shadow entirely filled the space. She was thrown sideways as Magus careened around a tree, and then they shot out of the woods onto a one-lane asphalt road. He was going over a hundred miles an hour.

She looked back through the window.

The shadow was gone.

His foot was to the floor as the engine whined. Katelyn held her breath and gripped the armrest. The view to her right was of a massive fire igniting towering trees one by one, as if a giant held an enormous match to each in turn. Smoke poured out of the woods onto the road like a layer of fog, billowing and pluming as the truck ran through it.

Katelyn had no idea how much time passed, but after a while, again as if by mutual consent, she and Magus both slumped back against the seats and sighed with relief. She detected something hard in the pocket of her jeans and pulled out her phone. It was on, and she checked to see who had called her while it had been in Cordelia's possession.

She expected it to be Trick, but it was a Los Angeles number. It took her a moment to realize that Detective Cranston, the lead detective on her father's murder case, had called her and left her a message. She slid a glance toward Magus and put it back in her pocket.

"You didn't need to kill that guy," she began.

"You're welcome," he retorted. "But really, Katelyn, there is no need to thank me for saving your life."

"He was no danger to me."

"We don't know that."

"We," she said. "Your pack. The Hounds of God."

He opened his mouth to speak, then pursed his lips and downshifted. Irritation flashed over his features.

"Did I insult you?" she asked.

"No. I had something for you. I lost it in the forest."

She remembered his outstretched fist

"What?"

"It doesn't matter now. And the Hounds of God are more than just a pack," he said. "We're an order of werewolves. We have a mission. A divine mission."

"To go down into hell and kill demons," she filled in. "Why doesn't it matter?"

He lifted his gaze from the windshield and cocked an eyebrow. "To kill demons *wherever* we may find them."

She went cold. Was he referring to her? Was this a trap? She was unarmed.

But not helpless, she reminded herself. *I can kick his ass.*

"Do you think the Hellhound is a demon?" she asked him.

To her surprise, a sour smile played across his lips. Covered with tattoos, he looked like a demon himself.

"Wiser men than I don't know the answer to that," he said. "We have endless debates about it. Some religious groups argue about how many angels can dance on the head of a pin. We argue about the place of the Hellhound in our world."

"Do you know who it is? Is it a person at all?" she asked. He didn't answer.

"In the sense that our founder was once a person," he said. "Thiess, tortured by the Inquisition in Livonia in 1691. He explained to them that God had changed him into a werewolf to go down into hell to vanquish wickedness, but they found him guilty of black magic. To us, however, he is a martyr. A holy man."

"How? How do you go down into hell?" she asked him.

"In visions and rituals. We use good magic, what you might call 'white.' Our present leader, Daniel, entered into a trance and witnessed the the carnage between the Fenners and the Gaudins at the bayou. He knew it was time for us to intervene."

She swallowed hard, wondering if they had seen her with the gun that shot silver bullets. Watched her leap into a bayou filled with silver to save Doug, Cordelia's brother-in-law.

"You have to stop the feuding. Now. Or we will destroy you." He looked over at her. "Don't think we can't. Ask the older werewolves about the Manarro family." He smiled grimly. "We wiped them out."

"How?"

He drew himself up and straightened his shoulders. "We made an earthquake."

"No, really," she said.

He gave her a look, then returned his attention to the road. A flash of lightning heralded a downpour. He put on the windshield wipers.

"What I lost was your safe passage, should you have decided to come to us," he said. "Maybe that's a divine sign that you should come with me now."

"Come with you," she repeated nervously.

"To where we are staying while we sort out this mess."

"Come with you because...?"

He moved his shoulders. "I have to tell you that my report to Daniel, my leader, won't be favorable. We don't believe the Fenners and the Gaudins will be able to make peace. They're savages, all of them. We predict that in the end, for the good of the world, we'll have to kill them all."

"That's not for you to decide," she insisted. But his answering look told her that he would never accept that. "Some of them are good." Like Doug, who had tried to look out for Katelyn, and had died a hideous death for his trouble. Or Justin's big brother Jesse, who had Downs syndrome, a sunny, sweet guy.

Except that Jesse keeps talking about breaking necks, she reminded herself.

"They're not good *enough*," he replied. He cocked his head, appraising her. "But I think that perhaps you're worth saving. Come with me now and prove it."

"I have to go home," she said. But Wolf Springs wasn't home. Los Angeles was. "I have to make sure that my family's all right."

"Your pack," he said dismissively.

"My grandfather. And someone else."

Trick.

A funny look crossed his face. She scowled at him.

"Stop trying to be all mysterious. What is up with you, anyway? You dress like a Renaissance Faire refugee and you're wearing Old Spice. I'm betting you don't have a day job unless it's being in a motorcycle gang."

He jerked in shock. Emboldened, she was about to lob more insults at him when his expression turned steely and he swerved to the side of the road and stopped.

"This isn't a game," he said. "I killed a werewolf back there. It's not my first. And it won't be my last."

She realized she was cowering against the door and forced herself to sit up straight. But when she tried to glare back at him, she broke into a cold sweat. Her stomach clenched and her face prickled. And she had to avert her gaze.

"So we understand each other a little better," he said with grim satisfaction.

"I don't understand at all."

"If you join forces with us, you'll understand everything," he said. She sucked in her breath as he held up his forefinger. "But only if."

Then he focused his attention back on the road, leaving her to sit in queasy silence. She thought of a thousand things to say and instead, pulled her phone back out. Instead of listening to the voice message from Los Angeles, she put her phone on mute and pulled up a video of Trick. He had been filming a play, *Dark of the Moon*, and in it he played a witch boy who falls in love with a human girl. Trick had translated it into Russian, which he spoke fluently, and in the video, he wore nothing but a pair of black footless tights and had feathers woven into his dark, curly hair. A spotlight was shining on his face, highlighting the sharp angles of his cheekbones, the warm brown color of his skin. His hair was pulled back from his forehead, accentuating his sea-green eyes, and he swayed like a snake.

Trick Sokolov, who had bewitched her. The only thing she wanted more than Trick was not to be a werewolf any more. So far, both were things she couldn't have.

She drank in his movements, his face. She remembered what it felt like to kiss him. To be held by him. The video was so sexy, and so Trick, that her heart skipped beats and she played it again, focusing on him, on how she felt about him. It was hopeless: he knew nothing about her werewolf world, and if he ever learned of it, he would be put to death.

Even now, he was in trouble. Mike Wright, who had bullied and terrorized Trick for years, had been found dead. Katelyn had been unable to confess that she'd beaten him badly after he rammed her car and tried to rape her. But she had left him alive. Of that she had been certain. Trick's only connection to the murder was his known animosity toward Mike—and the fact that he'd been in trouble with the law before. People had it in for Trick, because he was wealthy, and different, and of mixed heritage. Some of the girls who'd warned Katelyn about him were the same girls who wanted him to be theirs. People who detested him had crashed his amazing Halloween party on his family vast, sprawling property.

His parting image was a slow, wicked smile. It physically hurt to think of him smiling that way for someone else. But he would have to, one day.

"What are you doing?" Magus asked sharply. "Are you texting someone?"

"None of your business," she retorted.

His hand shot out as if to grab the phone, and she yanked it out of his reach.

"Hey, not cool," she said.

"Everything is my business," he retorted. "For you, that's a lucky thing."

"Why?"

He looked her full on, and his eyes glowed against the crimson firelight beyond. "Because I can save you, Katelyn, even if you can't save them."

4

Katelyn figured she had the rest of the drive back to Wolf Springs to learn all she could about the Hounds of God. She wasn't sure yet what she would do with the information—go straight to the pack? Call Cordelia first?—but the more she heard, the more convinced she became that the Hounds of God were just as crazy as the executives who attended Jack Bronson's Inner Wolf Center, with their drumming and their howling at all hours of the night. The Inner Wolf guys stirred up the animals in the forest, and made the locals resentful, hostile. Bronson urged them to let out their wild wolf side, and people were wondering aloud if one of them had gone too far, and committed the murders that were baffling the two officers of the Wolf Springs police department.

"So in your rituals, you drink this potion, and that's when you change," she said, recapitulating what he'd been telling her. With each revelation she had become more doubtful that the Hounds of God really were werewolves. It sounded to her as if they were a bunch of tattooed freaks who got high and then shared some elaborate mass hallucination. When he talked about the werewolf packs they had already "cleansed," she imagined them riding into town like an outlaw bike gang and physically blowing werewolves away with guns. But she remembered the names: Manarro, Lycanan, Verdulak.

"You're not initiated into our order, so I can't go into detail," he replied. "But yes, we derive our power from aligning ourselves with God and his avenging angels. The Fenners and the Gaudins are descended from monstrous creatures—the Fenners from the Fenris Wolf, son of Loki, and the Gaudins from the Beast of Gévaudan, who terrorized France in the eighteenth century."

He narrowed his eyes. "The Fenners claim descent from a god, and they say that the Gaudins are upstarts, possibly a mutated offshoot from their godly origins. But there is only one God! And the Gaudins are proud to claim a ravening monster as their forebear."

"Is that why they hate each other? Cordelia said they've been feuding for centuries."

"They've been feuding because they're sinful barbarians," he replied, as if the fact were obvious. "Only we who claim God as our Creator are free from sin."

Wow. They're total religious fanatics, she thought. She gave him a careful nod, not wanting to appear as if she were insulting him. She didn't want him to clam up.

"I think the Fenners would agree that the Gaudins are barbarians," she said. "They dumped silver in the water. That's not playing fair."

He looked at her in disbelief. "There's no such thing as playing fair in a war."

"They had traditions," she said. "Fighting only on the full moon..." She stopped. Tonight was not a full moon night. The Fenners had deliberately chosen it to launch a surprise attack.

Gazing at a light snowfall through the windshield, she wondered which of the Fenner werewolves had survived the battle and would be returning home. Who would be in charge? Justin had a good shot at it, especially given how much anguish Regan and Arial were going to be in over their father's death.

She hoped it was Justin. Even with her silver immunity she wasn't sure that either of Cordelia's sisters would be thinking rationally enough to know that they should work with her instead of against her.

Pack politics. They were confusing, exhausting. She ran her fingertips over the faceplate of her phone. There had been a time back in the bayou when she had planned to run, and she would never have seen Trick or her grandfather again. Now it looked like she could, at least, for a while.

She would get home and hope that everything would go okay. Her grandfather had no reason to think that she wasn't at a sleepover at Paulette's, as she had told him the day before. She'd still be able to make it back to his cabin by noon. Except that she had left her Subaru at the Fenners', and he would know something was up if she came home without it.

Magus shifted in his seat as though he had sensed her sudden unease. "What's wrong?" he asked.

"My car. It's at the Fenners."

He cursed under his breath. "I can get you there before they get back."

"There'll be people there already." Jesse, who was Justin's brother, and Lucy, Justin's fiancée. "People who didn't go to the bayou."

"Werewolves, not people," he corrected her, pursing his lips. He puffed air into his cheeks, such a normal-looking gesture of frustration that she almost burst out into nervous laughter. He accelerated and the trees blurred past. They had long ago put the forest fire behind them, and it was still dark out. What kinds of red flags would be raised if Lucy, who had only backed down from a challenge to the death because of the battle at the bayou, saw Katelyn with this weird monk werewolf?

"You should leave the truck there and come with me now," Magus said.

"I need to sort out a few things," she replied. Everyone wanted her to leave with them, first Cordelia and Dom, and now Magus.

If only Trick would ask me to run away with him. We'd run and never look back.

~

Katelyn woke with a start and it took her a moment to remember where she was. Magus's truck. She didn't know when she'd fallen asleep or how long she'd been out, but she'd been dreaming about Trick. In her dream, they'd been playing in the waves at the Santa Monica pier. Such a simple thing, and yet far beyond the realm of possibility.

The sun was up and she could feel warmth on her arm where it was pressed against the window. Her anxiety rocketed sky-high. There was no hiding under cover of darkness anymore.

She looked around to spot a landmark, something familiar. But the trees looked like the trees anywhere else. A premonition reared its head that Magus had decided to take her away after all.

"We have to be getting close," she said, clearing her throat.

"Yes," he said shortly.

"And you know the way," she said, failing to keep the suspicion out of her voice.

He cocked a brow at her. "I went to the Fenner compound once when I was very young," he said.

That took her aback.

"Why? Do they know you?"

"They wouldn't remember me," he said. "It was just a visit."

"A visit?"

He frowned at her. "It's got nothing to do with what's going on."

"I sincerely doubt that. They told me about your pack. They didn't like you."

"Why would they? We have the moral high ground. And the power to destroy them."

"Well, if you think they're so bad, why haven't you?"

"We wait to learn of God's will in all things," he replied with the confidence of someone who is convinced he is right.

"And God told you that he wants you to kill them now?"

He was quiet for a moment, and he didn't look at her. She waited.

"Once you've joined us, Daniel can explain this to you more clearly," he said. "Now, as to your question, I was here once, with my great-aunt. On a visit."

"Once. And all these trees aren't confusing you."

"You really are new at this, aren't you?" His smile was unbearably patronizing. "You'll soon learn that those of us with the gift have an excellent sense of direction, much like our wild brethren."

"Gift. 'Curse' is more like it," she said flatly.

"Not at all. It's an honor to fight for God, to destroy the demons that would overrun this earth. 'Blessed are they that go down into the earth for my sake.'"

"Is that in the Bible?"

"In our holy scripture, from the Inquisition trial of Thiess," he replied.

Justin thought of it as a gift as well. Katelyn hadn't gotten there yet. She doubted she ever would.

Then she studied his profile, his green eyes. The werewolf who had attacked her had had blue eyes. She'd been compiling a list of werewolves with blue eyes ever since. Justin was on it, and a few other people as well. Not as many as she would have expected.

"If you think it such a gift, why don't you bestow it on everyone?" she asked. Maybe that was exactly what someone in his pack—or group, or whatever they called it—had done to her. Who said her attacker had to have been a Fenner or a Gaudin?

Magus shook his head sharply. "The gift must be protected. The responsibilities that come with it can be overwhelming. The mantle is not to be taken up lightly."

"Wow," she said, aloud this time.

"And beyond that, we don't bring strangers in," he went on. "I told you that we're not changed through a bite. We become werewolves through a magic ritual, and one must participate willingly, or it won't work."

"So can you undo it with a magic ritual?" she asked hopefully. "If someone isn't doing too well with the gift, can you take it back?"

She held her breath as he fell silent, and tried to read his hesitation. She caught herself hopefully crossing her fingers, like she did when she was little.

Please, she prayed. *Please*.

"That's something that hasn't been revealed to me," he said carefully. "But I've never heard of it being done."

Crestfallen, Katelyn chewed the inside of the cheek as she resumed staring at the endless lines of trees. Maybe she could hold out a little hope there. He might be lying. Maybe their leader, Daniel, knew how to do it. Cordelia had been definite that you had to be bitten to become a werewolf. So were the Hound of Gods actually werewolves, or something else? This other world was much more complicated than Cordelia had led her to believe.

"Of all people, *you* should welcome the gift," he said.

She jerked. "Why is that? Why have you guys picked me out?" Did they know about her immunity to silver?

"Daniel will explain," he said. "I'm just his messenger."

"But you must know more than you're telling me." She tried a different tack. "Did you ever hear about the string of murders around here forty or fifty years ago?"

He nodded. "My great-aunt has spoken of it often. She grew up around here. That's why I've been to the Fenner house before." He added the last sentence as if he were giving in to her request to explain his past to her.

Katelyn's pulse sped up. "She did? How? Is she a Fenner? Are you?"

He grimaced; she'd clearly insulted him.. "That doesn't even make sense," he said. "She didn't receive the blessing until she was older...like you."

"But who is she?" she persisted, and when she watched his face glaze over, she realized that it didn't really matter at the moment. "Did she ever say who she guessed could have been behind the killings?"

"She didn't have to guess. It was a werewolf, and she survived an attack by the beast. That's how she first learned of our world."

"She was *bitten*?" Katelyn gasped.

"Just deeply scratched."

She blanched at the memory of her grandfather's scarred back. Two close calls. Why hadn't she gotten off that easily?

Because you got out of the truck, she reminded herself. *You left the party alone because you were mad at Trick, and you blew it.* A wave of bitterness soured her stomach, but she pressed on.

"Did she ever figure out who scratched her?"

He took his eyes off the road again to look at her. His eyes gave her chills as he stared her down like the wolf—*correction, werewolf*—that had leaped on the hood of Trick's car on her first day of school at Wolf Springs High. She should have taken that as a warning, been more careful.

He said, "It was the Fenner alpha, of course."

Katelyn felt like she was freefalling, and she dug her fingers into the spongy material of the armrest.

"Lee?" she whispered.

"No," Magus said abruptly, turning back to the road. "Tommy Ray Fenner. Lee Fenner's father."

She blinked, processing that information. No one had ever talked about Lee Fenner's father. But Cordelia had a distinct lack of older relatives.

"She saw him?"

"No, it took us years to piece it all together. By then he was dead and Lee was alpha. The matter was closed as far as we were concerned. We didn't stop to think that sickness of the mind might run in the blood."

She felt off-balance, as if the vehicle were spinning around her. *Sickness of the mind.* A pack forced to endure the rule of more than one demented Fenner?

"Did that…does your great-aunt have problems? With her mind?" She was trying to be tactful, but she supposed it was a little late to try for niceties.

"No," he retorted. "We would never have permitted her to become a Hound of God if that were the case."

"Do you think Lee's father was the one who killed all those people fifty years ago?" She hesitated. "Do you know about that?"

"Of course. Without a doubt."

She wasn't sure which question he was answering.

"That's likely why Lee challenged and killed Tommy Ray. We believe Lee's brother Tyler opposed the challenge."

"Tyler. I've never heard that name before," she said.

He slid her a glance. "Tyler Fenner. The father of Justin and Jesse Fenner. Who died mysteriously."

She shuddered. Lee had killed his own father. Justin had as much as accused Lee of killing *his* father, Tyler. What kind of man could do that? What kind of world required that?

I think my grandfather killed my father, she thought. And I think my mom knew something. So what kind of people does that make us? What kind of a family are we?

"The recent maulings," she said. "Did Lee do that?"

"So I would assume. However, we have a bigger situation to worry about," he replied.

She stared at him, but quickly had to look away when his eyes locked with hers. Locked onto her. "'For the Lord will send out his warriors, and they will cut down the unrighteous. They will smite the disobedient, and the sinners will sink into the earth,'" he said. "Thiess."

I have to tell Cordelia about this, she thought, *These guys really could be dangerous.*

"We're nearly there," Magus said. "And someone's coming toward us." When she jerked, he looked at her warily. "Don't you hear the motor?"

"You startled me. I was just about to tell you that when you started talking," she said defensively. The truth was, she hadn't heard it. Her heightened senses came and went, but there was no need to tell him that.

She almost shook her head in exasperation. She was a terrible liar.

They rounded a curve and she saw a car bouncing toward them. Fenners, most likely.

"Shit," Katelyn said, ducking down out of sight.

Magus squinted through the windshield. "There's a young woman and a man," he reported.

Lucy and Jesse, it had to be. She realized he didn't know who they were. So the Hounds of God didn't know *everything* about Wolf Springs—or at least, Magus didn't.

Katelyn listened in anxiety to the sound of the approaching motor. Then it was passing by them and slowly fading into the distance.

"Gone," he reported. "You can sit up."

Katelyn did; fifteen minutes later they pulled up outside the Fenner home. There didn't seem to be anyone else around, and she practically jumped out of Magus's truck.

"You know how risky it is for you here," he said shrewdly. "You should come with me. We can protect you."

"Not now," she said.

Not ever, she vowed.

"We'll be in touch," he said.

She didn't respond. The best news she could have on that score was never hearing from the Hounds of God again. As he idled, she made it to her Subaru and heaved a half-moan of relief when it started right up. She waited for Magus to go up the driveway and back onto the road, and then she followed, torn between putting distance between himself and her, and avoiding any returning Fenners. Magus might already know where she lived but she had no intention of leading him there if she could help it.

A few minutes down the road he turned west off the country road. As he disappeared down the dirt path, half a dozen enormous black wolves with hair tipped in red trotted across in a line, turned, and stared at her. The wolf in the middle of the line snarled at her and snapped its jaws. Though her windows were closed, she could hear the sharp clack of teeth. It was a warning. She knew enough to tell that. They would have let her through with Magus, but not following him.

"We'll do it your way for now," she said.

SAVAGE

She hit the gas and continued on her way, eager to put as
much distance between herself and the sinister new pack as
possible. Finally she slowed down, convinced that she'd
clocked enough miles to be safe.

Exhaustion was setting in, and she struggled to keep
herself awake. She blasted some music at full volume and that
made her think of Trick, whose whole life seemed to be
accompanied by a soundtrack. Thinking of Trick was good. It
kept her busy, occupied. She hoped he'd been cleared of
suspicion in Mike Wright's murder and freed, and that he
would be at her grandfather's cabin when she got there.

She glanced down at herself and realized that she had
forgotten that her clothes were ruined, covered with soot and
muck from the poisoned bayou. Pulling over to the side of the
road, she got her duffel bag from the backseat and quickly
changed into fresh clothes. She found a large bottle of water
and cleaned off her face, neck, and arms, then poured it over
her head. Snow was falling, but she relentlessly washed
herself, then ran a comb through her hair and grimaced as it
caught on knots.. She hoped she looked like someone returning
from a sleepover, and not a war.

Katelyn reached for her phone, remembering that she'd
gotten a call from L.A. When she played the message, she
realized it was from Detective Cranston, the man who had
investigated her father's murder when she'd been ten, and was

looking into the house that had destroyed her home less than six months ago

She put the phone up to her ear. He identified himself, then added, "I just wanted to let you know that the fire investigators finished their report on your house. Given what happened to your dad, the department wanted to make sure there was no arson or anything else involved. It turns out it was just an accident. Earthquake broke a gas pipe, there was a spark...you get the idea. I'm sorry.

. "There was one interesting thing they did find, though, that I thought you should know about in light of our recent conversation. They did find what appeared to be a bullet made out of silver. We're looking into that. Call me if you want to talk."

With a trembling hand, Katelyn deleted the message. She sat for a few minutes staring at falling snowflakes without seeing them, as she tried to make sense of what she'd just been told.

Why had there been a silver bullet in their house?

She thought about how dramatically her mom had changed after her father had been killed. Giselle Chevalier had become a broken woman. Afraid of everything, the poster child for post-traumatic stress disorder. Katelyn had had to grow up fast, raise herself, baby her mother.

Her mother, who had sent Mordecai McBride the newspaper article about Katelyn's dad being bitten by a wolf.

See, I told you so.

That was what her mother had written in the margin of the news clipping.

"Keep it together," she whispered to herself. "You'll figure all of this out."

She just wished she believed that.

~

By the time she pulled up outside the cabin, her heart was thumping *Just breathe*, she told herself.

Trick's car wasn't there and she was disappointed She closed her eyes tightly, got out, and slammed the door. She mounted the cabin steps slowly, her hand was shaking so badly she had to try twice to unlock the front door. She pushed it open and stepped tentatively inside, closed the door and leaned against it for a moment, struggling to catch her breath. She couldn't let him know anything about what had really happened in the last twenty-four hours.

Her grandfather appeared from the kitchen, wiping a butcher knife with a dishtowel. She stared at the glinting silver of the blade and began to sweat.

"What the hell happened to you?" he asked gruffly, eyes narrowing as they took her in from head to toe.

"Oh, hi, Ed," she said. That had been her nickname for him when she'd first arrived in Wolf Springs. He'd told her that when she was little, she hadn't understood what a grandfather was. He'd told her it was like having an extra daddy, and she had taken the initials—E.D.—and called him that. In the months since then, they had moved on to "Grandpa," but in her uncertainty, she'd reverted to the more distancing name. "I, uh, was at Paulette's. Like I said." Her voice sounded like a tiny squeak to her own ears. She thought of the wound at her temple. Surely it had healed by now. She could feel the sweat rolling down the middle of her back. It was beginning to bead up on her forehead and she clenched her fist, hoping that he didn't notice.

"Paulette live in a pigpen?"

She glanced down. There was muck under her fingernails and she could still smell bog water in her hair. She'd done a terrible job of cleaning herself up.

"No, she, uh—it's just that—"

Katelyn panicked as she realized she was stammering. She was an idiot. No one had been at the Fenner house. She could have used a faucet outside or probably even found her way inside to a shower.

"It's just that—"

"Just what?" he cut in, sounding angry.

He took another step closer and she smelled the poisonous, silvery tang. With a sudden sinking in the pit of her stomach she realized that he wasn't holding a kitchen knife but a hunting knife.

And it was made of silver. Hunting knives were usually made of stainless steel.

He knew. He knew, and now he was going to kill her.

Just like he had probably killed her father.

He took another step closer.

There was nowhere to run.

His eyes darkened and the towel fell on the ground, leaving the bare knife in his right hand, glinting wickedly in the light.

He was standing right in front of her now, close enough that she could feel his breath, hear his heart. His eyes burned into her; she could taste bile spilling into her mouth.

"Girl, you tell me right now what happened."

Strike first, said a voice inside her head.

5

Strike first.

Katelyn took a deep breath as some kind of switch turned on and adrenaline surged through her, pouring into her veins, feeding her aggression impulse. Ed practically tapped his booted toes on the cabin floor and waited for her to explain herself. Swimming in the river? It was snowing outside. Snowball fight. Snow wouldn't make her this filthy.

He crossed his arms, the wintry sun catching the sheen of the blade and throwing the reflection around the room. The rows of animal heads on his walls seemed to blink at her. This man killed things.

So did she. So would she. She knew it.

"Tree," she blurted out. "A tree fell and it was blocking me. And with the snow and all…"

"Did you even *try* to call me?" he asked her.

"No service." There was an excellent chance that that was true. "And it didn't look that big. But I slipped. In the snow." She forced a goofy, abashed smile on her face. "It was just a-a sapling but the ground is all muddy and, um, here I am."

He scowled at her. "You should have gone back to Paulette's and called me. I have a chain saw."

"Maybe I could keep it in my car," she said, and then she quaked, because saying that might remind him that she still had his gun that shot silver bullets. Justin had it now. Maybe if her grandfather asked to see it, she could say that it had been stolen.

His face worked as if he were about to say something, maybe about how ridiculous it was to continue to live in a cabin in the middle of a forest on a mountain where people were getting killed, and you had to think about packing a gun and a chain saw just to get home and back. And that he had forced her to move there with him. She knew now that he had had his reasons. She just wasn't sure what they were.

"So anyway, next time I'll call," she said, darting past him. Then she stopped. She had to know. "Is Trick okay?"

That made him smile. "Yeah, the boy's okay. Got sprung from jail. No evidence to connect him to Mike Wright's death. They're saying animal attack."

"Oh, Grandpa," she said in a rush. "That's good. That's so good."

They shared a moment. It felt as if Trick was practically in the room with them, and she looked down at her filthy fingernails. "Can I go take a shower?"

"Katie," he said, and then he pursed his lips together as if to prevent his saying something and gave her a nod. "Did Paulette's mama feed you at least?"

"Yes, Grandpa," she lied. She didn't remember the last time she'd eaten, and she was starving. But lying clearly was the better course of action. "Pancakes."

"Sure. Go take a shower. A long one." He cricked his head toward the stairs, and Katelyn escaped.

She checked her phone for texts and messages from Justin and Cordelia. Nothing.

She gave herself the gift—there was that word again—of a fleeting smile, took a long shower, and collapsed into bed.

Dreams came:

Katelyn.

Click click click.

Don't run from me.

In the room.

I marked you.

Hot breath on her cheek. In her ear.

Come with me.

~

Voices woke her. Moonlit snowflakes drifted down from her skylight and she got up. She peeled out of her pajamas and quickly dressed in jeans, a sports bra, and a plaid shirt, grabbing a pair of socks as she left her room and went to the top of the stairs.

She froze.

Men and women were milling in the cabin's front room. They were warmly dressed and heavily armed—shotguns slung over their shoulders, one man sighting down a handgun as he raised it toward the ceiling. Some of them were drinking coffee.

The front door opened, and Trick stood in the doorway in his sheepherder's jacket and a pair of leather gloves. Snowflakes dusted the crown of his black cowboy hat and he kicked the snow off his boots before he crossed the threshold. He was holding a rifle at his side.

He looked up and saw her, and hurried across the room toward her. She flew down the stairs as he set down his rifle and threw his arms around her, planting a kiss on her lips. That kiss loosened something inside her that she'd been holding onto very tightly, and she fought hard to stay in control. She wanted to crawl inside a little place where it was just she and Trick and nothing else, not a thing, certainly none of this.

"Hey, girl," he said softly, kissing her again. He pressed his cheek against the side of her head and she heard his thunder heartbeat. He smelled so good. He felt even better. She wanted to stay like this forever.

He whispered something against her hair, in Russian, and she looked up at him.

"What did you say?"

Her field of vision was nothing but his eyes. "I think you know," he murmured. And then the light in his eyes faded. Something had replaced his joy in seeing her.

"What's going on? What's happened?" she asked, indicating the crowd in her grandfather's living room

"Oh, darlin'," he said, and he wrapped his arms around her again. He cradled the back of her head and rubbed his cheek against her temple. She wanted to melt against him again but now she was too afraid.

"Someone's died. Someone's been killed," she said.

"Yes."

The news hit her like a punch to her stomach. More death. "Who?"

"I don't know. Your pappy didn't say. He called, I came."

She shut her eyes tightly. "Mauled?" she ground out.

"Neck broke first, looks like. Before the…mauling. So maybe this time it really was just a wild animal."

She looked at the milling crowd. Faces were vaguely familiar—she'd seen a lot of these people around town, but hadn't actually met many of them.

"Folks in Wolf Springs are used to taking care of things themselves," Trick said, following her gaze. "It's not like our police department can do much. We only have two officers."

"But it's dark out. It's dangerous. Guns, a big group—"

"Exactly why I am going," he said in a soft voice. At her look, he added, "Don't want Doc out there without me."

She was touched beyond words. Her grandfather was Trick's godfather, and Trick called him "Doc" because Mordecai McBride had a PhD in philosophy. He had taught at the University of Arkansas for many years.

"You don't tell him I said that, hear? Man's got his pride," Trick said.

"He told me you've been cleared of suspicion in Mike's murder." She made a little face in case it wasn't cool with him to talk about it.

His face hardened. "Official word is lack of evidence. Unofficially? I think my parents made a donation to the police officers' benevolent fund."

"Oh, my God, a *bribe*?" she blurted.

He rolled his eyes. "And you thought graft and corruption were just big-city values."

"But I met Sergeant Lewis. He helped find our silver. He wouldn't take a bribe."

He gave his head a little shake. "Your daddy was a district attorney, yes? I'll bet he knew some real nice police officers who took freebies now and then. First you give Officer

Friendly a cup of coffee here, a donut there, tickets to a Lakers game. Then she fixes your parking ticket. Next she withholds evidence so your kid stays out of jail." He blanched. "I didn't mean it that way. No evidence is being withheld on my account."

She flashed back to the first time she'd met him, when he had made a big deal out of having to be formally invited into the cabin before he entered. He'd said it was "a court thing." He'd been falsely accused of breaking into people's houses.

Just like he'd been falsely accused of murder?

And someone broke into our cabin.

She couldn't even believe she was thinking like that. Was she so twisted that she could even *suspect* Trick of doing anything wrong?

"Hey, it's going to be okay," he said. "All of it. We're going to figure it out."

"No. Just stop it," she said.

"You're shaking like a leaf." He put his hands on either side of her face. "I'm going to make these woods safe for you, Katelyn. Or...I'm going to take you out of them."

You can't, she thought, but a dozen images of life with Trick unfolded like flowers: getting away from here. Being together for the rest of their lives, with him knowing what had happened to her, and dealing with it.

SAVAGE

"Trick," she whispered, but she didn't know what to say next. She had almost bitten him out of sheer selfish desire to have him. She couldn't have him. Period.

"I'll watch out for him," he promised, misreading her tone. "I know he's all the family you've got left."

You. I want you to be my family.

She held her tongue and inclined her head as if in thanks.

"Trick," her grandfather called. "Time." Then the older man looked at Katelyn. "You stay home. With your gun."

If he asked to see the gun, she was sunk. She was too off-balance to lie convincingly. Holding her breath, she nodded and said, "Okay, Ed. Grandpa. But please, please tell me. Who was it?"

He came over to her as the front door opened and the crowd filed out. Truck engines began to roar.

"Was it Mr. Henderson?" she asked, so afraid of the answer. She had liked him, started to connect with him. He was a person to her.

"Another Inner Wolf attendee," he said. He smiled grimly. "This gets out, maybe that place will finally shut down."

She blinked. Given the immediate circumstance, that was a pretty cold-blooded way to think.

"Where's your weapon?" her grandfather continued. "You leave it in your car? I can fetch it for you."

"It's in my room," she said quickly.

"Let me check it out, make sure it's working." He looked so worried.

"We gotta go, Doc. She knows how to check her weapon." Trick said. He looked at Katelyn. "You'll get it out and stay put, right?"

She blinked. Was he covering for her? Uneasily, she nodded.

"There, you see?" Trick said. He turned to Katelyn. "Anybody knocks and tells you they're selling Girl Scout cookies, you blow 'em away."

She pursed her lips and nodded. "I will."

Trick and her grandfather joined the parade to the vehicles parked up and down their little country road. Trick climbed into the passenger's side of her grandfather's truck, unrolled the window, and gave Katelyn a wave as she watched from the window. She wasn't allowed to go outside after dark, not even on the porch. When she had first arrived in Wolf Springs, she had chafed at the edict. She'd thought her grandfather was super-overprotective.

Then I hated him for making me come somewhere that was so dangerous. But…am I safer here than I would have been in Los Angeles?

She texted Justin:

HUNTING PARTY 2NITE. SOMEONE ELSE KILLED.

She hesitated. She was assuming Justin was alive, that he had made it back safe. She didn't know the current status of the pack, let alone her own. But in the event that they were out in the woods, they had to know, to be warned. She hit send and waited.

She would have preferred never to speak to any of the Fenners again, but she was still connected to the pack. What happened to them happened to her. Justin didn't answer. She almost phoned him but she didn't know where he was, and if he was with Lucy, that might be enough for his almost-fiancée to renew her challenge to a fight to the death. Katelyn was probably alive now only because news of Cordelia's marriage to Dom Gaudin had interrupted their fight.

She texted Cordelia the same message. As with Justin, there was no answer. Katelyn pictured the raging forest fire and the Hellhound and worried. She would have thought both of them would be on tenterhooks waiting for word from her, and made plans to communicate back.

Sliding her phone into her pocket, she put on her shoes and socks, grabbed a flashlight and crept outside toward the garage. Her objective was to find another gun that shot silver bullets so she'd have one to show her grandfather next time. If she was lucky, he wouldn't look too closely at it.

She didn't bother with a jacket despite the light snowfall that piled drifts around the door to the garage. Werewolves weren't as sensitive to the cold as humans.

Looking left and right, she confirmed that she was alone and darted into the garage. She flicked on the flashlight and played the beam over the towers of dusty packing cartons as she headed for the section where she had found the ammo box filled with silver bullets and the incriminating newspaper clipping that had revealed the story of her father's wolf bite. And her mother's handwritten note: *I told you so.*

Detective Cranston had found a silver bullet in the wreckage of their house. Her grandfather had come to Los Angeles for her father's funeral, so maybe he had brought some silver bullets with him.

But he hadn't come to her mother's funeral. Why was that?

She put all that aside for the moment, trying to concentrate on what she was doing. The cardboard boxes in question appeared as dusty and untouched as the night Katelyn had stumbled upon them. She had done everything she could to avoid tipping off her grandfather that she'd found them. Setting down her flashlight so that the light bounced off the ceiling, she explored several boxes new to her. She found more baby things of her father's and a photo album filled with old black-and-white pictures of her grandparents. There were no more boxes of silver bullets; she had begun to despair of ever finding another gun when she smelled a hint of silver. Eagerly she moved aside a light blue crocheted baby blanket and looked down at a gun very like the one she'd lost. Cracking it open to see if it was loaded, she smelled more silver and figured it for residue from the silver-laden bullets.

She slipped it in the pocket of her jeans and carefully put everything back the way it had been. Then she boldly went to the ammo box and gathered up several handfuls of bullets. She'd been afraid to disturb everything last time. But now she loaded the gun slowly, deliberately, defiantly emphasizing the fact that the silver didn't bother her at all. Justin had had trouble holding the gun even though the firearm itself wasn't made of silver—the bullets inside were enough to bother him.

She took another handful of bullets and stuffed them into her jeans. She'd taken enough for her grandfather to notice, which was foolhardy. But necessary.

The stakes were higher now. The threat was closer.

And for all she knew, she was arming herself against him.

Her phone rang, the ringtone the dog bark she'd assigned to Justin as a sort of in-joke. She took the call.

"Hey," he said. "Who died?"

"Inner Wolf guy." She heard how shaky she sounded, how needy, and cleared her throat. Werewolves despised weakness. "Where are you? What's going on?"

"We're still on the road. We think the Gaudins are trailing us and we're resting up in case they launch an attack. They rammed my truck and Al got killed."

"No," she began. She'd seen what happened. It had been the Hellhound, not the Gaudins. But how could she tell him that without revealing that she'd run from him?

"Don't shed tears for that one, darlin'. He was no fan of yours," he said. "Where are *you*? I've been looking for you everywhere."

She had prepared for this. "I'm back home. I started running and I wound up on this road. A trucker pulled over and I-I tried to call you but I guess it didn't go through. I went to your house but no one was there. So I came back to my cabin."

"Huh," he said, and she realized he'd bought it. "There's a power vacuum now, with Lee gone. It's making everyone insane and folks are gearing up to issue challenges for dominance. You best stay away."

"No problem," she said tartly, and he chuckled.

"Kat McBride, respectful as always."

"Don't start. Please. *Sir,*" she added in the same acidic tone.

"You're right. Now's not the time for an etiquette class. We're in crisis. Let me tell you what's going on. I sent Lucy and Jesse away to a hunting cabin way up in the hills to keep them both safe and out of things. I don't know how Jesse will take Lee's death. He loved that man."

He wasn't a man, Katelyn thought. Then she had a sickening thought: that Jesse may have already found out, and broken someone's neck in his rage.. That he might have transformed—he was older than Justin, and physical maturity determined when you could will yourself to change—and killed the Inner Wolf attendee.

That the hunting party might find him.

"Are you sure they reached the cabin?" she asked.

"What's this? Concern for the welfare of fellow pack members?" he asked softly. "Are you finally getting it?"

"These being the same pack members who stood by while Lucy nearly killed me in a challenge," she retorted. "The same ones you've sent Lucy and Jesse away from, because you're all running amok without someone to tell you what to do. The same werewolves who were cheering her on when she was trying to kill me could turn on her at any second."

"Kat, I'll excuse that because you're scared. You're new at this," he said.

"I don't care. I never want to get used to this. It's sick and you're all crazy. I hate this. I hate you!"

"It doesn't matter. You're stuck with us. And with *me*."

"No," she said, and before she could stop herself, she disconnected the call. For a moment she was breathless, realizing how disrespectful it had been, and then she was fiercely, exuberantly glad she'd done it. She was immune to silver. He wasn't. The Hounds of God had come to her, not to him. And she had a garage filled with silver bullets, and another gun that shot them. She wasn't going to be some wimpy little coward sniveling at his feet.

"Bring it, Fenner," she sneered at the phone.

Then she shook a little, because she wasn't stupid. Justin might become the new alpha, which meant that she might have just pissed off the most powerful werewolf in Wolf Springs. She might have a gun with silver bullets, but he would have an entire pack of werewolves to do his bidding.

And he had her other gun. He had only been able to hold it for a couple of minutes, but it had been long enough to take down Luc Gaudin.

"Yeah, with what, three bullets?" she muttered, and got herself another handful. But he would never actually hurt her, would he?

Once everything was back in place, she crept out of the garage and was heading for the porch when she noticed a shadow stretched against the wall. She sucked in her breath and flattened herself against a darker section of the wood siding as she tried to force her werewolf senses to kick in. Adrenaline seemed to activate the change. But nothing happened.

It's just a tree, she told herself, but the same feeling of dread that she'd experienced when the Hounds of God had formed a line earlier stole over her. Ice pellets slapped at her cheeks and wind buffeted her ears.

A metallic creaking noise jerked her attention to the right, to the porch. The wind was pushing on the front door, which was open.

A butterfly lodged itself at the base of her throat.

I shut it, didn't I? Is there someone in our cabin?

She scrutinized the door, dialing back mentally, replaying her actions. No. She had shut the door tightly, carefully.

There was someone in the house.

Her phone rang with Justin's ringtone. He probably wanted to read her the riot act for hanging up on him. Fumbling in her jeans, she tried to turn off the ringer but succeeded only in declining the call. That meant he would probably try again. Panicking, she turned off the phone, not meaning to, but it was too late.

The wind caught the door and slammed it against the front of the house. Then a gust blew it the other way, and it crashed shut.

Now there was no way to quietly sneak in the front door. She licked her lips and her heartbeat kicked into overdrive, pounding so hard she could feel the pressure in her head. She transferred her gun to her left hand and wiped the icy sweat off her right palm, then gripped it and held it close to her chest, pointed upward, pushing the air from her lungs slowly, her body so taut it was nearly impossible to make herself exhale.

Maybe it's just the thief who took our stuff.

She didn't believe that.

The best course of action was to wait.

Except...she heard a rustle in the shrubs along the garage. So there was someone in her house, and someone behind her. A wave of fear made her sway. She pressed her lips together to keep from making a sound and forced herself to think. Whoever was outside with her was closer, more dangerous.

She snaked her hand up the side of the gun to prevent it from glinting in the moonlight as she cautiously swiveled toward the sound. Bushes rustled. The wind blew her hair in front of her eyes and she shook her head to try to clear her vision.

A stronger wind blew snow around her ankles. The ice pellets tinked on the garage roof..

She heard a footstep. Another.

Directly behind her.

A hand came over her mouth. Something hard–the barrel of a gun–pressed against her temple.

She had miscalculated, badly. Somehow someone had concealed themselves between the cabin door and her. The roof. She forced herself not to whimper as the voice of an older woman rasped into her ear:

"Arial Fenner sends her greetings," she said. "And she sent me, too. To kill you."

6

"You're making a big mistake," Katelyn managed to get out. Was there just the one or were there more werewolves? Her own gun was in her hand, but she would never be able to move it in time before the woman shot her.

"I don't think so," the woman said with a short, sharp laugh that sounded more like a hyena than a human. It set Katelyn's teeth on edge.

"The new alpha wants me alive and wants to see me now." Katelyn deliberately refrained from identifying who that might be.

The woman laughed harshly. "There is no new alpha yet, and if you think for a moment that Justi—"

"Regan," Katelyn interrupted. "Regan is the new alpha and she knows I risked my own life to save her husband, Doug. She knows the value her father placed on me and why. And she understands that I'm the pack's best weapon in this war."

"You're lying. When Arial sent me here she was very clear that no one had won, no alpha exists. Yet."

Katelyn continued to lie through her teeth. "Arial's dead. Justin called me and told me just before I came back outside. Regan fought her and killed her."

It was plausible. After all, Katelyn had no idea which of the sisters would have the upper hand in a fight and she was hoping that the woman holding the gun to her temple wouldn't either.

"So I'd distance myself from Arial and anything she told you to do as fast as I could," Katelyn pushed, sensing hesitation and seizing upon it. "That's the losing side. You need to honor the new alpha."

"You're lying," the older woman retorted.

Katelyn felt the gun barrel move a fraction of an inch. Good. She had the other woman off balance and distracted, which was exactly what she needed her to be.

"Oh, come on. Surely you know the secret," Katelyn pressed.

"What secret?" the woman asked. The gun barrel wobbled slightly more.

"I can't be killed by bullets." Katelyn let herself fall, straight down, sliding through the woman's grasp. She threw herself back, slamming into the woman's knees and the woman tumbled with a gasp. The gun discharged harmlessly in the air, then hit the ground and Katelyn kicked at it, sending it skidding away. Miraculously her own gun was still clamped in her hand. She twisted around and pointed it at the woman's head, but something was wrong. She was having a hard time holding it, as if her fingers were too short. She tried to wrap her index finger around the trigger but it was also thickening.

She brought her other hand up to keep hold of the gun when she got a good look at it—it was turning into a paw tipped with razor sharp claws.

The woman was terrified. "You-you shouldn't be able to change!"

Katelyn opened her mouth to say that there were a lot of things she shouldn't be able to do, but all that came out was a hideous growl.

The gun fell from Katelyn's fingers. Her bones snapped, reformed. Before her eyes the older woman began to shift in response.

With a roar Katelyn leaped on top of her, trying to keep her pinned to the ground. Pain seared through her body and instead of screams, howls tore loose.

She was changing, all the way this time. She waited for the inevitable, where her humanity slipped away from her and only the wolf was left.

Save your life, she told herself as the pressure in her head mounted and her thoughts squeezed together into a tighter and tighter ball. *Survive.*

And then...the squeezing stopped...and she was still herself. Or rather, she was still aware of her human self, even as the wolf switched into high gear. She exulted, alive, vibrant, stronger than ever before.

It felt like...

...freedom.

She stared in fascinated horror as the other woman finished her own change. Katelyn snapped at her, teeth grazing her cheek. It was a warning: *stay down.*

But the other wolf wasn't heeding it. Instead, she wriggled below Katelyn and champed her fangs down on Katelyn's left front paw.

The yip of pain was ripped from Katelyn's lungs even as hatred surged through her.

Must kill.

The other wolf kicked out with its back legs, catching her in the stomach and lifting her up and off. She contorted in midair and landed on her feet, snarling, even as the older wolf struggled to her feet.

They circled each other, snapping, feinting, looking for an opening.

The throat could be torn out and that would be a kill, Katelyn knew, understood on a deep level. The same was true with the soft belly.

Brown eyes glared at her. Brown. Not the wolf who had bitten her.

The attacker lunged forward and Katelyn, leapt to the side, spinning and slashing at the other wolf's flanks as it overshot her. The smell of blood filled the air and it stirred a hunger deep inside. Time to kill. Time to eat.

Her foe yelped, a cry of injury, and more, of fear. Yes. It was afraid. It reeked of it. Katelyn would teach it to fear. She would make it sorry it had ever set eyes on her.

The other wolf attacked again and Katelyn vaulted over her, but then tucked her head and bit into the other wolf's back, fangs puncturing skin and cracking bone.

More blood, more yelping, as Katelyn landed safely on the other side. She turned and looked back at the other wolf, daring her to take it one step farther, daring her to attack again.

And Katelyn's challenger stood, whining, uncertain.

Its mistake.

Katelyn leapt forward. She was going to rip out her enemy's throat. She could do it, she had closed on her, and the stupid wolf was holding her head too high, leaving her throat exposed.

She was foolish and she would die.

No!

Katelyn turned her head at the last and sunk her fangs into the other wolf's shoulder, slicing through muscles and tendon. Katelyn shook her head hard and then threw the weakling ten feet.

It was fantastic to be so strong.

She tensed, ready to attack again, but something was different. Something had changed.

The stench of fear in the air was now more pungent than the scent of the blood. The challenger's chin was brushing the ground and she was backing up, making strange, pained moans.

Katelyn stepped forward, claws cutting into the dirt.

The other wolf retreated again and then threw itself down on the ground. Katelyn stood for a moment. This gesture was one of submission, of surrender. It felt right.

The creature rolled onto her back, exposing her stomach. The moaning became frantic whining. And Katelyn could almost swear she heard the words "Please don't kill me" in the sound.

Katelyn stalked forward, her legs powerful, head and tail high. She was the victor. She answered to no one. Life or death. The power was hers. The choice was hers.

The defeated wolf continued to cower and then slowly began to morph back into a human, naked, whimpering and writhing in agony. Katelyn blinked at her, watching, waiting for her to be fully human again. Part of her was hoping the other would make just one false move so she could rip her throat out. The older woman's body went slack and her eyes rolled back in her head. Then, when the transformation was done and it was clear that she wasn't going to do anything, Katelyn felt her own body begin to shift back.

She blinked in astonishment. The pain was somehow even more intense as her consciousness expanded rapidly, her thoughts filling every nook and cranny. All her glorious muscles, her strength and speed were being stuffed back into a body that couldn't handle them.

She wanted to cry out but every muscle seized and she couldn't force open her mouth to get out the sound. She had always assumed that at the end of the full moon the pack fell asleep and somehow shifted back while they were sleeping. She realized now that wasn't the case. They didn't go to sleep. They passed out from the sheer torture of being forced back into bodies full of limits and boundaries.

She collapsed onto the ground as bones broke and muscles began to rearrange themselves. She lay quivering in anguish.

Darkness swam in front of her eyes, but she couldn't, wouldn't succumb to it. She had to stay conscious. If she didn't, she was as good as dead.

She curled her paws and her nails cut into what were becoming palms again. Her left hand throbbed where it had been bitten. Her nails began to shrink and her bones were knitting themselves back together.

And then she was human again. She could feel it. She had the overwhelming urge to cry at the unfairness of it and she blinked rapidly, trying to settle her mind and grasp and hold her thoughts.

She was human.

And that was a good thing.

Naked, she pushed up off the ground and forced herself to a standing position. Her knees were weak and rubbery. For a terrible moment she thought there was something wrong with her and then remembered that her human body would bear the brunt of her battle until it healed.

She stared down at the other woman who was still lying unconscious on the ground, covered in blood.

I did that, Katelyn realized. *I hurt her.*

It was more than that. Katelyn hadn't just fought her. She had fought her and won. She looked down at her own injured hand, already healing itself. She hadn't just *won*, she'd beaten the other woman nearly senseless. She'd come off with just the one injury. How had she gotten so lucky in her first challenge?

Then she realized it hadn't been luck, but skill. She might not have spent years learning how to fight, but she had spent years learning how to contort her body, how to demand the most of it while still keeping it safe. In the end, that self-awareness had saved her, had helped her beat the other werewolf.

How long would it take for the woman to wake up? However long it was, Katelyn couldn't wait. Every minute that passed could be bringing fresh dangers her way.

And with every minute that passed her enemy's body had a chance to heal just that much more.

She reached out and shoved the woman in the ribs with her foot. The assassin groaned, then slowly blinked several times. Her eyes finally seemed to focus on Katelyn and she paled.

Katelyn registered her reaction with a mild sense of shock. It was the first time another werewolf had been truly afraid of her. The unfolding of the next minute was completely crucial to survival for both of them.

Her legs still felt shaky but she forced herself to sound calm, confident. "What's your name?"

"Wanda. Wanda Mae."

The name sounded vaguely familiar. She knew she had met the woman before, right after her first transformation, but there had been so many new names and faces.

"Wanda Mae, I'll let you live if you swear allegiance to me."

Katelyn stared directly into her eyes. She had beaten her, won fair and square. She told herself there was nothing to be afraid of.

Unless there are more of them. If someone's in my cabin.

But she refused to give any sign of her own uncertainty. If there were any more werewolves skulking around they hadn't chosen to reveal themselves or intervene in the fight in any way.

Which meant that they didn't want to get any more involved than they already were.

"I swear allegiance to you...my alpha," Wanda Mae said, lowering her head.

A thrill zinged through Katelyn when Wanda Mae addressed her as alpha. Was this what it had been like for Lee? What the new Fenner alpha would feel when others addressed him or her that way?

She tried to give herself a reality check. She had a pack of two. That wasn't truly a pack. And what did she gain by having Wanda acknowledge her as alpha?

I need more werewolves to acknowledge me as their alpha.

She was stunned by the turn her thoughts had taken. It was preposterous, unthinkable.

But why couldn't I be the new Fenner alpha? After all, Magus told me to end this war. Me. Not Justin, or either of Cordelia's sisters. What does he know that I don't?

"Alpha?" Wanda Mae whined very softly.

Katelyn looked down and realized that the other woman was still huddled on the ground, bleeding from a dozen wounds even though they were starting to heal.

"Who came with you?" Katelyn asked. "Call them out of my cabin *now*."

Wanda Mae took a breath, let it out. "You and I are alone, alpha. There's no one here but us."

Katelyn heard the change in her voice—ingratiating, trying to please. Providing her superior with information.

"The door was open," Katelyn said.

"I went inside," Wanda Mae said. "I could smell you coming. I went out your kitchen door and jumped up on the roof." The hand that pushed her gray hair out of her eyes was shaking. "I swear I'm telling you the truth. Now that I'm yours, any other werewolves would be my enemies too."

That was massively convenient. Katelyn was thrilled. Except for the lying about Arial being dead part.

"Okay," Katelyn said. "Listen, I lied to you about Arial." The woman looked stricken. If you see her…" She stopped. "If you see her, tell her that you haven't seen me." She wondered if her scent would be on the woman. Lucy had challenged her because her scent was on Justin after a hug. "You'd better lay low."

"Yes, alpha," she murmured, her voice shaky. "I know you'll look out for me."

Katelyn was taken aback. She knew that was the role of an alpha, but it hadn't occurred to her when she'd forced Wanda Mae to declare her loyalty that she'd be assuming an obligation as well.

"Try to avoid her as best you can, but if she asks you what happened, tell her that you tried to take me on, but humans arrived unexpectedly and you had to let me go. And if a new alpha is declared, pretend to be loyal. But you're mine."

"Pretend…" Wanda said, looking shocked. Then she quickly nodded as Katelyn narrowed her eyes in displeasure. "Understood."

"Things are in chaos, but it'll be all right soon." She looked at the woman, realizing that she wasn't as embarrassed that both of them were undressed as she had been in the past. "Did you bring some clothes?"

"Yes, I did," Wanda Mae said proudly. She pointed to the forest. "Hid 'em good."

"Then get dressed and go," Katelyn said.

"Yes'm, alpha," Wanda Mae said, bowing her head. "Thank you. I'll do everything you say." Then she scrambled to her feet and disappeared into the darkness.

Katelyn stood for a moment, breathing deeply of the cold night air. Things had just changed irrevocably and she didn't know what it meant for her future, but she was grateful that at that moment the overriding fear she had been feeling for weeks seemed to have evaporated.

"There's a new alpha in town," she whispered to the darkness, partly to hear herself say it aloud and partly as a show in case there were more werewolves lurking somewhere in the darkness.

SAVAGE

The Fenner pack knew she was immune to silver. She wondered if Wanda Mae had bought her lie about not being able to be killed by bullets of any kind.

Somewhere in the distance a wolf howled and she knew that it was Wanda Mae.

She picked up her gun and the remains of her tattered clothes, then hurried into the house as life, her other life, flooded back in.

What if her grandfather or Trick had come back and seen everything? She sighed as she closed and locked the cabin door. For one minute an overwhelming, ecstatic freedom had lifted her and now she plunged back into her prison.

This is why the others take such joy in being wolves.

She buried her shredded clothes at the bottom of the trashcan and then hurried upstairs to shower and dress. She took her new silver bullets and gun and put the bullets in some socks, then slid the gun and the socks beneath her mattress.

Then, completely wired, she went downstairs to wait for the hunters to return. She fixed herself some pasta, continuing the myth that she was still a vegetarian when she was dying for meat. After cleaning up, she found herself pacing the living room. She should have asked how long this was going to take, how long until they came back.

But of course they wouldn't have known.

Finally she wandered over to the bookshelf and the Jack Bronson book, which she had reshelved there, caught her eye. She pulled it out and took it back to the couch with her.

Another Inner Wolf executive had been killed. She thought of her run-in with Jack Bronson. The man had been powerful, charismatic, and intimidating. She wouldn't put murder or much else past him. It was possible that it wasn't a werewolf who had been killing people in the woods, but rather some of his attendees who'd gotten a little too in touch with their inner wolves? And why was it she had found a piece of her grandfather's stolen silver outside the Inner Wolf Center?

Maybe Jack Bronson or one of his disciples had broken into their house to steal the painting that revealed the entrance to the lost silver mine, then covered it up by stealing other valuables too. The legend of the mine was no secret, and why else come to some place like this to build a fancy retreat center? There were loads of places he could have built that were still in the woods yet closer to civilization.

She cracked open the book and began reading from the beginning. The introduction provided a mini-biography of Jack. Apparently he had grown up in the mountains in Arkansas. That could help explain the appeal of the area for him.

She kept reading, hoping that at any moment she'd hear Ed and Trick returning. She pictured Jesse lying dead in the snow, and then Justin, and resolutely kept reading the book, trying to drive away images of their mangled corpses.

The more she read about getting in touch with her inner wolf and Jack's theories about the primal savage lurking within everyone, the more she was convinced that if he hadn't killed anyone in Wolf Springs he must have at some point in his life. There was so much glorification of savagery, of the brutish nature. He even urged his readers to eat their meat raw whenever practical. Katelyn was alarmed that her stomach actually growled when she read that section.

"'Deep in his psyche, man has never lost his instinct to kill, and that's a good thing'," she read aloud.

She put the book down. Whoever, whatever, Jack Bronson was, he was a sicko, and moving to the top of her suspect list. She stood up and stretched her back and glanced at the clock. It was midnight.

She crossed to the windows and peered out. No one, not man nor beast seemed to be stirring outside. She couldn't decide if she was relieved or disappointed.

She flexed her left hand. It seemed to have healed completely from Wanda Mae's bite. Belatedly she wondered if there was blood on the ground outside from the fight. There had to be, she realized—Wanda's, at least.

She stiffened. What would the hunters make of that when they came back? Still, she wasn't sure what she could do about that. Maybe she could say she'd seen some kind of animal kill a rabbit outside if anyone asked. That would be less suspicious than the smell of freshly dumped bleach outside.

She glanced back at the book. Jack Bronson seemed to be smiling at her from the cover. And it wasn't a nice, warm smile. It was an I'm-a-psychopathic-killer kind of smile.

On a sudden whim she sat down at her computer, launched a browser and did a search for Jack Bronson. Thousands of hits came back and she gritted her teeth in frustration. She began to scroll through, automatically dismissing all the bookseller sites and promotion sites.

Finally she tried adding the word "criminal" to the search. The fifth result from the top of a smaller list looked promising. She clicked on it and found a rant by an angry guy named Eric Custer who claimed that Jack Bronson had brainwashed his boyfriend. The tirade went on for pages and Katelyn skimmed it, hoping that the man might have actually dug up some dirt on Jack.

Finally, quite a ways in, Eric started dishing about what he'd found in his own investigation of Jack Bronson. A couple of disappointed customers. No big surprise there. But there was another surprise: Jack Bronson had mysteriously appeared out of thin air a decade before the man's article. Before that, there had been no record of him.

That was because "Jack Bronson" had changed his name so that people wouldn't know he'd been charged with three assaults. Apparently there was also a string of hunting violations. Katelyn read the section eagerly, hoping there was evidence that would point to him as the current killer.

And then she read a sentence that stopped her cold.

Jack Bronson's birth name is John McBride.

7

Katelyn stared in shock at the name for several seconds before her heart started back up. Jack Bronson's last name was McBride? Her last name? The name etched in the stained glass window on the landing of this very cabin? Her brain shot off in a hundred directions at once, seizing puzzle pieces and trying to fit them together. Her father, shot with a silver bullet. Her mother, knowing. A piece of stolen silver just outside the Inner Wolf Center.

Did Trick know about Jack Bronson? Was that why they'd broken into the Inner Wolf Center instead of coming through the front door?

The name Eric Custer was highlighted in blue letters, signifying a link, but when she clicked on it, she got a 404

Error—no such page. She typed in his name and more links popped up—dozens of them—and she tried some of them. There were all broken. Wearying of the dead ends, she searched for John McBride. As with Eric Custer, there were dozens of John McBride's. Jack Bronson definitely wasn't the John McBride who was married to the country singer Martina McBride. She looked for something, anything that linked the Inner Wolf Jack Bronson to John McBride, and to her grandfather. She found nothing. Maybe Eric Custer had been wrong.

She decided to ask her grandfather about it when he got back, but then she hesitated. If he hadn't told her that he was related to Jack Bronson, he didn't want her to know.

She tapped her fingers on the table and reread the article. Why didn't more people know about this? Or if they did, why didn't they care?

Doggedly she returned to the search, trying keywords— "Inner Wolf," "author," "criminal record"—but nothing else came up. Just the Custer article.

By then it was almost two in the morning.

Frustrated, she dialed and redialed Trick, pacing, swearing at the phone, jumping at every noise. It was hard to believe that back in Los Angeles, she and her then-best friend Kimi had helped Kimi's mother work on the Handgun Control Initiative. They'd been stereotypical peace-loving, tofu-eating California girls who washed cars at fundraisers for People for the Ethical Treatment of Animals. Katelyn hadn't even liked to watch violent movies.

But tonight, she had seriously considered killing someone. *I really wanted to. What have I become?*

She trembled as she walked to the window and looked out. She felt different, as if her human skin was no longer real and her wolf body was what she belonged in. As she scanned the snowy forest, a little part of her was hoping for prey. Were more assassins coming? If she understood pack behavior, what Arial had done was cowardly and underhanded: you were supposed to issue your own challenges, fight your own fights—even if you were the daughter of an alpha.

The former alpha. The crazy, dead alpha. She felt a rush of empathy for him as she remembered the one time she had seen what he might have been. Two Gaudins trespassing on Fenner territory had attacked the two of them in the forest and he had put his own safety on the line, nearly dying rather than letting the enemy werewolves know that they had a gun that shot silver bullets. She couldn't deny that she'd been impressed by his self-sacrificing bravery.

But that was the same alpha who had banished Cordelia and threatened to kill Katelyn and her grandfather every single day since she'd been forced to join the Fenner pack.

"Where are you, Grandpa?" she said aloud. "Trick, damn it, call me." She thought about getting in her Subaru and searching for them; she fantasized for the one-thousandth time about just leaving. If something happened to her grandfather, they would have to let her move in with Kimi and her family. She didn't have any other relatives, not that she knew of, anyway.

Her lips parted. Her entire life, she had assumed that her mother had had a falling out with her family, possibly over marrying an American. No one on the Chevalier side had gotten in touch when either of Katelyn's parents had died. But maybe Giselle Chevalier had been the one to cut off contact. But why?

I need to know what happened to my father.

She moved to another window. Starlight frosted the falling snow; there seemed to be as many snowflakes as there were possible reasons for her father's murder. Like the snowflakes, she couldn't count them all; and she finally turned away and sat back down at the computer.

She jumped at the little trill on her phone as a text came in. It was Justin.

YOU SAFE?

WHERE ARE YOU? she texted back, which wasn't an answer.

He texted back, OUTSIDE YOUR CABIN.

She ran into the kitchen and peered through the curtains, his silhouette was dark against the falling snow. She threw open the cabin door and he was on the threshold, stomping his boots on the boot rack, shaking snow off his shoulders.

Droplets clung to the ends of his dark hair. His blue eyes were stormy, and he looked gaunt and tired. Thick stubble accentuated the hollows of his cheeks. The wolf in her responded to his presence, and she looked away so that he wouldn't see the rising hunger in her expression.

"You shouldn't be here. My grandfather will be back any minute," she said, taking only a couple of steps back as he came inside and shut the door.

"Kat," he said, and he bent down and offered his cheek to her in a werewolf greeting. She still wasn't used to it, but she brushed her lips across the stubble on his face. Then she offered her cheek, and he molded his hand gently against the side of her face while he pressed his mouth to her cheekbone, then slid his lips toward her ear. She caught her breath and gave her head a little shake.

He kept hold of her and whispered, "Let's go upstairs."

To her bedroom, he was saying. She quivered. The wolf in her wanted to obey him.

Wanted him, plain and simple.

"Lucy," she said. It was the magic word that always stopped him when he started coming onto her like this.

Trick.

That was her magic word.

He was quiet for a moment. Then he said, "There are going to be some changes in the pack."

A thrill shot through her. Was the fighting within the pack already over? Had someone been declared alpha?

"Are you—did you win?" she asked.

He gave his head a shake and came close again. "I mean about Lucy. And me."

"Justin, she's your fiancée," she said deliberately.

He looped strands of her blond hair around her ear and studied her face. "You were amazing today. Ferocious. Brave. And you put your life on the line for Doug. Gotta admit, I had my doubts about you. But you're a hell of a werewolf, darlin'. You're going to make…someone…a fine mate."

His pupils dilated and she saw pure desire there. Justin was one of the most important, if not *the* most important, werewolves in the Fenner pack. In terms of pack politics, being Justin Fenner's mate would be like winning the lottery.

"When I'm twenty-seven, maybe, but not at seventeen." Her voice cracked. She was excited and nervous, and she was flooding with guilt. Trick was out there somewhere in the snow, chasing after a killer.. What the heck was *she* doing?

He reached out his hand, and she protectively crossed her arms over her chest.

"Lucy called me out," she reminded him. "She would have killed me. And you just stood there and *watched*."

"Ssh, honey," he murmured, stroking her cheek, like someone trying to gentle a wild animal.

She pulled away and got a glass out of the cabinet, turned on the tap, and filled it. Just as she began to put the rim to her lips, Justin clasped her wrist and forced her to set it down.

"You know that I've broken rule after rule for you," he said. "You don't know how hard it was to do nothing while she beat the crap out of you. The only consolation I had was knowing that no matter how bad it hurt, you'd heal.

"And I also knew that if I moved to help you, Lee would have taken my throat. What help would I have been to you then?"

"That's easy to say *now*." She made a point of lifting the glass. His hand moved, and for an instant she thought he was about to bat the glass out of her hand. She was scared. She was playing with fire. His uncle had nearly ripped the hair from her scalp when she hadn't been submissive enough.

"Remember who you're talking to," he said between clenched teeth. His eyes blazed. She could hear his heartbeat thundering. Feel the tension rising between the two of them.

I never forget. She remained mute. Unsteadily, she took a defiant sip of water.

Justin watched; then he swore under his breath, stomped to the kitchen door, threw it open, and left.

Holding the glass with two hands to keep from spilling it, she moved to the kitchen window, but the snow was coming down too hard to make out Justin as he left. She turned on the tap again and splashed water on her face.

SAVAGE

A wolf howled and she jerked because it sounded like Justin, who shouldn't be able to transform at will.

She made sure the back door was locked and walked back into the living room. She sprawled on the sofa, watching the flames dance in the fireplace. When she had first moved in, she couldn't come near the fire. Her house had burned to the ground, and her mother had been inside it.

"Mom," she murmured, "what really happened to Daddy?"

She lifted the phone to try Trick again, but it slipped from her grasp as her eyes closed. She drifted.

Running.

Leaping.

Attacking.

Blood on your paws, silver girl.

Blood in your mouth.

Mine.

Click, click, click.

Soft pelt sliding across her cheek. Hot breath on the crown of her head.

Click, click, click.

The back door, shutting.

Again.

~

Katelyn jerked awake the next morning to find herself still on the couch. She looked out the front window, fingers crossed that she would see her grandfather's truck parked outside. It wasn't there. She dashed upstairs and knocked on his door. It was locked, and there was no answer.

She ran back downstairs and tried Trick's phone. Nothing. She burst outside, standing on the porch as the sun began to peek through the trees, and caught her breath.

The snow in front of the cabin had been tamped down by dozens of paw prints. Someone—possibly more than several someone's—had come visiting last night.

She shut the door. Realizing that part of the reason she was shaking was from sheer hunger, she made herself a salami and cheese sandwich, not caring that digging into the meat might bring questions later.

She showered, brushed her teeth, and changed into clean clothes. Then she got her gun and her backpack, cocked the trigger, and dashed to her car. Leaping in, she peeled out, heading for school. Once she was on her way, she pulled over and called the police station. But there was no coverage. She connected her phone to the charger in the car and drove like a demon.

Trick wasn't at school. There were signs up in memory of Mike Wright, as there had been for Becky and Haley, the two girls who had been killed in the woods. No one had liked Mike.

She saw Beau in the hall and ran up to him. His father had been among the hunters in the cabin's front room, and when Beau saw her, he paled and shook his head.

"My dad hasn't checked in," he said by way of greeting.

"Where could they be? Shouldn't someone be notified?" she asked, her voice shrill and anxious. "Like the FBI or something?"

His worried expression softened. "Kat, these are the hills. Things like that don't happen here."

"But other things do happen. Are happening," she argued. She thought about calling Detective Cranston. Doing *something*. But just as quickly, she realized that she couldn't. The first law for werewolves everywhere was to protect the secret of the existence of werewolves. Breaking that law brought instant death. But surely some people in Wolf Springs *knew*.

Everyone at school was distracted and anxious. Katelyn spent most of the day trying to reach Trick, and as soon as the last bell rang, she drove straight to his family's place—a former dairy; she supposed you called it an estate—and found no one home. His parents traveled almost constantly, and they usually left Trick to manage things.

Trick had his own little house on the property. The door was locked and she thought about breaking in. Enough was enough. She didn't care if she pissed him off. He was her grandfather's godson; maybe he knew the truth about her family. Now was the perfect time to find out.

She had a werewolf's strength and she turned the knob on his door too hard, breaking it. She didn't care. She went inside and flicked on the lights, instantly enveloped by a cloud of scent—Trick's shampoo and soap, leather and cotton, his oil paints and clay. Books were piled in towers on the coffee table in front of his movie projector, and a sketchpad lay on the couch along with a plaid throw and a pillow. Behind the black curtain that divided the large room, she crossed to the table that he used for sculpting, and saw a new piece he was working on—emerging from the hunks of gray was a bust of her. Her long neck, her hair, her eyes, a smile—her throat tightened as she stared at it. She looked pretty. No, beautiful—more striking than she was. Idealized.

He loved her.

"Trick," she whispered, touching the clay, running her fingers over his sculpting tools. Amazed that he was a boy just a little older than she, who could do art and speak Russian and make movies and move like a trained dancer, and drove recklessly and had gone out in the snow with a posse to track a killer.

Who knew how to use a gun. How to take down something that had once been alive.

We have that in common, she thought.

She crossed to his bed and lay down on it, resting in the indentation his body had left, pulling the sheets up to her chin. It was as if he were lying on top of her. She rolled onto her side and buried her face in the pillow, imagining his chest against her forehead, the bridge of her nose, her lips.

She didn't know how long she lay in Trick's bed. She didn't want to leave, ever.

But that was a luxury she couldn't afford. How many times had the Fenners threatened to kill everyone she loved?

As many as there had been paw prints in the snow.

And she realized then and there that she loved her grandfather, even though she didn't know if he had killed her father. Her life was a tangle; she was overwhelmed with the chaos of her own emotions and she lay still, while her mind and heart battled for dominance. She could want Trick for the rest of her life. Nothing had to prevent her. She could be happy that she knew what it meant to love him even if she couldn't be with him.

Even if Justin chose her for his mate?

No, she thought, but the wolf in her howled with triumph.

She flung herself out of Trick's bed and went to the door. Then she got in her car and drove, tempted to pull to the side and compose herself, except that she knew no good ever came of stopping in the woods above Wolf Springs. It was cursed land, and it had cursed her. So she drove, wondering if she would ever see her grandfather or Trick again.

~

It was dark by the time she made the last turn before the cabin. When she saw the porch light shining on her grandfather's parked truck, she blinked hard, making sure it was really there. Then she pulled up behind it and scrambled out, charging up the stairs and, finding the front door locked, pounded on the door with both her fists. Her keys were in her hand, but she was too frantic to try and use them.

"Grandpa! Grandpa!" she shouted.

The door yanked open and he stood with his rifle to his shoulder. She screamed and he immediately lowered the weapon.

"I thought—" he began, and she flung her arms around him. He staggered backwards, then righted himself and shut the door behind her.

"I was so worried," she said. "What happened? Where's Trick? Is he all right?"

He eased her away from himself, and she was shocked by his appearance. He seemed to have aged a decade since she'd last seen him. His eyes were bloodshot and there were dark rings under his eyes. He looked like someone who had been locked up in a prison cell for years.

"He's okay. No one got hurt. The snow came and we hunkered down, waited for it to pass."

As she listened, she texted Trick. He didn't reply. She punched in his name and put the phone to her ear. "Did you find anything?" she asked her grandfather.

"No. I don't know what we thought we would find, anyway," he replied, sounding irritable and exhausted. "Bunch of damned fools. That's what we are."

SAVAGE

"I wish you'd called me," she said. Trick didn't answer. She figured he was out of cell reception range. "I've been so worried." She hugged him again, and he cocked his head as he patted her shoulder a bit awkwardly in return. They hadn't found a comfortable place with each other yet. She wasn't sure they ever would. Now that she knew he was safe, her wariness of him reasserted itself.

"You really were worried," he said in a low voice.

"I really was. Did you camp in the snow? Where did you go? Did you see anything?"

He led the way into the kitchen. "I'm cooking up some soup. There's enough for two. And yes. We camped in the snow. Trick complained all night." He chuckled and shook his head. "You want grilled cheese, too?"

"Sure," she said. "I'll make it. You sit down. I was so, so worried." She went to the stove and stirred the soup.

"You really were."

She looked at him. He'd been through so much. He looked exhausted. But he said, "You play poker?"

"No."

"Good. Then I can fleece ya." He gave her a wink and disappeared into the living room. He came back out with a big plastic wheel of brightly colored poker chips and a double set of playing cards. He set them on the kitchen table and she lifted an eyebrow.

"Aren't you too tired?" she asked him.

He took the lid off the box of cards and gathered the two decks together. He shuffled them with the finesse of a seasoned cardshark. "I had a lot of time to think up there," he said. "About things that matter."

"Poker," she said, but she knew he meant her.

He pulled out a stack of white poker chips. "We'll start with a thousand bucks. Cheese is in the fridge," he added.

"Right. Sorry. You must be starving." She tried Trick again. Still no luck. Her mouth watered as she bypassed the salami and got out the block of cheddar cheese. "Mom hardly ever bought cheese, except for that six-cheese macaroni she used to make." She stopped talking. The last time Giselle had made that dish had been the night Katelyn's father had been murdered.

"Your mama had some odd notions about food," her grandfather said as he pulled out a stack of blue plastic discs. "These are worth the most. It goes blue, red, white. Got that?" He began dividing them into two stacks.

She had so many questions. She wanted to talk about John McBride. And her father. And all the silver bullets. But she wanted this moment even more. She might have lost him.

He stopped as she tried Trick again.

"He's probably asleep," her grandfather said.

"Oh." It seemed odd that he wouldn't call her right away. Maybe that was the reason. She began to slice the cheese. "I was kind of hoping he'd come home with you."

"His folks wanted to see him," her grandfather said, and she thought a moment. When she'd broken into Trick's room, the rest of the property had seemed deserted. She pictured Trick home alone, wondering who had broken into his little house, and felt a twinge of guilt. The last thing she had wanted to do was freak him out.

"You get by okay without your grandpa around?" he asked her, stirring her from her reverie. His tone was deliberately casual, but she detected the uncertainty.

"Of course not. I forgot how to drive my car and I starved to death." She smiled gently at him and turned on another burner on the stove. She set a small frying pan on the burner. "But I missed you. It scared me when you all went out like that."

"Scared me too, danged fools. Half of 'em would shoot their own shadow if they could get it to hold still long enough."

She smiled. "They didn't have you to teach them."

"Katie..." He searched her face. Then something changed in his eyes, and he turned away from her. "After the blue ones, the reds are the ones you want."

"Got it." She buttered two slices of bread and put them face down in the frying pan. She covered them with pieces of cheese.

He began to deal the cards. A text message came in, but it was from Justin, not Trick. It said, HUNTERS R BACK?

Why bother asking? He already knew the answer. She finished making the sandwiches and flipped them.

"Hands are dealt," he said. "I'm going to wash up."

She heard him go down the hall to the bathroom. A call came in on her phone. Jumping, she took it,

"Katelyn, it's me," Cordelia said. "Are you all right?"

"So far," Katelyn replied, realizing that sounded cryptic. "I'm fine. How are you?"

"Dom found me. He was slashed in the fighting but he's going to be okay." She lowered her voice. "What happened with Magus?"

"He told me more about their history. He'd been to your house, Cordelia. Your grandfather attacked his great-aunt. Did you know that?"

"*What?*"

"Yes. She wasn't a werewolf yet," she began, then realized what she was saying. It was against pack laws to attack humans. "Listen," she began, as she heard the door to the bathroom opening, "

"My grandfather did *not* attack humans," Cordelia interrupted. "Ever."

"Okay, okay," Katelyn said. "But there was another mauling tonight."

"Oh, God. They can't find out about us. Or about the mine. My daddy said it's got piles of silver bullets. Silver knives."

Like the silver knife her grandfather had.

"We have to find it first," Cordelia went on. "You have to find it. Then no Fenner will dare lay a hand on you." She exhaled. "Or on *me*."

"We could make the peace happen," Katelyn said hopefully. "Us two."

"We'd definitely have a shot at it," Cordelia agreed. "Promise to keep looking?"

"I do." Her grandfather walked into the room. "So, yeah, they're all back and safe," she said into the phone. "Bye, Beau." She disconnected. "School friend," she told her grandfather.

He raised his brows and nodded at the stove. "Sandwiches are burning."

She whirled around. A column of smoke was wafting from the pan. She groaned and lifted it off the fire.

He walked up beside her with a fork and inspected the underside. "It's just a little singed," he said. He looked at her. "Everything all right?"

Katelyn nodded, but she was replaying her conversation in her head. She realized she hadn't told Cordelia about Wanda Mae. But she also realized she'd had no plans to. Everyone in Wolf Springs had secrets. Maybe that was the nature of life. The secret of surviving in this world, or any world. There were things you could never tell anybody. You just had to find out what they were.

"Everything is fine," she told her grandfather.

You had to keep secrets, and you had to lie.

~

Trick didn't show up at school until Wednesday. Katelyn spotted him climbing out of his Mustang in the school parking lot and rushed over to him. He looked worse than her grandfather, his green eyes flat and lifeless, his cheeks hollow.

"Trick, what's wrong? Why haven't you called me?" she asked.

He looked at her hard. She blinked, waiting for his answer.

"I was sick," he said. "I lost my phone."

All the blood in her body crept up her neck and spread to her cheeks in a hot, angry flush.

"Are you kidding?" she said, as they faced one another beside the open door of his Mustang. "You can lie better than that. You could have reached me if you'd wanted to."

He remained silent, and she was stung. Deeply hurt, she took a step away from him, and he didn't make a move to close up the space. He bit his lip as if he were considering what to say to her, then gave his head a little shake and closed the door of his car.

"What is going on?" Then a light went on. "Hey, so, I was the one who broke into your room. I'm sorry. I was so worried."

"Okay."

"*Okay? Just 'okay'?*" She reached out a hand. He visibly stiffened, and she pulled it back. "What happened out there? What's wrong with you?"

He started to speak. Then he grimaced and shook his head. Shadows ringed his eyes and he balled his fists as if just standing there with her was a monumental effort. She stood her ground, waiting for an answer.

Finally he said, "Katelyn, please, just trust me."

He was scaring her. "Trust you how? To do what? And I guess with the way you're acting, the better question is why? Why should I trust you?"

"Because you have to trust somebody. And it sure the hell better not be Justin Fenner."

She went cold. *He doesn't know,* she told herself. *He's just jealous of Justin in a guy way.*

Trick brushed past her and headed for the entrance of their gingerbread-house school. In shock, Katelyn watched him walk away.

She whispered at his back, "Please trust me too."

~

The snow bucketed for the next hour, drifts piling against the doors so fast that teachers took up shovels to keep them clear. Kids began to chat eagerly about snow days and a cheer rose up when classes ended early so they wouldn't be stuck there overnight. Katelyn tromped with the others to her car, her friend Paulette giving her a tutorial in how to rock it free of the snow as Katelyn looked everywhere for Trick.

"Good thing you have four-wheel-drive," Paulette said.

Katelyn paid her scant attention. Around them, students were checking the chains on their tires and making plans to get together. She lingered, hoping for one more shot at talking to Trick, *really* talking, but there was no sign of him Snow began to pile on his Mustang, and she gave it up. As she climbed behind the wheel Justin called and told her the snow was a good thing, giving her another reason to steer clear of the pack.

"Folks have been asking after you," he said. "Where you stand. If you want to issue a challenge. Come full moon, decisions will be made. And you and I need to talk way before then."

"Okay," she said vaguely, scanning the lot one more time for Trick as the last trickle of kids emerged from the school. "Wait. What?"

"Be ready," Justin said, and then he hung up.

She scowled through the windshield and turned on her wipers. They did nothing to clear away the icy buildup. She got out, shin-deep in the snow, and used her scraper. She winced at the grating sound and got back in. Her grandfather called and she assured him that she would hurry as fast as she could.

She joined the exodus out of the school lot. Trick's car was still there. She reminded herself that Trick had always kept secrets from her, and that he was unpredictable. She shouldn't be disappointed that he was staying true to form. Cordelia had warned her to steer clear of him from the beginning. But she thought they'd reached a place where it was different between the two of them. Where Trick let her in.

But I can't let him in, she thought. *I've just been kidding myself. It would never work.*

Wolf Springs was barely visible out her windows. She reached the forest and drove slowly. There was so much snow that it reminded her of a tide washing over her. The world was white. She didn't know how she would ever get home.

She inched along until yellow beams pointed straight at her, then blinked. She stopped the car, barely able to make out the shape of a truck, someone getting out of it and walking toward her.

Katelyn reached under her seat for her gun and put her hand around it. When there was a knock on her window, she realized she couldn't unroll it and cracked open the door instead.

"Katie, it's me," said her grandfather. "I've come to get you. We can leave your car here."

She was touched beyond words. After having been utterly ignored by Trick, she appreciated the sweetness of his gesture even more.

But if she took him up on it, she would be stuck at the cabin without her own transportation. She smiled at him and said, "Thank you so much, Grandpa. This is so sweet. I'll follow you. Okay? I can do it."

It was obviously too cold to argue with her. He got back in his truck and drove slowly. She kept his taillights in her view and together they made the tortuous drive back to the cabin. She was exhausted by the time they went inside, to find the fireplace blazing and lanterns and candles flickering everywhere.

"Power's out," he said. "I've got the generator going, but we've got to conserve. Blizzard's coming."

"Coming?" she echoed. "It's not here?"

"Nope," he replied, and he smiled at her. Actually smiled. "Just you wait."

She did wait. All night she listened to the banshee howling of the wind, and the fierce pounding of the snow on the roof. Her grandfather had covered her skylight with a storm window and she huddled in her room, staring at the NO SERVICE message on her phone. They were cut off. Isolated.

"Snowed in," her grandfather announced in the morning, inexplicably pleased.

"How long?" she asked, trying to keep the tremor out of her voice.

"Could be a couple of days. Could be a couple of weeks."

Trapped, maybe even until the full moon. Katelyn clutched her phone.

NO SERVICE.

SAVAGE

And the walls closed in.

8

"So, how about some hot chocolate and some board games to kick this winter off right?" her grandfather asked cheerfully.

"How can you be so happy?" she asked. "This is…" She trailed off as his shy smile broadened.

"I've never much minded being snowed in. It's a beautiful time of the year. But, I have to admit this year it's special. I've got someone other than myself to share it with."

He wasn't joking. His eyes were twinkling. He was positively grinning. Part of her began to respond.

Maybe it wouldn't be so bad. And if it was only a couple of days then everything would be okay. "Yes to the board games and an even bigger yes to the cocoa," she said and was rewarded by an even bigger grin from Ed.

Grandpa, she reminded herself.

He trounced her in Monopoly in what had to be the fastest game in recorded history. When they switched to Scrabble she struggled to hold her own, and surprised even him with how inventive she got with some of her words. By the time they moved on to Trivial Pursuit they were evenly matched and she found that she was really starting to have fun.

Doubts and fears about him, the storm, even herself slowly began to fade away as they chatted and played. Still, part of her knew that she should use the time to get information out of him. She was hesitant to do so, though, because they were both having a good day and who knew how long they were going to be stuck together?

"Penny for your thoughts," he said. Then, more softly, "Missing your mom?"

"Missing them both," she replied.

"Your dad was a good man, focused, and dedicated. Stubborn to a fault. Once he set his mind on something, there was no dissuading him."

"That I do remember," Katelyn said, feeling a bit wistful. "I remember I got this swing set for Christmas. I was like three, and it had like a million pieces, and Mom kept telling him that we could wait and get the handyman who lived on our block to put it together. But he just kept insisting he could do it himself. It took all day, Christmas dinner got cold, and Mom was furious with him. Then he worked all night on it, but he finally got it done."

Her grandfather chuckled. "I remember. I was there."

"You were?" She didn't remember him, and low-grade anxiety played across her shoulder blades. It was too late to keep her grandfather out of her father's life. It was done.

"Yup. Who do you think gave you the swing set?"

"You? Oh, thank you! Thank you so much. I played on those monkey bars constantly. It helped give me my first taste of gymnastics." She put her hand around her cocoa mug, letting the warmth penetrate her bones. "You started my dream of joining the Cirque du Soleil."

"Well, you're welcome," he said with a grunt as he straightened up the stack of Trivial Pursuit cards. "But you want to hear a secret?"

"Sure."

"Your parents had suggested a much smaller swing set, one without all the monkey bars and everything."

"And you got me the big one? That's so awesome! How come?"

"I knew you'd love it, of course, but, to be honest, I wanted to watch him put that thing together. I never laughed so hard in my life as when he put half of it up backward and had to start over."

"Grandpa!" she cried, batting at his hand. He yanked it out of her reach.

"Yup, your dad was like a dog with a bone when he got his teeth into something. He just wouldn't let go for love or money."

He took a sip of cocoa and more walls crumbled. It was a flash of humor that she rarely got to see. Plus, she owed her own dreams to him, even if it had all started out as a prank on her father.

"I used to embarrass the heck out of him," he added. "He traipsed off to the big city to go to college and I'd show up in Los Angeles and put on my best Ozarks accent. His hick daddy, as backwoods as they come. He wouldn't be able to convince any of his frat brothers that I had a PhD until he showed them proof in black and white. When he met your mama, he told me he'd pay me twenty bucks to speak like a normal human being around her."

He guffawed and she grinned at him. Shadows of memories darkened her own mood; she wanted to talk about the night her father died. But she couldn't make herself bring up anything that might hurt either of them. Trick was right; her grandfather was her only family. The phones were out, and it was just the two of them. It was a good time. She wanted to cherish it while she could.

~

The second day brought back a twinge of concern as the storm continued to rage. The silent snow fell in cascades. She'd never lived in the cold before, and had always pictured snow as soft, fluffy whipped cream. But it was wet and cold and heavy. They played more games and drank more cocoa and she tried to shut out her fears, but they kept gnawing at her. They played more board games and talked about going somewhere on her spring break. She knew she would have to check in with Justin and the pack, and see when the full moon would rise. Her grandfather noticed her seeming lack of enthusiasm.

"Katie? Is something wrong?" he asked.

It was the perfect moment to ask him some questions.

"Grandpa," she said, and then she exhaled and shook her head. She couldn't bear to ruin the moment. "I'm good."

"The snow will melt," he said, patting her. "And we have lots of food. We're fine. We're safe."

"I know," she said.

By the third day, anxiety had taken firm hold. When it stopped snowing mid-afternoon, she struggled to hide her hope that that meant that soon life could return to normal.

On the fourth morning her grandfather came inside after stamping his feet on the porch. He didn't look pleased.

"How does it look out there?" she asked, holding her breath for the answer.

"The snow's melting. You'll probably be able to drive fine by tomorrow," he said.

Mingled with her relief was a flash of sorrow. As worried as she'd been, this had been the most fun she'd had with him since she was a little girl. The more time they spent together, the more she caught fleeting memories of being with him when she was young. There was a trip where he had come out to visit them when she was five and they had all gone to Disneyland together. He'd held her hand when they'd gone down the waterfall in the Pirates of the Caribbean and she hadn't been afraid of the pirates because she knew her grandfather could kill them all singlehandedly.

Who knew, maybe he could have. But no one was living in a fantasy world these days. The world was stranger and crueler than she could have imagined.

And the sweet space of time where they had been like a normal grandfather and granddaughter was melting like the snow. It was time to return to that more brutal world.

To ask him what he knew about the night her father had died.

Her mind cast back, remembering. Her dad had been late coming home, and he'd been coming home progressively later for a long time. He'd said he was working on something big, something important.

Her mom always set a place for him every night at the table anyway. "Just in case," she said every time Katelyn asked her why.

But not that night. That night when Katelyn had gotten home from her gymnastics practice there had only been two places set at the table. Her mom had made her own version of mac and cheese, a delicacy because she hardly ever served cheese. She'd made Katelyn's favorite dessert, chocolate soufflé, as well.

Her mom's eyes had been puffy, like she'd been crying, but she'd said she'd been dicing some onions for dinner. And Katelyn had believed her even though there were no onions in mac and cheese.

But Katelyn hadn't questioned. She'd been so thrilled to be able to have the things she loved. She hadn't questioned her mom's red eyes, or the lack of a third place setting, or the meal.

Then, late that night, the doorbell had rung, and she had gotten out of bed because it was one in the morning and who came by the house that late? She had peered through the banister railings, watching as her mom opened the front door.

Her mom wasn't in her pajamas. She was dressed like she'd never gone to bed, like she'd been expecting someone to come by the house. Two police officers had come by. One of them had been Detective Cranston.

They had said something to her mother, so softly that Katelyn couldn't hear. Then Giselle Chevalier, the great ballerina, the most graceful woman in the world, had fallen on the floor and began to sob.

Katelyn remembered creeping down the stairs, terrified, but her mother wouldn't even look at her, wouldn't touch her. Detective Cranston had taken her into the kitchen, found the rest of the chocolate soufflé in the refrigerator, and had given it to her while he'd told her that a bad man had shot her dad.

Could it be *this* man?

In the cabin, the landline rang. Katelyn jumped. She hadn't realized the phone was working again.

Her grandfather raised his eyebrows in mild surprise. "It's gotta be for you. Not many folks call me."

She sprang up from the couch and ran into the kitchen to get the phone. Her heart beat a little faster. Maybe it was Trick or Justin.

Preferably Trick.

"Hello?" she asked somewhat breathlessly.

There was a pause and then a familiar voice said, "This is Sergeant Lewis. Can you put your grandpappy on?"

"Oh, sure." She covered the mouthpiece. "Grandpa, it's Sergeant Lewis for you," she called.

A moment later his frame darkened the doorway. Jekyll and Hyde: he was scowling, a different man than the one who had been teasing her just a minute before.

He took the phone from her and she retreated a couple of steps, but didn't leave the room. She could hear both sides of the conversation clearly.

"What can I do for you, Pat?" her grandfather asked.

"There's been another one."

Her grandfather glanced at her, but she refused to move.

"Who is it?" he asked.

"Wanda Mae Peterson."

Katelyn gasped and her grandfather's eyes narrowed as he studied her face. She turned away, struggling to compose herself, straining to hear the rest of the conversation.

Wanda Mae, the werewolf assassin Arial had sent who had sworn allegiance to Katelyn. She was dead. Katelyn's head swam. First Mike and now Wanda. Both had attacked her. She had beaten both of them. Now both were dead. Could that possibly be a coincidence? The twisting in her gut said definitely not.

"Is that the retired librarian?" her grandfather asked.

Librarian? She stiffened. Could Wanda Mae have been helping Lee Fenner find books dealing with the mine, like the Switliski book? "That's the one. Something different about this, though." He paused. "She was found in the woods all right, but she was naked."

"Beg pardon?" her grandfather asked.

"Not wearing a stitch. And she'd been pretty slashed up. Whatever killed her took a few chunks out of her, too. As in, ate."

Cannibalism. Wouldn't that be what it was if one werewolf ate another? Katelyn's stomach roiled more fiercely. Or maybe it was the Hellhound who had gotten to Wanda Mae. After all, if she had known something about the silver mine, maybe she had gotten too close to discovering it.

I lost my ally. Whoever had killed her, whether it had been because of Katelyn or the mine, the woman was gone.

"Another posse is forming up. They found tracks in the snow leading away from the body. Something big. Jed Crane's bringing his hunting dogs along for this one. Those hounds have never quit a trail."

"I don't think that's such a good idea," her grandfather said, his voice tight. She blinked. He almost sounded angry.

"Jack Bronson's even called in to volunteer."

"No!"

She definitely wasn't imaging the anger this time.

"You leave that man out of it and I'll come. I won't be in any hunting group with that idiot."

"You got it, Mordecai. Rather have you than that city boy. We're going to meet at the old Miller dry creek."

"I'll be there as soon as I can."

Her grandfather hung up; he crossed the kitchen and clamped a hand down on her shoulder, turning her to face him.

"So you heard," he said, and she nodded, not bothering to deny it. "How do you know Wanda Mae?" His tone, instead of being sympathetic, was harsh, suspicious.

"I-I don't," she lied. "But there's a guy at school with the same last name. Maybe they're related."

She had no idea if there was a guy with that last name at school.. She hoped her grandfather didn't check.

"Oh," he said, after a moment. "Grandson, maybe."

"Poor guy," she muttered, feeling disingenuous.

"I got to go. Hunting party's forming up," he said as he moved toward the living room.

"*Why* do you have to go?" she asked him.

He pursed his lips. "Honey, a lot of the people who will come are from town. They've lived their entire lives on the edge of the woods but not in them. They're good marksmen, good people, but they don't know the forest like I do. And with everyone so jumpy about everything that's going on, they need someone with them like me so that no one accidentally gets hurt."

"Why do you hate Jack Bronson so much?" she asked, pushing it.

His back was to her—his back that was covered with scars. "I've told you, the man's a damned fool."

He pulled his rifle down from the wall, cracking it open, checking it. Not looking at her. She just couldn't let it go.

"I don't think you're telling me everything."

"Katie, I don't have time for this right now. Look, the man's a moron. That's all there is."

He moved to a cabinet in the family room, opened it, and she heard the sound of a creaking lid, like on an old box, and then rattling, like bullets being jostled together. She blinked. She hadn't known he kept bullets in there.

"How come you never told me that his last name is McBride?"

He swore and she heard a couple of the bullets hit the floor and roll. She walked into the room just as he was scooping them up.

He straightened slowly, slipping the bullets into his pocket. He sighed, a deep, bone-weary surrender. She could see in his eyes that he wanted to lie to her. For a moment she thought he was going to.

"Where on earth did you hear that?" he asked.

"I read about it online, how he changed his name. That he had a past."

Her grandfather swore again. "He turned his back on his family a long time before he changed his name. I didn't tell you because it wasn't important. He's no kin of ours." He said the last in a dark, vehement tone that left no doubt exactly how he felt.

He walked past her and she cast her gaze down to avoid looking at him head on. There, on the ground, halfway under the couch, was one of the bullets he had dropped.

"You forgot one," she said, bending to pick it up before she could think.

And as her fingers closed around it she could smell the stench of silver even as her skin tingled. She froze for a moment. A silver bullet. He had them in the house, too, and she hadn't known it. He was taking them with him now, which meant he must know he was going after a werewolf.

Her mouth went completely try. She had to do something, say something. She couldn't just stay bent over indefinitely. Slowly, she straightened and looked at him.

She held out the bullet. As if in slow motion, he reached out to take it from her, their fingers touching on the silvery metal. He pulled away, tucked the bullet in his pocket.

"What are you?" she whispered.

The words had just slipped out and hung in the air between them, fraught with meaning. She sucked in her breath hard. She hadn't meant to say that, hadn't meant to give voice to one of the many questions that had been plaguing her.

He had stopped, his whole body gone very, very still, and she knew that he understood what she was asking.

He took a ragged breath and looked her straight in the eyes. "I know that you can't live here, especially not with all that's been going on, without hearing things, rumors." Something flickered in his eyes. "I am your grandfather. And I pray to God that's all you ever need to know."

He turned abruptly and strode out the door, closing it firmly behind him. Katelyn sank down on the couch, staring into space.

"What just happened?" she whispered.

Seconds later, she heard his truck start up and drive away from the cabin.

Had her grandfather really just admitted to something? . The very fact that he had gotten out silver bullets was proof.

The bullets did belong to him and not his friend who had died. And the only thing you needed silver bullets for was werewolves.

She shuddered.

Her grandfather was hunting werewolves.

She had to call Justin, to warn him. The pack had to stay hidden, safe.

Her cell still wasn't getting reception. She ran over to the kitchen phone and dialed Justin's number. It went straight to voicemail. She took a deep breath and redialed. This time she left a message.

"My grandfather just left. There was another person killed. It was…" she hesitated, still not sure what to reveal, "some woman named Wanda," she said at last. "There's a bunch of people going out hunting. I wanted you to know."

She hung up and waited fifteen minutes, hoping he'd call back. He didn't, so she tried him again but it still went to voicemail. Cell reception was nil. Maybe he wouldn't even get the message.

I should let my grandfather kill them, she thought. But she couldn't do it. Whether it was pack instinct or just being moral, decent, she had to intervene.

Decision made, she grabbed her keys and put her new gun and lots of bullets in her backpack. Then she locked the cabin and climbed into her Subaru. She didn't know how deep the snow was on the roads, but she had to try to get to the

Fenners'. The snow was melting, but it still covered the roads, and she forced herself to drive slowly and carefully even though it felt that each second was a year.

The woods were dark and deep; and just as she finally reached the turnoff for the Fenners' house, she hit her brakes with a shout.

An impossibly tall man stood, seemingly immovable, in the center of the driveway as she practically plowed in to him. He was dressed in a robe identical to the one that Magus had been wearing, and the bumper of her car stopped mere inches from his body. Slack jawed, she gaped at him; he had to be over seven feet tall, built for basketball, but she'd be willing to bet money from the look of him that he'd never played a game such as that in his life.

He was tattooed all over his face, like Magus, with crosses over his high, pronounced cheekbones and gaunt cheeks. His abnormally large eyes were black and she couldn't detect pupil from iris. A shock of white hair swept his high forehead, which seemed out of keeping for a face as young as his.

She waited for him to move out of the way, but he didn't budge, just stared at her through the windshield. He had to be another one of the Hounds of God.

She debated what to do. Part of her wanted to throw the car in reverse and get the heck out of there. Another part wanted to stomp on the gas and run him over. The logical part of her triumphed and instead she opened the door and stepped out to face him.

"I'm Katelyn McBride," she said, not sure why she needed to announce herself so clearly.

"I know who you are Ms. McBride," he said, his voice deep as an ocean. "I'm Daniel Latgale. I'm the alpha of the Hounds of God."

And she understood in that moment everything that an alpha could, *should* be. She had an intense, implacable urge to lower her head. Because she wanted to do it so badly, instead she forced herself to stay upright, head straight forward, looking him squarely in the eye.

He stared back at her, unblinking, and she again had the urge to show submissiveness. It was more than just his imposing height. There was a presence about him that felt regal. He was someone who commanded respect and was so used to it he didn't even stop to think about it.

"Aren't you going to lecture me for being disrespectful?" she asked when he remained silent.

"There's no lack of respect when one alpha doesn't bow to another," he said slowly.

She blinked. "I'm not an alpha."

He shrugged one shoulder. "You are. You just don't know it yet."

She didn't have a response to that.

"Why are you here?" she asked.

"To remind you that you must act swiftly to end this conflict before it goes any further. More have died and there's been another Hellhound attack already."

Wanda Mae. That had to be who he was talking about.

"Cordelia and I want to end this. We're trying."

"That's not enough. There's been too much blood, and there will be more. With no Fenner alpha in place, things will only become worse."

He took a deep breath and it was if all the oxygen had left the air around her. She swallowed. Her mind was just playing a trick on her.

"We're still willing to offer you sanctuary. One way or another this war *will* end. You don't have to die with the others."

The certainty in his eyes chilled her. She had seen fanatics back home—religious guys on street corners, people a little too into the redwoods and keeping the beaches clean. But Daniel Latgale had them beat—his brand of intensity held more menace.

"I understand you, I really do. But I can't. I can't leave my grandfather alone," she said. It had been the excuse she had given Magus and she was sticking to it. Besides, despite everything, she couldn't leave him alone. If he knew that werewolves existed, odds were good he would wind up on a werewolf hit list to keep him from revealing the truth. She couldn't let that happen.

She did understand Daniel's point of view, too. What the Fenners and the Gaudins were doing was dangerous, destructive, wasteful. They risked all their lives because they couldn't end their longstanding hatred and mistrust of each other. It was childish and unfair of them. Lee and Dom. They should have been able to put aside their own feelings and make peace for the good of their packs. That's what alphas did, took care of their own.

So it fell to her and Cordelia to straighten out their mess. But the Hounds of God were impatient. "We don't bring outsiders into our pack," Daniel said gravely. "But we'd be willing to make an exception, just this once."

"Exception," she said carefully.

"You're special, Katelyn McBride. Worth the risk."

She was so tired of being that kind of special. But neither was she stupid enough to burn her bridges. Options were the only things she couldn't afford to run out of.

"I have to talk with my grandfather first. He doesn't know what I am, about any of this," she lied.

Whatever happened, she needed Daniel and the other werewolves to keep on believing that Mordecai McBride was in the dark when it came to their kind.

He nodded, agreeing far more easily than she had expected. He reached inside his robe and pulled out a card, which he handed to her. There was a phone number printed on it and nothing else.

"Call when you've decided. We'll be able to pick you up within an hour."

A chill rippled up her arm as his fingers brushed hers. An hour meant they were definitely sticking around, probably gearing up to take the others out.

"Okay."

He locked his gaze on her; something about his eyes pushed down hard on her diaphragm. She couldn't take a breath.

"If you are coming to us, call quickly. You have three nights. Then it'll be too late."

9

All Katelyn could do was nod in mute shock as Daniel disappeared into the forest. Three nights. Why such a short time? It was impossible.

Maybe they want it to be impossible. They need to justify exterminating two packs to someone else, but they had to give us a chance.

She stared down the Fenners' drive. She was almost certain no one was at home.

Maybe they had caught wind of the hunters and gone into hiding. Justin had sent Lucy and Jesse away to some cabin. She had no idea where it was—possibly out in the wilderness like the warming hut Dom and his brother had forcibly removed Cordelia from.

In any case, it was useless to look for them. She decided to switch her priorities to the mine.

And to do that, she needed to find the painting that had been stolen from their house. And since it hadn't been found with her grandmother's silver in the bog, that left one other place someone had taken the silver:

She was going to break into the Inner Wolf Center again.

Katelyn put the car in reverse and headed out

Trees and darkness; the woods had frightened her when she'd first moved here; now they terrified and enthralled her. But they stayed dark: her werewolf senses had not kicked in in a long time, and she wondered if Daniel Latgale would still think she was an alpha if he knew that.

A little over an hour later, Katelyn rolled up to the chain link fence where she and Trick had parked on their first trip to investigate the center. It was eerily quiet.

There were two sections, the modern, new area, which fronted the ruins of the old spa buildings. Rather than bother with tearing the ramshackle structures down, they had simply been declared off-limits. That was how she and Trick had snuck in before—a trip cut short by the arrival of a ferocious German shepherd guard dog.

The fences and berms were crusted with snow, which hadn't startled to melt in this part of Wolf Springs. She wondered if the attendees at the retreat were resting up in their rooms for a big night of howling.

SAVAGE

She got out of her car and gingerly picked up her backpack. The bullets clinked against the gun.

She shut the car door quietly. She had to do this as quickly as possible. It wasn't good to be out like this. And she didn't want her grandfather to return to an empty cabin. Given how long the last hunting party had taken she probably didn't have to worry about that. But there was plenty more to worry about.

Briskly, she moved over to the fence. She scanned the ground to see if there were other pieces of silver. There were none. Next she inspected the fence. There was the hole Trick had cut, but the fabric from his shirt was gone.

She didn't step through the opening, because no way was she going back into that decrepit, terrifying ruin. If nothing else, she wanted to steer as clear as possible from the German shepherd if it was on patrol.

She returned to the patch of ground where she had originally found the knife. Her grandfather had said that only half the silver service had been recovered, so that left a lot of pieces to be found.

All she saw in the snow were scattered leaves and stones, and the shattered fragments of an amber-colored beer bottle.

Then something glistened, and she honed in on it as if it were prey: another piece of silver.

She picked it up. It was a large spoon, nearly black, with the same pattern peeking from the brown filmy residue. She put it in her jacket pocket. Walking slowly, she stayed parallel to the fence, glancing up as another ramshackle structure came into view. It wasn't as tall as the other one, but it was topped by a tower, and in it, something seemed to be sitting hunched over. Slumped over.

A body, she thought fearfully, taking a step backwards. But she didn't know if that was what it was. And why would anyone stuff a body into a tower?

Why does anyone do anything in Wolf Springs?

She moved to the right, trying to make out the shape as the sunshine fell on it. And her foot came down on another piece of silver. It looked like some kind of skewer.

It looked like it could do some damage.

She picked it up but didn't pocket it. Instead she held it like a weapon or a magic wand. If only she could wave it, and make all this go away.

She climbed up a rise, keeping the fence in view, skirting around a tree. Nervously, she glanced up, recalling the story of Hangman Jack that she had read in a book of Ozark legends: the thief who hid in the trees and dropped nooses to hang unsuspecting passerby.

Another piece of flatware. A fork this time. It was the filthiest piece yet. Grimacing, she put it with the others, and considered starting a collection in her backpack.

Then she looked up to check on the shape in the tower again. What had seemed like a body was an old bell. Her gaze moved and she saw a break in the hillside, a black circle; as she approached, she realized it was a tunnel.

She crept up to the entrance and peered in. It was too dark. She had brought a flashlight, and she clicked it on.

The floor was littered with debris except for a narrow strip of cement floor that had been swept clean. Lying on the concrete was what appeared to be a piece of maroon velvet. A bag that had come with the silver service? She approached cautiously, not really wanting to touch it, so she poked at it with her silver skewer. Gathering up one corner, she lifted up the fabric and flopped it over. There was gold writing on the other side. She cupped her flashlight again, and squinted at it. There was a *B* and then some missing letters, then a *ville,* and *Jewelers. Pine Bluff, Arkansas.*

She scooped it up with her skewer.

Then she heard the drumming. Loud, and fierce; and then howls, barreling through the tunnel, bouncing off the walls. The Inner Wolf guys howled and howled, as if they were in some kind of competition. Didn't they care that one of them had died? People kept dying in Wolf Springs. Wolf Springs had to be the mouth of hell.

Water trickled, echoing off the hard surfaces. She heard the squeak of a rat and her mouth filled with saliva, in anticipation of the hunt. The anticipation instantly morphed into disgust.

Then her werewolf senses kicked in. She could smell the rat. Hear it skittering away. And she could see perfectly, without the flashlight, so she clicked it off. And she could hear, beneath the howling and the drumming, more rats, and scraping insects.

Then the tunnel opened to a flight of concrete stairs. Katelyn peered upward. It was dark; but faint, ambient light was coming from someplace, enough to reassure her that the stairway was empty.

Clutching her backpack tightly to her chest to keep the silver from clanking, she started up, searching for more of her grandfather's stolen property.

At the first landing she hit pay dirt: another spoon.

She climbed three more flights and saw nothing more. Then at the top of the stairway, she opened a door and stepped out into the empty lobby of a modern building of tinted glass panels, each etched with a wolf paw. The place appeared to be deserted, but she stood quietly just in case. The drumming was deafening; the howls seemed desperate.

. As soundlessly as she could, she glided down the hall. To her left was a rustically decorated reception area—rough-hewn furniture and couches upholstered in gray with more wolf paw prints, and the words *INNER WOLF CENTER* in letters made of timber wood behind a long varnished wood desk, on which stood a trio of computer stations.

So she was in the belly of the beast, the place she and
Trick had hoped to investigate together. Pulling out her phone,
she snapped some pictures. She wasn't sure why. It was
probably a stupid thing to do, proof that she had been
trespassing, but who knew what might be important to
remember later on?

Across the hall, there was a carved door of an enormous
wolf's head with the words *Jack Bronson* emblazoned above
it. The head was perfectly rendered, and she quivered a little as
its eyes gazed at her, so lifelike.

I shouldn't be doing this, she thought as she
experimentally tried the knob. *A man like this wouldn't break
into our house and steal our painting. But maybe someone on
his staff would.*

*Then again, if he is family, maybe he thought it was his.
That's...crazy. But maybe so is he.*

The knob turned.

"Huh," she muttered.

Cautious, she cracked open the door and waited. No
burglar alarm? No security guard? You could just walk right
into the CEO's office?

Guess so.

She pushed the door open wider, and crept into the room.

Her enhanced vision was still in force, and she could see
through the darkness that the space she entered was very
minimal, holding only a large wooden desk and an austere

looking chair. An enormous oil painting of a wolf, head back howling, hung on the wall. She resisted the urge to look more closely at it.

Go back, she told herself, but then…

…then she smelled silver.

Not too far from where she stood, there were two closed doors. She chose the nearer one and crept into a conference area dominated by a large rectangular table.

And on that table:

Oh, my God.

There, sitting right out in the open, were half a dozen pieces of her grandmother's silver.

And the painting of the heart-shaped rock.

Why did it seem too easy?

When she heard a step behind her and swiveled around, she realized it was a trap.

Standing there, staring at her, an amused expression on his face, was the Inner Wolfman himself. Jack Bronson. Silver hair, trim silver beard, fine wool trousers, a white shirt and a sports coat. In his own element, he seemed even more intimidating than he had that day in town when he'd sent those two drunk businessmen packing.

Sweat broke out on her forehead. *Wait. I have a gun*, she thought. She glanced down at her backpack. *I'm not going to shoot this man. Why would I even think that?*

"Can I help you?" he asked, amusement in his voice.

"Oh, hi, Mr. Bronson. I-I-I'm Katelyn and I'm doing a school paper and it's supposed to be a biography and I came here wanting to ask if I could interview you since you're famous and all."

She was shocked at how easily the lie rolled off her tongue.

And she was more humiliated than frightened when he laughed.

"On a dare," she added.

"Cut the crap, Katelyn. I think we both know why you're here."

She was stunned and had no idea what to say to him in response.

"Why don't you just admit that you're here looking for something?" he asked conversationally.

She struggled not to let her eyes fall on the things on the conference table. She'd gotten to go to court a few times with her father, sitting in the first row of spectators and watching him pull information out of criminals with ease. Facing Bronson, she felt like he could easily do the same to her. If they were talking and he hadn't already called the police or gotten out a rifle, then maybe he would just let her go.

"I don't know what you're talking about," she said, hoping that she sounded naïve and innocent, but willing to settle for stubborn.

"You took your time," he said. "Wasn't sure he would let you out from underneath his...thumb, shall we say, long enough for you to come looking."

"Why did you steal our stuff?" she asked.

"Who says it belonged to you in the first place?"

"Because it does," she said, irritation flooding her as she stared at his smug face. She understood intensely at that moment why her grandfather didn't like him.

"Ah, I don't suppose your grandfather has told you who I am."

"He has, actually," Katelyn said.

"He actually admitted to you that he's my brother?" he asked, sounding surprised.

"He did," Katelyn said, masking her dismay.

It wasn't exactly true. Family yes, but she'd thought maybe a cousin. But his *brother*? Why hadn't anyone told her? Why hadn't Trick?

"Interesting," Bronson said. "And what else has my dear old brother told you?"

"Everything important, Uncle John," she bluffed.

He blinked, then chuckled, sure of himself again. "I very much doubt that." Bronson looked at her. "You ever notice that everyone around here is lying about something? You ever look deep in their eyes and see that underneath everything, they're scared as hell? Like you, right now?"

His question took her by surprise, and she couldn't help but answer him. "Yes," she whispered.

He raised a brow.

"That's because everyone who lives here has secrets." He walked toward her, and she stiffened. "Of course, some are darker than others. But *everyone* hides something in Wolf Springs."

He waited a beat. Then he smiled broadly at her, as if he were savoring the moment.

"Even your precious grandfather."

What could he possibly want from her? He had made it clear that he had left the silver lying around, like a trail of breadcrumbs, hoping to lure her in. Whatever his motivation for doing that, it dawned on her that it couldn't be good.

She fumbled in her pocket, trying to get her phone. She could call for help. She could dial 911. Except that would be a total waste of time in Wolf Springs. The two police officers they had were over an hour away.

Then she heard the signal tone that a new text message had just come in.

"Mordecai is not hiding anything," she said quickly.

"Sure he is. From you." He took a step toward her.

Her flight instincts were grabbing hold. She was getting jittery, panicky.

"Um, I don't know what you're trying to do—"

"Your grandfather murdered someone," he said. He gazed at her levelly and took another step. "A werewolf."

She knew that she didn't want to hear this. She wanted to run.

"A-a *what?*" she stammered, backing away from him. She came up against the edge of the desk.

"Someone from your neck of the woods," he said, closing the space between them in a fluid, easy motion. "An attorney. Maybe you knew him."

Everything exploded. Everything.

He nodded at her. She hadn't believed it until then.

My grandfather killed my father.

10

"I knew," she whispered, wanting to deprive him of
whatever sick victory he thought he had.

He raised a finger. He smiled at her, gloating. He had won.
What, she had no idea.

"Ah! You might have suspected, but you didn't *know*.
And knowing is so much clearer, isn't it?"

"Shut up," she said. She had known. Of course she had.
She just hadn't believed.

"Did you know who begged him to do it? Your mother—"

The word galvanized her into action. Before she knew
what she was doing, she grabbed the painting and pushed him,
hard. He flew backwards and slammed against the floor.

She hit the lobby and ran, terror lending her speed. She yanked open the door and half-ran, half-fell down the stairs. She flew through the tunnel. She got to her car.

She drove.

"It's not true. Mom didn't call him," she repeated to herself, over and over. Tears and screams ripped out of her. It wasn't true. It didn't happen.

She had known deep down that her grandfather had killed her father. He killed him because he was a werewolf. She had known; she was prepared.

But she hadn't known that he'd done it because her mother had asked him to.

Her mom had never recovered after her father's death. She had been fragile, broken, leaving Katelyn to fend for herself. No wonder. She had her husband's blood on her hands. No wonder it had taken her weeks to touch Katelyn after the funeral, months before she could look her own daughter in the eyes.

She hadn't even had the courage to do it herself. She'd made Mordecai murder his own son instead.

The cell phone trilled again. She yanked the car to the side of the road and opened up the text window.

Justin had finally responded.

GOT YOUR MESSAGE.

That was it. No "thank you." No, "we're safe, don't worry."

Well, Justin Fenner and his entire family could go to hell.

Before she even knew what she was doing, she called Trick.

He answered on the second ring, his voice barely more than a whisper.

"Katelyn? What's wrong?"

"Everything. Where are you?"

"I'm with your pappy. On the hunt."

Katelyn slammed her fist into the steering wheel.

"Darlin'?" he asked, his voice filled with concern. "Do you need to talk?"

She nodded, then cleared her throat and ground out a yes.

"Go ahead."

She took a shaky breath. "Not like this. Not on the phone." *Not when my grandfather might hear me.*

"I'll come back to the cabin right now. Doc can get a ride—"

Her eyes fell on the painting in her passenger seat.

"Not tonight. Tomorrow."

"But—"

"I'm okay. I'll be okay," she amended, because there was nothing about the way she sounded that could possibly be taken as okay.

"Still thinking I should get over there," he said, sounding doubtful.

"No." She took a deep breath. "And you-you have to be there for me tomorrow. You have to, or I will never, ever forgive you."

She could hear the pain, the hurt in her own voice and she didn't bother to disguise it.

There was a pause on the other end and then she heard him whisper, "Don't you worry."

She hung up before he could say anything else. She picked up the painting and as she did so she couldn't help but see Jack Bronson's self-satisfied smirk. What on earth would drive someone to tell a seventeen-year-old girl what he had and to take such joy in the telling? Wiping her eyes, she stared hard at the landscape. Flecks of paint had been scraped away in the bottom corner and she thought she could make out what looked like a number underneath.

She blinked rapidly to clear her vision. One of the books had mentioned that the location of the mine was underneath the artist's signature and she began to scrape at it. One number, then another; in less than a minute, she had cleared a small strip of them. She stared at them, remembering the first time she had looked at this painting—her first night in Wolf Springs, when Trick had dropped by to meet her. All that time the painting had been right under her nose.

Shaking, she plugged the coordinates into the GPS app on her phone, glancing repeatedly in the rearview mirror for signs of her uncle. She had no clue what his motivation had been to lure her to the Inner Wolf Center. She was sure now that he had stolen the painting, or had it stolen. But he hadn't scraped off the signature to get to the coordinates.

She kept to the road until the GPS informed her that she had to take the Subaru off road. She realized it would be no help for her if she got stranded, but she had to carry on.

The trees grew together more densely, vines hanging down; branches swaying as the snow melted away. She had often thought of this as a Snow White forest, the trees reaching out to grab her as she passed. Now they scraped at the sides of her car and she flinched at the sound.

After a mile, she knew she had to abandon the car.

She saved the GPS route and emailed it to herself, then opened up the message because she would probably lose coverage. By opening it now, she would be able to look at it once that happened. This was so idiotic. It was like those movies where the stupid blonde got out of the car exactly when she shouldn't.

I've already done that, she thought bitterly. And I've paid the price.

She climbed out and locked her door.. At least no one would be hiding in it when she returned.

She walked into the forest, forcing herself to put one foot in front of the other. She kept going. A mile, then another. She remembered that she was a werewolf and broke into a trot. It felt good to move. More than good: it felt right.

The sun was slanting toward the horizon, warm on her face, and the ground became spongy as the last traces of snow liquefied.

She checked the picture of the map on her phone, veered to her left, and froze.

The heart-shaped boulder. And behind it, a tiny trickle of a waterfall, created by the snowmelt.

Her phone trilled and she jumped, so startled she dropped it. She hadn't realized she still had bars. She bent to scoop it up with a shaking hand. It was a text.

R U OK - C

Cordelia. Still trembling, Katelyn called the number, hoping her friend would answer. The line picked up, but there was silence.

"It's me. Kat," she said, in case Cordelia was hesitant to identify herself.

"I was just checking in but there's something wrong, isn't there?" Cordelia asked.

Katelyn almost laughed, but she knew it would come out as a wail. She didn't even know how to go about catching Cordelia up, or even if she should. Once upon a time she had thought Cordelia had a screwed-up family, but was nothing compared to what she had just learned about her own.

"I just found the heart-shaped boulder," she said instead, cutting to the chase. "Just now."

"Kat!" Cordelia cried, and Katelyn winced, hoping she was alone. The last thing she wanted was for Dom to know about this.

"I'm staring right at it. There's a little waterfall running behind it."

"How did you find it? What about the cave?"

"I'm looking for it," Katelyn said as in her mind she saw the layout of the painting, and scooted backwards, then left, right, as she searched for the cave entrance.

She tried smelling the air. If the mine was as loaded with silver as legend said, maybe she'd be able to smell it from there. Silver might not affect her as it did other werewolves but the smell was still unpleasant.

She walked back and forward, then side to side, trying to line up the angles.

Then, as if by magic, there it was.

She stood frozen in mute astonishment. It couldn't be that easy.

It hasn't been. None of this has been easy.

"I think I found it," Katelyn said.

"Oh, Kat, are you sure?" Cordelia said.

"Let me get a closer look."

"Be careful. It's full of silver. Bullets and knives. So my father said."

Katelyn steadfastly kept her mouth shut about her immunity. "I'm not smelling anything from here. We have to know if there *is* silver."

"And the-the thing that guards it…" Cordelia trailed off. "We saw *that*. We know *that's* real."

"We know it's real," Katelyn affirmed. Her chest constricted so tightly she couldn't breathe, and her pulse sounded in her eardrums. Peering left and right, she stayed on alert for an attack. If ever there was a time when she needed to be able to transform, this was it. But she stayed Katelyn, as if the werewolf inside her knew to hide.

She picked her way carefully over the rocks toward the entrance. Movement caught the corner of her eye and she turned her head farther. There, about forty yards from the boulder, something fluttered in the breeze. It looked like cloth.

"Cor, I see something," she said, dropping her voice.

"Oh, God, what?"

"I'm going to check it out."

Katelyn took a couple of steps forward and a sickly sweet smell assaulted her. She jerked hard. The same scent had clung to her when she had awakened after her first full moon, to find a deer carcass in the clearing and blood on her face.

A cramping fear twisted in the pit of her stomach. Every instinct she possessed cried out for her to flee.

Hellhound.

But she had faced down the Hellhound, it hadn't smelled like that.

Death smelled like that.

Dizzily, she stared at the entrance to the mine and shook her head in refusal. Nothing was worth going there. Let all the Fenners and Gaudins die.

I have the gun, she thought.

The gun that she had never fired in her life.

The stench of death wafted toward her. An instinct kicked in: she wanted, needed, to know what had been killed. It went beyond an impulse. It was a directive from deep inside her.

An animalistic drive.

I'm not really doing this, am I?

But she was. As if she had lost all mastery of herself, she walked a few more cautious steps, and she saw the remains of a campfire that had burned itself out. A sleeping bag, duffel bag, shovel, pick, and other supplies appeared to be untouched. The camper had come with a mission.

A hundred yards from the cave entrance she spotted a lump, something lying among the rocks. The death smell billowed up from it like a cloud of smoke.

Too rotten to eat, she thought. And then when she saw it, she began screaming.

Hollow eye sockets. A chest cavity emptied of all the organs.

Mr. Henderson.

"What is it?" Cordelia was shouting over and over in her ear.

"Kat? Damn it, what?"

There was a book shoved partway in one of the duffel bags. Breath hitching, she yanked out a book that said *U.S. Geographic Survey Northwest Arkansas.* A page was marked with a sheaf of papers and she pulled them out.

It was a photocopy of the history report she and Cordelia had written. Next to their concluding paragraph where they claimed the story was a myth, he had written LIE and underlined it.

She crumpled the paper against her chest and began to rock. "I'm sorry, I'm so sorry," she wept. They had given Mr. Henderson just enough information to complete his own research. They had led him there.

And a werewolf—or worse—had killed him.

"It's Mr. Henderson," she forced out.

"Oh, God," Cordelia said. "Kat, you have to get out of there."

A snuffling noise landed on Katelyn's ear just a little too softly to hear, as if warmth breath, invisible, nearly undetectable, was spraying the back of her neck.

Something is here, she thought, riveted to the spot, trembling slightly. *Gun, I have the gun.*

She threw down the paper and reached for the gun. But she didn't see it. It had been right there, at her knee. Wildly, she felt the ground. It wasn't anywhere. It was gone.

She sprang to her feet and ran for all she was worth. Over brambles, under branches. Fleeing.

But she was running the wrong way.

It was coming straight for her, from the underbrush. She could hear it crashing through.

"No!" she screamed. "No, please!"

11

A deer burst out of the trees, took one look at Katelyn, swerved, and darted away. Katelyn collapsed on the ground, panting; she looked over her shoulder as she scrabbled into the brush, waiting for a monstrous black shape to fill the sky. Then one by one by one, flocks of birds erupted from the tops of the pine trees, cawing as they wheeled and soared into the gray sky until at last they were nothing but black dots. A squirrel flashed past her and leaped onto a branch, cracking the frost that sheathed the wood. As she heaved and gasped for air, the earth itself seemed to expand, contract, as if it were breathing.

Wrapping her hands around the nearest tree trunk, she pulled herself up to a standing position and inched her way around it, using it as a shield. Her phone seemed to be glued to her hand; she could hear Cordelia shouting her name over and over. Katelyn tried to drop the phone's volume to its lowest setting but accidentally disconnected Cordelia instead. Just as well; she had to focus. She tried to inhale a steadying breath, and peered cautiously around the trunk. There was nothing there, no monster. The back of her neck was damp, as if something had breathed on it, but she was covered in sweat. She remembered the night she had been attacked, when the werewolf that had bitten her had melted into the darkness in a bizarre and unnatural way—not running, simply vanishing. At the time, she had thought she'd imagined it because of her trauma.

Now she knew better.

Her legs were barely holding her up as she clung to the tree. She looked through the middle distance, careful not to drop her gaze toward the campfire as she squinted at the mouth of the Madre Vena cave. The horrible memory of Mr. Henderson's savaged corpse sent fresh bile gushing and she snaked up a hand to cover her mouth. A wind bowed the branches of her sanctuary and she glanced upward. Then she remembered how she'd used her gymnastics skills before and experimentally grabbed a branch higher up wanting to climb to a higher vantage point.

On the other hand, she would be easier to spot.

She decided to chance it. She leaped and caught onto a branch with ease. It felt good to be in control of her body, and it helped her manage her jitters. Soon she had climbed up more than halfway and she stopped. Below, her own footprints had gouged the snow, and fresh powder was beginning to fill them. There were no other prints, no evidence of anything having approached the campfire. She wondered how long Mr. Henderson had been there.

The sun had sunk lower, and streaks of orange bled into the slate-colored horizon. The mine proper was in an outcropping of rock that rose like a stairway up against a mountain. If she could travel from tree to tree, she could climb down the side of the mountain and enter the cave from the right side, instead of head on. If something lurked inside, then she might have a shot at concealing herself in the shadows and—

She groaned softly as the sunlight glinted on a small object lying in the snow a few feet in her direction from the campfire. She should be glad that she'd located her gun, but now she had to retrieve it. That either meant climbing down now and going back the way she had come, or continuing with her plan to creep down the mountain. She could still do that, then break cover and grab the weapon. Whatever she decided to do, she had to do it fast: the daylight was fading much more quickly than she had anticipated. She didn't want to be out here in the dark. Wanted to go into the mine at night even less.

If her wolf senses kicked in, she'd have a much better advantage. Steely-eyed, her jaw set, she moved to another tree and held on for a moment as the wet snow slid off her new perch and splatted on the ground. She was giving herself away. Frustrated, she hopped down and charged forward to grab the gun. She swiped it up and before she could tell herself to stop, she dashed to the side of the cave and flattened herself to the right side of the entrance. The metal was icy in her hand. She breathed in and out very shallowly to keep herself from panting too hard. What did it matter how noisy she was if the Hellhound was inside? It would smell her.

She inched toward the cave opening and darted quickly inside. It was dark; she clicked on the faceplate of her phone and cupped it, exposing just enough light to figure out a route forward. Now she was a moving target.

She sniffed the air for the smell of silver and caught instead the horrible odor of Mr. Henderson's corpse.

The cave floor canted downward and she angled her steps like a skier to keep herself from sliding.. Then the light played over something white and branch-like on the ground, and she realized it was a bone. Animal or human, she couldn't tell. She swallowed hard and her left foot came down on something hard. She lost her balance and windmilled her arms; and as she did so, the light from her phone washed one of the walls. Two spindly stalactites hung in front of what appeared to be a cave painting of wide black brush strokes crisscrossing the rock. She took a few steps back so she could take in the entire, enormous picture. The formations had been incorporated as fangs in a grotesque, misshapen face with dragon-like eyes and a snout like a pig. It didn't look exactly like the Hellhound, but it glared from the rock with such hatred that even though she knew it was just a painting, she shivered. Maybe the Hellhound changed shape. Maybe there were different kinds of Hellhounds. But she knew in her gut that the thing on the wall was killing people. Had killed Mr. Henderson.

Had almost killed her.

The image was smudged in black except for the eyes, which were a lighter color. On closer inspection she realized they were reddish-brown handprints. She took a deep breath and inhaled. Dried blood?

Yes.

And…finally…she smelled silver.

The metallic tang made her teeth feel jangly. She uttered a strange feral sound deep in her throat. She went on alert, bracing herself for the torture of transformation, afraid of how vulnerable she would be while she was changing. She took slow, deep breaths, trying to calm down.

Find the silver now, before it happens, she told herself. *Find it now and get out of here.*

She raised her chin and sniffed. Her jaw was aching. She looked down at her hands; they were still just her hands. Following the scent trail, she took a few steps deeper into the cave, gripping her phone hard. Her shoes crunched on gravel as she shuffled as quietly as she could. Her heart was beating so loudly that surely it could be heard. Then everything began to glow. Her vision was shifting. The cavern became luminescent, a fairyland of stalactites and stalagmites. She saw more paintings on the walls, of other hideous monsters. There were rows of strange angular Scandinavian runes from the Old Country. Cordelia had shown her some before. The Fenners were Norse. Their patron werewolf god was Fenris, son of Loki, nephew of the great god Odin— and his prophesied assassin during the Viking version of Armageddon.

Each rock she dislodged as she crept forward sounded like an avalanche. Silver stunk up the air, so thick it felt as if someone had stuffed silver bullets up her nose. It was sickening.

The odor urged her to turn left and she entered a low, narrow tunnel. The walls were coated with drawings of human skulls, and wolf skulls superimposed over them. Some of them were crossed over with more blood—human. She could detect the unmistakable scent and to her horror, her mouth watered.

She gripped the gun and kept going. Something was hanging at the end of the tunnel. It looked like an overgrown mass of Spanish moss—

God!

It was a human skeleton dangling from a noose.

Her hands covered her mouth so that she wouldn't scream. Swaying left, right, she staggered backwards, tripped over something—a human skull—and fell hard onto her butt.

. She covered her head with both her hands as if she were protecting herself from an attack, grabbed the gun, and began to awkwardly crawl back through the tunnel. She realized she was slinking away like a coward. It was instinctual. Her wolf self knew this was a bad place, this cave of silver.

As she forced herself to stand firm, deep, bone-chilling pain seized in her knees and ankles. Her hands were still normal. Her face was human.

She turned around reluctantly and looked at the hanging figure at the end of the tunnel. There was something tied around its neck—what appeared to be a sign. Nothing in her wanted to walk toward it. But it hung in the path to the silver. She had no choice.

A shock of colorless hair was stuck to its head and a few tatters of clothing draped loosely over its shoulders. The sign, which looked like a piece of wood, was twisted and smelled of blood; she would have to reach out and touch it to read it.

No, she protested, reached out, grabbed the wood, and flipped it around.

DeAndrew, the sign read. The legend of the Madre Vena said that Jubal DeAndrew had forced a man named Xavier Cazador — a Spaniard who had rediscovered the lost silver mine in 1868 — to reveal the mine's location. Cazador was supposed to have painted the picture of the heart-shaped boulder and the waterfall that Katelyn had in her car. And then both he and DeAndrew had gone missing.

SAVAGE

She didn't smell the musk of werewolf on the body. A human had done this, then. The silver smell pulled at her; she hurried toward it, around a corner and then another, realizing that she should have done something to mark her way, keeping track of all the twists and turns. Everything around her was bathed with the filter of her enhanced vision—

—and then the glow became an explosion of light so bright that she covered her eyes. She grunted, forced her hands down, and blinked as a hole in the ceiling of the cave emitted the last rays of the sun, and her werewolf vision revealed the treasure of the Madre Vena mine:

To the right against the wall rose stacks of gray bars— tarnished silver, she guessed; and beside those, a parade of mining carts brimming with what smelled like silver ore. Stacked against the carts were dozens of wooden boxes, many of them rotted, and hard metal objects had slid from the holes to the ground, most covered with cobwebs. She ran to one, wiped the sweat off her forehead and kicked at the cobwebs, then fished out what she already knew was a gun.

She set both it and her other gun down on a box. Silver rose like incense and she wrapped her hands around the lid, preparing to yank; but the desiccated wood crumbled to sawdust in her fists.

Inside the box lay silver bullets. At least a hundred. She grabbed a handful and let them slip through her fingers. Then she wiped her hand on her jeans and cracked open the gun. She jammed a bullet into the chamber. It went in reluctantly because of the dirt and grime, but it was clearly the correct caliber. She tried to load the second gun, but the bullets were the wrong size.

She pushed open another box. There were more guns. More bullets. Wicked silver knives with serrated edges. Swords. Bayonets.

Weapons no werewolf but she could withstand—or use. Just holding the gun with the silver bullets inside it had hurt Justin's hand.

"I did it," she whispered to herself

She held onto the gun and examined the swords and bayonets. They had to be old—no one used things like this in combat any more. She wanted to know who had brought all this here. She knew why.

To kill werewolves.

She skirted the ore carts to reach a cluster of square boxes and opened the topmost one. What she saw stopped her dead:

It was an animal trap made of silver—the same kind of spring-loaded trap she had fallen into out in the forest. That was how she and Justin had learned that she was immune. Justin had hidden it, and never told anyone about it.

If he sees this, he'll completely lose his mind, she thought. She couldn't help one triumphant little cackle. She'd done it. She'd found it.

"Me," she whispered, nearly pinching herself. She stared down at the wicked-looking device, with its serrated teeth and heavy coiled spring. So many questions. But for now, she had to take what she could carry and get out of there. In her moment of victory, she had almost—but not quite—forgotten the danger she was in.

She scanned for a box in semi-decent condition, opened it, and found another trap inside. She placed her new gun inside, then added another. One aspect of her werewolf nature—her strength—never left her. She would be able to carry her treasure with ease. She added a box of bullets and wrapped her arms around the container. She turned to go—

And heard something moving behind her.

It was coming up fast behind her. Sucking in a breath, she dropped the box, whirled around and aimed her gun.

Her vision almost completely shut down; but something black and scarlet was filling the entrance into the cavern.

Katelyn's heart fluttered in her throat like a moth; she made a strange jerking sound as the thing howled and lurched toward her. Its stench was so foul her eyes watered and she gagged; all she saw were rows and rows of fangs and glowing red eyes; it was slathering and drooling and each time it howled, every bone and muscle in her body cramped. She pulled the trigger.

Nothing happened.

She pulled it again.

It was jammed.

I'm going to die. She was too calm. She had to be in shock.

Guns and silver bullets littered the ground. The Hellhound had caught her red-handed with stolen treasure.

"I-I…" she stammered. She wanted to tell it that she would never come back. But as she tried to form the words, her thoughts evaporated into sheer terror. Facing the Hellhound in this cave, with no one else around, no way to call for help.

And she saw…

She saw…

As she stared into the eyes of the Hellhound, which was pushing rotten breath out through its nose, behemoth claws scraping the earth—

Her world shattered. It shattered and it would never come back together, ever again.

Its pale green eyes were so familiar, and so very, very sad.

And she knew that her grandfather, Mordecai McBride, was staring back at her.

12

Katelyn knew she was screaming because that was the only explanation for the high-pitched shrieks that bounced off the cave walls and assaulted her ears.

The Hellhound stood, monstrous, its huge jaw clacking at her.

She leaped forward, flashing past the beast. She expected to feel its razor sharp claws slashing into her back, grabbing her, ripping her from limb to limb.

But nothing touched her.

She sprinted through the darkness, past the hanging skeleton and into the claustrophobic tunnel, struggling to remember where she was going, her own gasps of terror the only thing she could hear.

Finally she made it out of the cave. The sun had set, and this time she could feel the cold winter air. It seemed to pierce her very heart, chilling her all the way to her soul.

She ran to her car, her eyes averted from the corpse of her history teacher. The Hellhound killed all who found its cave. It—*he*—had killed her father. Why not her too?

She made it back to her car before she would have thought it possible. Somehow she got the door open and threw herself inside. She laid her gun onto the seat. Her shaking hands fumbled with the car keys. She jammed the right key into the ignition; the engine roared to life and she slammed the gas pedal to the floor.

This time she forced the car through the walls of branches. They squealed as they scraped off the paint, cracked as they broke.

My grandfather is the Hellhound.

The words kept echoing round and round.

She pounded the steering wheel as she pushed her foot on the gas pedal and the car lurched forward. The wheels spun in the muddy earth. She had to stop; she had to think clearly, figure out what to do, where to go.

Because if her grandfather was the Hellhound, she most certainly couldn't go home.

She grabbed her phone and hit Trick's name. She would tell him everything. He'd help her make sense of it.

Doubts and fears churned.

Trick had been born in her grandfather's cabin. He was Mordecai McBride's godson. He *must* know—about the Hellhound and werewolves and all of it.

Did he know about her? Was that why he was always acting so weird?

The cell connected and it was as though time slowed down, every ring chiming hours apart. Trick would help. He had to.

Finally she heard his voice and her heart leapt—only to come crashing back down into her chest when she was realized she was listening to his voicemail message. She licked her lips and forced herself to breathe before she spoke.

"Trick, call me, please. Something..."

She didn't know what to say. She was afraid of sounding crazy or revealing too much.

"Just call," she whispered and then hung up.

She took another deep breath, trying to steady herself. What if she was wrong? What if that hadn't been her grandfather looking at her through the Hellhound's eyes?

It was possible the stress of all the lying and sneaking around was getting to her, but she didn't think so. It made too much sense. Her father's death, the silver bullets, the picture that had been stolen from their house.

Quickly she rolled down the window and let the cool air blow on her face as she drove. She was shaking hard.

She didn't want it to be him. She wanted him to just be her grandfather, nothing else.

She didn't know what to do, where to go. She couldn't just keep driving forever, either. She didn't have any money on her and she only had half a tank of gas. She couldn't get very far on that. Certainly not to California. Maybe not even to wherever the Fenner pack was holed up.

She called Cordelia.

"Kat! Are you okay?" Cordelia burst out as she picked up.

"No, I'm not okay," Katelyn said, pushing down the urge to cry.

"What's wrong? Did you...did you find it?" Cordelia whispered.

Katelyn shut her eyes. The Gaudin pack would likely murder her if she went to Cordelia. And with Regan and Arial vying for control of the Fenner pack, Katelyn was just as likely to be slaughtered by Fenners. And if either side found out that she knew where there were hundreds, if not thousands, of silver bullets...

"Kat?" Cordelia said.

She had to stay well away from both packs. Her best chance of survival lay with the Hounds of God.

"Cordelia, promise me you'll be careful."

"What's happening?" When Katelyn didn't answer, Cordelia pushed harder. "Tell me. Where are you? What are you doing?"

"I'm going to put an end to this." Katelyn hung up. "One way or another," she breathed.

She pulled out Daniel's card and called him. He answered on the first ring.

"I'm ready," she said.

"Do you need us to come get you?"

"No, I'll come to you."

"As you wish."

He gave her coordinates and she punched them into her GPS.

"You're doing the right thing for everyone," he told her.

"I hope so."

She hung up.

~

Katelyn had been driving for well over an hour and she was getting anxious. The Subaru was running on fumes and she'd never make it to the rendezvous point. She didn't want to abandon her car. A vehicle gave her some small amount of autonomy, a chance to leave when she wanted. But only if it had gas in it.

She saw a light flash through the trees and put her foot on the brake. A moment later it appeared again and she realized it had to be coming from a building—most likely a cabin.

If the lights were on that could mean someone was home—and there was likely to be a vehicle with gas. She hesitated for only an instant and then turned up a dirt path leading toward the light.

She didn't want to attract attention to herself by begging for fuel that she couldn't pay for. She didn't have anything to siphon it off with, and she wasn't sure she knew how anyway.

She set her jaw. Somehow, she was going to have to manage it if she wanted to go any further. She pulled over and parked, turning off the engine. Until she had scoped things out she didn't want to alert anyone to her arrival.

She considered taking her gun, then thought better of it and slid it underneath the passenger seat. Regretfully, she thought of the weapons and bullets that she had left behind. If her gun was jamming, she didn't need to wave it around. Better to try to fix it before she wasted precious ammunition.

She got out and walked up the dirt path. As she rounded a turn, a log cabin came into view. It was larger than her grandfather's, but it was not as finished. It was more like a cabin at a sleepaway camp than a home.

There were no lights on, but a faint orange glow suggested a fireplace fire; she could smell the wood smoke drifting out of the chimney. She walked as silently as she could. She was holding her breath.. Her vision was beginning to shift, the forest around her coming alive with infrared and platinum lights.

Not now, she thought as she forced herself to keep moving forward.

There was a truck parked to the right of the rough-hewn cabin and she tiptoed toward it. She checked the bed of the truck when she reached it, hoping to see a gas can.

No such luck.

With a grimace, she turned her attention to the gas tank. Even if she could find a hose to suck the gas through, it would be moot without something to put the gas in.

She could wait until they went to bed and then she could rummage around in their garage. People were nervous from all the murders. What if they shot at her?

"Kat!"

On high alert, she swung around. Jesse Fenner stood on the front porch waving at her. She stared at him, stunned,. It finally hit her: this was the safe house, the cabin in the woods Justin had told Lucy to run to.

Lucy.

A twig cracked.

Katelyn whirled back around.

She stood face to face with Lucy, whose butter-soft features were contorted in a mixture of hatred and fear.

Katelyn tensed, waiting for Lucy to lash out at her, for that battle that must surely come, that could no longer be postponed. She thought about the malfunctioning gun loaded with silver bullets.

"What are you doing here?" Lucy asked.

Katelyn realized that there was far more apprehension in the other woman's voice than anger, and she forced herself to relax.

"I'm here to check on you and Jesse," she said. Lies. They came so easily these days. No surprise. Everyone in Wolf Springs lied.

Lucy looked fearfully into the forest. "Who's with you?"

"No one, I swear," Katelyn said even as an image of the Hellhound filled her mind—and Lucy's promise to fight her to the death rang in her ears.

Lucy grabbed Katelyn's arm and dragged her toward the cabin. Although Lucy held her too tightly, Katelyn allowed her to lead her. When they stepped onto the porch it finally registered that Lucy was carrying a rifle in her other hand.

"Jesse, honey, you greet Kat proper and then go to your room and watch a movie. She and I have some girl stuff we have to talk over," Lucy said firmly.

Jesse made a face and whined deep in his throat, but he obediently kissed Katelyn's cheek and shuffled into the cabin. Then Lucy led Katelyn inside.

Her impression of the cabin had been accurate. It was crude inside, with some furs covering the primitive plank floor. A massive fireplace was the only light source.

"I figure it'll be best if Jesse is occupied while we talk," Lucy said, her voice tight.

Katelyn nodded. Lucy's civility was unnerving.

"No phone, and no cell signal out here," Lucy continued. "We've been cut off since we got here."

Lucy was isolated even more than she had been. Impulsively Katelyn reached out and grabbed the other girl's hand.

"Let go of me," Lucy snapped. She was shaking. Lucy was always the level headed one, the one in charge. Katelyn couldn't help but think about the disastrous Thanksgiving dinner when Lee Fenner had accidentally started to shift into wolf form at the table. Lucy had taken over, ensuring that Katelyn's grandfather hadn't seen what was happening.

Katelyn had been so worried about his discovering that werewolves existed, afraid for her grandfather's safety. All along she should have been terrified for the safety of Justin, Cordelia, Jesse, and, most of all, herself. She should have been worried about protecting them from her grandfather.

The irony made her want to laugh and sob at the same time.

"What's happening?" Lucy whispered.

Katelyn assumed she was lowering her voice to keep Jesse from overhearing.

"What have you heard?" Katelyn asked.

"Not much." Lucy shook her head. "Justin called, said it was going badly, that I should take Jesse and come here. Wait for someone to come get us."

She looked at Katelyn hopefully and despite everything, her newly-revealed fragility softened Katelyn's heart.

"Let's sit down," Katelyn suggested.

Lucy nodded and led her over to a couple of pine chairs with threadbare cushions. The place was such a marked contrast with the comfortable elegance of the Fenner home that Katelyn couldn't help but notice. Lucy caught her at it.

"This place was built by Justin's great-grandfather. The family hasn't lived in it full time since before Lee took over the pack."

Katelyn nodded, the mention of Lee's name reminding her of all the unpleasant things she had to tell Lucy. She cleared her throat, but kept her voice low because of Jesse.

"Last I heard, Justin was okay," she began.

Twin tears slid freely down Lucy's cheeks and she wiped them away with hands that shook even more. "Thank God."

"The battle...it was chaos. The Gaudins poisoned the bayou with silver."

Lucy gaped at her and finally found her voice. "So Uncle Lee was right about them. They were the kind of snakes who'd do something so evil. Did anyone...did they die from that?"

Katelyn dipped her head. "The Gaudins set fire to the trees too. People were running everywhere. We would get separated only to meet back up someplace completely different. The order was given to fall back and regroup."

SAVAGE

"But Justin is safe?" Lucy asked, clearly needing to hear it again.

"Yes, at least he *was*. I haven't heard anything for hours and hours."

Lucy knit her fingers together. She looked as if she would burst. "Okay," she said. "All right." She clenched her hands. "What about everyone else?"

The moment of truth. "Doug and Al," she said. "And...Lee."

Lucy stared at her. Katelyn was surprised by the lack of reaction.

"There were others, too, I just don't know—"

A high-pitched wail rent the air. Katelyn and Lucy both jumped to their feet and spun around.

There, standing at the foot of the stairs was Jesse, his face wild with grief and rage. He threw himself from side to side, smacking into the banisters, howling like a wolf.

"Jesse, honey, I told you to stay upstairs," Lucy said, the distress in her voice overwhelming as she and Katelyn rushed to him.

"Uncle Lee, Uncle Lee!" Jesse savagely pushed her away. He glared at Katelyn, the heartbreak in his eyes killing her. As Lucy stumbled backwards and fell, he bolted for the front door.

"Jesse, no!" Lucy shouted.

It was too late. Jesse tore open the door and then he was outside, making terrible, half-howling sounds as if he were strangling. Lucy threw herself after him and Katelyn followed.

With no time to adjust to the darkness, Katelyn could still easily hear the two of them crashing through the trees. She trailed after, night-blind, hoping she didn't run into a low-hanging branch or trip over a root.

She glanced off a tree and she heard a snapping sound as her arm broke. She let out a curdled shriek of pain and fell to her knees.. She hunched over, panting in agony.

"Come on, heal," she begged her body. "Damn it."

And then, miraculously, she began to feel better. Bones started to knit; she raised her good arm and wiped a sheen of perspiration off her forehead. As the throbbing subsided, she stared into the darkness, listening to Lucy calling for Lee Fenner's adoring nephew, seeing nothing. Slowly she got to her feet, and staggered one step forward, then stopped. She would be good to no one if she slammed into a tree trunk and knocked herself out. If ever she needed the enhanced night vision, it was now.

If she was lucky, Lucy would catch him. Or Jesse would calm down enough and return to the cabin under his own steam. Surely he could find his way back.

Still, Katelyn shambled forward like a zombie. Her eyes began to adjust to the darkness, but her view was a mere shadow of what she could have seen with the eyes of a fully mature werewolf.

In the distance Jesse howled.

And, then, mid-howl, he was cut off.

A chill danced up Katelyn's spine.

Lucy caught up with him; that has to be what happened, Katelyn thought.

She couldn't stop her thoughts from flying to the Hellhound. What if instead of Lucy, it, *he*, had caught Jesse?

Fear drove Katelyn to go faster. She stumbled, her foot catching in some roots, and fell. Gritting her teeth, she picked herself up, and when she did, the forest became alive with light and colors. Brilliant scarlet, orange, shimmering with auras of purest white.

She leaped forward, running, her enhanced vision guiding her safely around and over obstacles that sprung up in her path. She could see glowing footprints on the ground—Jesse and Lucy's tracks.

And then, coming out of nowhere, there was a third set of tracks. Wolf tracks.

Katelyn careened to a stop, nearly crashing into a tree.

She studied the ground, light and heat steaming off the tracks as if they had been burned into the soil. They were running on top of Jesse and Lucy's human footprints, so neither of them had shifted into wolf form.

She thought of Jesse's choked-off cry and her heart
pounded so hard the vein in her forehead throbbed. She should
have grabbed something from the cave when she'd fled,
something silver. She hadn't been thinking. She'd been trying
to escape.

She forced herself to start moving again, following the
three sets of blazing indentations in the snowy ground. As
suddenly as they had appeared, the wolf tracks vanished after
about a quarter mile. The hair on the back of Katelyn's neck
stood on end. Instead of knowing the wolf was in front of her,
it could be anywhere.

"Jesse? Lucy?" she whispered hoarsely.

She kept going. Where was it? What was it? She scanned
the illuminated trees, the coasting ground, even the windy
night sky.

Then she heard quiet sobbing. She slowed, wanting to
approach cautiously, see before she was seen.

Finally she made out two glowing images. Jesse and Lucy
were on the ground, backs against a large tree. Curled in fetal
position, Jesse was crying, and Lucy was rocking him, trying
to soothe him.

Slowly Katelyn's vision began to fade, returning to
normal, and she wanted to howl in frustration. Just because she
had found them didn't mean they were out of danger yet.

Lucy looked up at her, her own face wet with tears. "I've
got this," she said harshly.

Katelyn shook her head and moved in close. She whispered into Lucy's ear, "There's someone else out here. I saw wolf prints tracking you just like I was."

Lucy stiffened. "I haven't seen anyone."

"They disappeared a while back. I don't know what that means."

Lucy slowly disentangled herself from Jesse and stood up. She turned slowly, sniffing the air. Then she locked gazes with Katelyn.

"It means that we're surrounded."

Jesse sat up. "It's Justin. He's coming to get Kat. He's going to marry her."

"No, he's not," Katelyn said firmly. Her face was hot. "He's marrying Lucy." She looked straight at Lucy. "And I really do hope that's him out there."

"He didn't send you for us, did he?" Lucy asked.

"No," Katelyn admitted.

Lucy growled deep in her throat.

"Can you tell who's out there?" Katelyn asked. "Are they on our side?"

"Can't *you* tell?" Lucy asked savagely. "You're such a two-faced—"

"Justin *is* going to marry, Kat," Jesse said, wiping his face. "You'll see. He's trying to make me a mate, but I only love Lucy."

Katelyn blinked. Lucy cocked her head and peered at him, clearly just as taken aback by what he'd said as Katelyn.

"You're so sweet, darlin'," Lucy said. "Sweet as sugar. But what do you mean, 'make you a mate'?"

Jesse put his finger to his lips. "It's a secret."

And before Katelyn could say anything, all hell broke loose.

13

Howling werewolves transformed in midair from human to wolf as they dropped from the trees. Huge growling werewolves with black and gray pelts exploded out of the darkness and rushed Katelyn, Jesse and Lucy.

"Run, Jesse!" Lucy screamed. "They're Gaudins!"

The trio wheeled around, fleeing for the cabin, but their attackers had the advantage of surprise.

Hot breath flashed across the back of Katelyn's neck and she jogged left. There were wolves everywhere, bursting out of hiding places and charging.

Katelyn put on a burst of speed as she realized her change in direction was taking her farther away from the cabin—and her gun. Fangs flashed between her and sanctuary and she zigzagged to throw off the enemy. But the invaders kept coming at her. She had to shift to wolf form so she could defend herself, wolf to wolf. She had to turn and fight. It was her only chance for survival.

Unless I can get the gun and make it work.

Her breath expelled in hard, misty pants as she tried to circle back around. There were so many werewolves she couldn't count them. A howl vibrated against her eardrums and something deep inside her, primal and unconscious, registered that it was the call of a friend.

Jesse must have recognized the howl. Katelyn heard him bellowing, "Help! Help!" and Lucy shouted, "Gaudins!"

A river of fearless werewolves, tawny, gray, and white, poured into the battle. One of the oncoming werewolves dove at another. She knew it was a male; his massive teeth sank into the throat of the enemy and he shook his huge head, ripping flesh.. There was blood everywhere, spraying the trees; to Katelyn's enhanced vision the blood glittered and glowed as if it were being shot with flamethrowers.

Blood dripping from his muzzle, the werewolf that had taken the throat of the attacking Gaudin looked hard at Katelyn. Katelyn's vision telescoped, as it often had when she'd first been bitten and her body had begun to change. The Fenner werewolf had blue eyes.

She'd been attacked and changed by a werewolf with blue eyes.

He dipped his head in recognition but she didn't know who it was. Arial had put a price on her head. Many wanted her dead. There could be Fenner werewolves ready to save Lucy and Jesse but not her.

As if he had read his mind, the Fenner lunged at her, jaws wide, snarling, and Katelyn backed away as fast as she could. She tripped over something and fell, hitting her head so hard the world went black for a second.

A second was all it took for the Fenner werewolf to sail into the air at her. Then another werewolf sprang between Katelyn and the werewolf that was targeting her and took it down. The two rolled, howling with fury, biting and swiping at each other with their sharp claws. Katelyn's attacker pinned her champion and clamped down ferociously around its neck.

Blood geysered into the air.

The victorious werewolf raised its head and looked at her.

Katelyn bolted. Her arms pumped as she forced herself to pour on speed. If she could get to the Subaru, she could lock herself inside and drive. She didn't have a lot of gas but she had some. Maybe the gun would finally shoot.

The car, where was the car? She grunted, terrified, fighting down panic as she searched the landscape for it. If she went the wrong way she was dead.

Then she spotted it. One moment it was a glowing rectangle and then her enhanced vision shut down. A werewolf sailed over her head. She huddled close to the earth, straining to pinpoint the car again, afraid to move. She had lost sight of it and she stayed where she was, panting, afraid. But she couldn't let fear hold her down. The fight was savage and brutal, and she'd be taken down just like a deer if she didn't leave the killing field.

For the second time that day she scrambled toward her Subaru.

But this time she didn't make it.

Beside her car, a werewolf she didn't recognize transformed into human shape. It was a woman, naked, and she yanked open the car door. Katelyn grimaced, remembering that she had left her gun inside. A werewolf would smell the silver. The stench might encourage her to leave or to investigate. Not everyone knew about Katelyn McBride's secret weapon.

The woman climbed into the car, cutting off that avenue of escape. Disheartened, Katelyn veered off into the trees and ran as fast as she could. She kept running, knowing that although she was still physically strong and had superhuman endurance, at some point she would tire. She couldn't double back for Jesse and Lucy. She couldn't falter.

She couldn't rest.

So she kept going, and it started to snow. Flakes drifted, then fell, then sleeted. The downfall would cover her old tracks but possibly reveal her new ones. She kept going as icy branches whipped her cheeks and snowflakes clumped eyelashes. The howling of the wind mingled with the cries of dying werewolves.

Finally she had to stop. Pressing her back against a tree trunk, she yanked the phone out of her pocket, saw one bar, and tried to call Daniel again. The call failed. Failed again.

She was taking in huge gulps of air. Sweat iced her skin as she pushed desperately away from the trunk and took a few stagger-steps forward. Her clothes were soaked. If she'd been merely human, she'd be half-frozen by now. But the cold was sucking up her reserves of energy.

She was in trouble. Deep trouble.

She tried to redial. Nothing.

There were fewer howls. In her ears, her heartbeat roared. She couldn't seem to suck in enough air.

Lurching forward, she grabbed a branch and used it to drag herself along, then clung to another one and called on her reserves to put one foot in front of the other. The direness of her situation was sinking in—alone, in the forest, no car, no gun, no contact, and no friends.

How had the Gaudins known to attack here? In her mind's eye she saw Cordelia. She'd had Katelyn's phone in the bayou. Had she somehow jacked it? Werewolves possessed a loyalty instinct, she'd been told. Once they identified their superior, they felt compelled to follow them. Cordelia had mated with a Gaudin. That would make her feel loyal to them. But she had married outside the pack of her birth. She must still feel loyal to the Fenners on some level—even if the Fenner alpha had banished her.

Then Katelyn circled back to her own sense of loyalty— not to packs, but to people. To a person. To her friend.

Would Cordelia still be her friend if she knew that Katelyn's grandfather was the Hellhound?

I don't know that for sure, she reminded herself, as her stomach did a flip and her throat tightened. *And I don't know if he killed Daddy. I don't know any of that.*

She wasn't going to go there now. She was losing it, getting more scared and desperate by the minute and yes, feeling the cold. It was seeping into her bones and they were stiffening, aching. There could be Fenners searching for her. Gaudins, too. Where was Justin?

Slushy snow on the ground was icing up, covered by the powdery white sprinkling overhead. She walked on pinecones and pine needles as she kept moving. Where were Daniel's gang of bodyguard werewolves? She'd been worried before that they'd been following her. If only they were following her now.

Then she realized that something was pricking at her awareness. There was a sensation between her shoulder blades, like someone poking her with a long, frozen finger.

Someone watching her.

She pretended to drop and glanced around as she bent over. The blood rushed to her head and a wave of dizziness sent the world swirling. She forced herself to breathe slowly until the sensation passed. She saw no one, wolf or human, and she looked just as hard for places to run.

She was out in the open in a vulnerable position. If only she had her gun. She had changed so much from the girl who had first arrived in Wolf Springs. Her grandfather had had to bribe her with tickets to Cirque du Soleil to get her to pick up a rifle and learn how to shoot. Now she was wishing she could blow someone away.

Only if I'm in danger, she thought.

But she *was* in danger. She could still feel fingers between her shoulder blades, walking up her backbone and wrapping themselves around her neck. It was almost a physical sensation, terrifying, and she touched her neck just to make sure there was nothing there. The Hounds of God claimed that they used magic to turn themselves into werewolves. Was somebody using magic on her?

She stood rooted; then she looked up at the trees and told herself to climb them, as she had to save herself before. Then she burst into action, bounding through the snow and bending her cold, sore knees, leaping up and grabbing a branch. Her recently broken arm throbbed with pain, but she grabbed another branch. And another. Climbing. Putting her hand around another branch.

Finally hearing something: the branch cracking. Her shout as she began to tumble toward the ground. She was a werewolf. She'd be okay. Her arms flailed until her gymnastics training kicked in and she pulled her hands against her chest and executed a twist in the air, sticking the landing as she slid into the snow like she was entering the water after a high dive.

A shadow pooled around her. It spread and blossomed, the cold swirling toward her knees. Her breath hitched in her chest and she looked around for the source as it expanded, spreading over her head like a net, blocking out the sky.

She looked up, up, then fell backward and crabwalked as fast as she could. Her hands pushed into the snow and she got her legs underneath herself. Her palm flattened on a sharp rock and she grabbed it. She yanked another stone out of the snow and held it against her chest. She got another one, and a fourth, and soon she was cradling six or seven of them as she used one hand to get to her feet. She staggered backward as the shadow kept coming. There was nothing but the dense, oily blackness crawling over her.

"Go away!" she shouted, and she threw a stone. There was nothing to hit. She threw another and another, then all of them as she got to her feet and began to run.

She heard something loping behind her, huge paws crunching the crusted surface of the snow, wind ruffling through its hair. The back of her neck grew hot and wet and she ran faster as a shriek of pure fright ripped out of her body.

Then something grabbed her and she screamed and screamed and screamed. Arms were around her tightly, as she struggled.

"Katelyn!" Trick said, grabbing her hand and breaking into a run. He dragged her behind himself and his cowboy hat flew off. He had a rifle looped around his shoulder but he didn't stop to use it. "What's after you?"

"Trick, Trick," she said wrapping her hand around his to keep herself linked to him, "it's... run, oh, God, please, run as fast as you can!"

They barreled along together until Katelyn thought her lungs had burned up. Then he moved in front of her and turned to face the way they had come. His shoulders were heaving. He stood with his legs wide apart and raised his rifle.

"No, that won't work, it's..." She looked past him to the trees as snow sprinkled down on them. "Bullets won't hurt it."

He glanced at her over his shoulder but he didn't lower the rifle. She could hardly stand still.

"Where's your Mustang?" she begged him. "We have to get out of here."

"Brought a truck," he said. "Bullets won't hurt it," he repeated.

Hysterical laughter bubbled to the surface but she kept herself together. "The truck. Get to the truck," she said.

"Okay, okay. It's just..."

He didn't re-sling his rife, but carried it against his side as she took her hand again and he turned sharply to the left. His truck lights were on, revealing a ribbon of road, and he practically threw her inside, then ran around to the other side of the truck. He handed her the rifle and started the truck, peeling out.

"Katelyn," he said, but she was staring out the window as they put distance between them and the forest. She closed her eyes and thought of Jesse and Lucy. She pulled out her cell phone. No service.

"Trick, do you have bars," she began, and then he was yanking off the road and pulling to the side. The lights on the dash revealed his green eyes and sharp, mocha-colored features; then his hands cradled her face and he covered her with quick kisses, a river of them, his lips touching, moving; he gasped and put his mouth over hers and eased his tongue inside.

She set down the rifle and filled her hands with his soft hair, grazing his earlobes and the back of his neck, unable to believe he was there, and that he'd saved her, and that she was alive.

"What the hell, darlin'," he said, and she kissed him some more. Her nerve endings sizzled and she couldn't kiss him enough, couldn't get close enough; she wanted him as much as she had been afraid. Trick seemed to know; he lifted her as close to his body as he could and molded her against his chest.

She wanted to growl and grab his head and kiss him so hard it was almost a bite.

Don't bite him. Don't, she reminded herself.

Then he gently took both her hands in one of his and pulled them off himself, then cupped them under his chin. He kissed her forehead and whispered, "Hush now."

"Trick, oh, Trick," she said, alternating between sobbing and laughing. "I thought I was dead and-and why did you stop talking to me and why are you *here?*"

"I *am* here," he said. He cradled her head and kissed away more tears. She hadn't even realized she was crying. "You called me, and I'm here."

He kissed her temple and the side of her face; she closed her eyes and he kissed her lids. She dug her fingers into his sheepherder's jacket, smelling the soap and leather scent that was Trick. There was something else, a piney fragrance that registered somewhere in her brain, if not her memory.

"Talk to me," he said. He looked hard at her, eyes nearly glowing in the light from the dash, lashes so heavily fringed they almost didn't look real.

"Tell me," he insisted. "I can help you."

"Trick," she began, and hope lit up inside her. Yes, he could help. Of course he could. He was Trick.

"I think...I thought there was something in the forest, like with all the killings." She remembered how close they had been to the road when he had run with her out of the woods. "I was going for gas and I ran into this…feud, like a mountain feud. The hill people …" She trailed off, seeing the disbelief in his eyes.

"Some of that is actually true," she said quietly. "Oh, God. *God*, Trick, I want to tell you but…" She took a breath. ""But I can't because if something happened to you…"

He placed the flat of his fingertips against her mouth. Something tingled at the base of her spine and caught fire in her chest. They looked at each other in silence. His chest rose and fell. He was struggling with something, just as she was.

"If something happened to me," he echoed, and she nodded.

He said, "This has gone on long enough. You've suffered way too much, carrying this secret. I *know*, Katelyn. I know."

Her face went completely numb. Everything fell away. Her chest constricted; she was floating. Trick squeezed her hands.

"What-what do you know?" she asked him. She didn't even sound like herself. She felt like she wasn't even there.

He blew out a breath and gave his head a little nod. "I know that something happened to *you*, darlin'." He squeezed tighter. "I know that you're a werewolf."

She couldn't breathe. Her lips parted. But before she could speak, Trick spoke again.

"I know all that.

"And I know that it's my fault."

14

"What are you saying?" Katelyn whispered. He looked as if he had been holding his breath ever since she had come to Wolf Springs, preparing, defending. As if he had been dreading this moment. His eyes were shiny, as if tears were welling, and that frightened her more than anything else could have.

"That night. I should have been with you. I shouldn't have let you drive home by yourself. I knew better. I...I was too caught up in my own head to think straight. If I hadn't, you wouldn't have left the party and it wouldn't have attacked you."

He knew. She didn't have to carry her secret by herself any longer. And she could share it with Trick. She was almost giddy with relief, light-headed.

"It's not your fault," she said.

"It is. I was meant to protect you."

"But how could you have protected me? How could you even have known?"

He leaned his head back against the seat and closed his eyes. A groan of misery escaped him. "Because, Katelyn, it's my job."

"It's not your job to protect me. I know Grandpa laid that on you but…" She stopped speaking as he cleared his throat and looked at her from beneath his long eyelashes.

"Actually, it's my job to protect everyone."

She frowned. "I don't understand."

Don't you? the voice whispered inside her head. The voice that had been whispering to her since she had come to Wolf Springs. The voice that had threatened, promised oh, so much.

Trick's voice.

Her hand flew to the door handle, but he was faster, grabbing her hand, holding it tight. Fear squeezed her chest. The voice that had haunted her dreams. It had been Trick all along.

"How? How can you be in my head?" she whispered.

"Oh, Katelyn, how do you think?" he answered.

She panicked.

She threw herself hard against the door, breaking his hold on her hand. She tumbled outside and ran. But something hit her around the knees, sending her crashing face first into the snow. She flipped over, blinking the powder out of her eyes, and looked up to see Trick above her. He pinned her with his hands on her shoulders. He might know she was a werewolf, but he could never guess how strong she was.

She brought her knee up into his stomach and tried to heave him off her. He grunted but didn't budge. His hands tightened around her shoulders and she registered that he was stronger than she would have expected.

Too strong for an ordinary guy.

"Katelyn, listen to me, listen," he said. His expression was serious, his green eyes intently boring into her very soul. "We've *both* kept secrets from each other way too long."

"I think my grandfather is the Hellhound," she burst out. She blinked in surprise. She hadn't expected, hadn't planned to tell him.

He nodded slowly. "He is."

And there it was, the final confirmation. She thought of her nightmare and waited for the free-fall into this terrible truth. For Trick to have to catch her.

She'd once heard someone say that the truth could set you free. She lay still.

"Does he know what happened to me?" she asked.

"I've never told him."

"But how do you know all this? How can you talk to me? So you know about everything? The war?"

"War," he echoed.

Trick would help her, be with her. They'd figure out a way out of this whole mess.

He let go of her and kissed her, his lips warm and soft against hers. Every sense clicked into *need* as she kissed him back.

"Run away with me, Trick, far away where they'll never find us."

He went completely still. He eased himself up to a sitting position and looked down at her, pain twisting his features. "I can't do that, darlin'. I can't leave Wolf Springs."

"My grandfather would like that. I'd be out of here. Safe. Since he doesn't know, he won't care. He doesn't know that I know that he..." She stopped herself. Trick didn't need to know about her father. Fresh secrets, beginning to mount up?

She began to sit up, too, and he took her hand to help her. "You can tell your parents you're going away to college, early acceptance, something, anything—"

He shook. "It has nothing to do with them. The minute I was released over Wrights' murder, they flew back to Europe. I can't leave because I have commitments, a job that I'm sworn to do."

"I don't understand," Katelyn said.

He laughed, the sound hard and bitter. "How could you? Because I haven't told you yet, haven't explained." He sighed. "Everything else being equal, we still couldn't leave without your pappy's permission. And that'll never happen."

She blinked at him, bewildered.

"He's the Hellhound," she said. "We don't need his permission. We need to get away from him before he finds out what I am." *Before he tries to kill me like he killed...my father.*

Trick pressed his fingertips against his forehead. "Oh, Katelyn, this is all so screwed up."

"That's why we have to get away from here, go someplace no one knows us where we can be alone, start over." She thought of how wealthy he was. He could make it happen. Her imagination shot into overdrive. She made herself ignore the pained expression that clouded his features, but her pulse was jumping.

"I can't." He sounded...haunted.

"Why not? Of course you can," she said, allowing the tide of her urgency, her euphoric hopes, to wash over him. "Trick, I want it to be you. I love you."

He stared at her with the strangest expression. He looked both young and very old, joyful, defeated. "And I love you. More than anything in this world. More than *anything*," he said again.

"Then come with me. Come *now*, Trick."

He took her hands in his and they felt icy. He squeezed tightly and she got panicky, because she knew he was going to tell her more things she didn't want to hear.

"Katelyn, werewolves aren't meant to be without a pack. It can drive them a little...crazy."

She thought of her father, a werewolf alone in Los Angeles. Madness? There had to have been a good reason for his actions. And his death. She shook her head.

"But I won't be alone. I'll have you."

Except...her father had had his wife. And his daughter.

"You can't turn me into a werewolf," he said.

"Is that what you thought?" she responded, gasping. "Trick, I would *never* bite you, *never* do that to you."

He nodded as if to assure her that he believed her. "I didn't say you wouldn't turn me. I said you *couldn't*. As in, it would be impossible. And a single werewolf, even one surrounded by family and friends, is still very much alone."

He was wrong about that. She would have to show him, convince him, but what he'd said about it being impossible to turn him into a werewolf gave her pause.

"Why couldn't I?" she asked.

There was another stretch of silence. He was staring downward as if he was trying to figure something out, make a decision. "Katelyn, there's only one creature that can put thoughts into the mind of another."

She breathed slowly through her nose, feeling her breath hitch, her pulse flutter. She couldn't feel his hands around hers anymore.

"At first I thought that it was the Hellhound talking to me," she said.

He kept his eyes lowered. "That's because it was."

"But I don't," she began, the fluttering turning into a lit fuse. She could almost feel it burning inside her chest. "My grandfather—"

"Is the Hellhound," Trick said. "And I am his apprentice."

"No," she said flatly, as the fuse ignited.

You know it's true.

His lips weren't moving. They weren't, but she could hear him.

"No," she said again. "Trick, this isn't funny. You think it is—"

He pulled her against his chest and pressed her head against his shoulder. She tried to lift her head but she couldn't. Inside she was imploding. Outside, she was as still as the bust of her mother that Trick had sculpted for her birthday.

Me.

"You spied on me from the skylight? You've been sneaking into my room while I was asleep, like a stalker?"

Yes. Because I love you. And because it's my fault a werewolf bit you.

She struggled to get away. He was a monster. A killer.

"I'm new as a Hellhound," he said aloud. "I can't control what I think. What you hear isn't always what's in my head. Sometimes it's what's in my heart. A Hellhound's heart."

"Let me go," she said, trying hard to free herself.

He held her fast. "You have to listen to me. Me here. Now."

"Those girls in the woods. Your own friends," she said. "Mike Wright."

He locked gazes with her and slowly shook his head. "Look at me, darlin'. *Not* me. None of them. I swear it, Katelyn." When she pushed against his chest, he kept his arms around her very tightly. "Katelyn, it was not me."

"Oh, God," she whispered. "Then it was—"

"We have nothing to do with humans, except to protect them," he said. "From werewolves who break their own laws." He looked hard at her. "Do you believe that of me? Do you believe I could do that?"

"Why didn't you tell me?" she whispered.

"Why didn't *you* tell *me?*"

They both smiled weakly.

"I'm new at this," he said. "Sometimes I can't control how I act. Even Doc struggles. The change comes on us like a whirlwind. We're violent. Werewolves are smart to fear us." He grimaced. "It's what I am."

She swallowed hard and nodded.

"And we're ugly."

They were. Hideously ugly. Hellish.

"Doc entrusted me with your safekeeping when you first came here because there's nothing stronger than us," he said. "That I'd keep you away from whatever was killing those girls in the forest."

"Do you know who bit me?" she asked.

"No, but trust me I've been trying to catch him. It's the same werewolf that jumped on the hood of my car." He let out another breath, warm on her hair. "When you told me you heard two wolves growling I wanted to kick myself. Second one you heard was me."

She nodded. "Catch *him*," she said.

"Definitely male," he said.

"But no one knew me. Why attack *me*? To get at the Hellhound?"

He gave her a skeptical look, and she shook her head.

"I guess the last thing you would want to do is piss off the Hellhound."

"Ironic, isn't it," he said. "All those morons at school beating me up. I couldn't fight back."

"God, Trick. That's so awful."

"No more awful than it's been for you. With *your* big secret life."

"Do you know who...the other werewolves are?" she asked,. "When they're people?"

He bared his teeth and his eyes narrowed slightly. "Doc didn't and neither did his predecessor. But thanks to you, now we know the Fenners are running the pack."

Despite herself, she grimaced, and she knew he saw it. She told herself she did *not* feel loyal to the Fenners.

"You and Cordelia always hated each other," she said.

He smiled sourly. "Werewolves can't even tell their own kind when they're in human form. Same goes for Hellhounds and werewolves. We don't sense each other as people. Still, who knows? You're right. I never liked any of the Fenners." He looked at her. "But I know there's more than Fenners in the pack."

She flushed and pulled away slightly. Was he asking her for names? Would she give them to him? What would he do with them?

"If you know the Fenners are werewolves, why haven't you killed them?" *Or me?*

"We don't just kill people for being werewolves. We kill them for breaking the laws, for endangering humans. Killing *them.*"

"The man we found," she said, her stomach churning at the memory.

"I don't know who did it," he said. "Or killed those other people. I think it was that crazy old alpha, Lee Fenner."

"He's dead," she murmured. And had been, when Wanda Mae had been killed.

"I know."

She took that in. "You know about the war."

"The Fenners and the Gaudins. Just like the Hatfields and the McCoys. We have to adjust our sights in a huge way."

"What do you mean? 'We' us?"

He gazed at her as if he were trying to memorize every inch of her face, every eyelash.

As if he were saying goodbye.

"Darlin', I can't be with you. I'm a Hellhound. You're a werewolf. We're two very different things. There's nothing about us fits together."

She gave her head a quick shake. "But my grandfather wanted you to be with me," she said, waves of anxiety rippling through her. "And he knows you're a Hellhound."

"He never dreamed you were a werewolf," he reminded her. "And you were talking all the time about going to audition for the Cirque du Soleil once you graduated. He figured if you liked me, you wouldn't mind me hanging around all the time. But that when the time came, you'd move on." He scowled at a far-off place in his memory. "And it backfired. I didn't protect you."

Trick's head swiveled around and he rose swiftly to his feet.

"Someone's coming," he said, his voice much deeper. "Get behind me and stay there."

"What-" she began, but she lost track of all thought as he pushed her behind himself and then a deep, agonizing groan tore out of him as he shrank down into a shadow. She ran in front of him to see what was happening, and she made two fists and bit down on the flesh of her forefinger to keep herself from screaming.

A living silhouette, Trick writhed and shuddered, and then he began to convulse. Black spun around him as he crouched with his hands over his head; he panted hard, then gasped and threw back his head. Katelyn shot toward him without thinking, to help him.

"No!" he ordered as he became a black explosion of fur, fangs, and scarlet, smoking eyes. Bones cracked and snapped; skin stretched and popped and bled; black reedy hair sprouted in tufts over the tortured surface of his increasingly grotesque body. He wagged his head from side to side as all traces of humanity disappeared, leaving a nightmare in their wake.

"I'm not afraid of you," she told him. His eyes were the most unnerving part—deeply red, with smoke issuing from them. Part of her kept denying that this was Trick.

But impossible as it was to believe, part of her liked his power and ferocity. His duty was to keep humans safe. Not to maul and kill. To *help*.

The Hellhound towered over her, but the monster was the guy she loved. Justin was always dark and seemed so dangerous, but compared to what loomed before her, he was nothing. She was both terrified and exhilarated as she took in the magnificence and horror that was Trick in his unnatural form.

"What's happening?" she asked after a moment.

Others are coming. His voice was clear in her head. Inside that body, Trick was still there.

"Who?"

He didn't answer and so she waited what felt like an eternity.

At last Daniel, the leader of the Hounds of God, stepped from the bracken. He was wearing nothing but his simple brown robe in the snow, and he held his bare hands open, palms upward, as though to show he held no weapon.

Katelyn had the crazy urge to laugh. What weapon could he possibly imagine could harm the Hellhound?

"Hellhound," he said.

Trick dipped his strangely shaped head.

"We come in peace, my brothers and I," Daniel said, stepping forward. "We seek your counsel." He looked quizzically at Katelyn. "You're allies?"

Any answer she might have given was interrupted by the Hellhound as it issued a low, menacing growl. Uncertainty flickered over Daniel's face.

He said to her, "We speak in an archaic way when we address the Hellhound. Don't be surprised."

Almost a dozen other robed figures stepped forward. Together they made an incredibly imposing, threatening group. Magus was one of them. He glanced briefly at Katelyn and then fixed his eyes on the Hellhound. In his gaze she saw awe and wonder, but very little fear.

Smoke poured from the Hellhound's eyes as it threw back its head and howled. The large group jumped visibly, and Katelyn hugged herself. Then black light seemed to streak from the figure, like dissipating energy, and the head began to shrink. Hair gave way to human skin, and the large, distended limbs to arms and legs. The thing that was rapidly becoming Trick was wearing the jeans, T-shirt, and jacket he had been wearing before the change.

When it was over it was as though Trick had never changed in the first place. She was surprised that he was letting the Hounds of God see his true face.

"Hounds of God, and Daniel, their servant," Trick said. "I will listen."

Daniel fell to his knees, beside him, and the others quickly followed suit.

"We serve the hand of God and will follow him into battle wherever he leads."

Trick straightened his shoulders and raised his chin. He stood over everyone there even though in stature he was not the tallest. Was that what it felt like to be in the presence of

SAVAGE

royalty? Katelyn wondered as she studied him closely. His face was inscrutable, as though he were wearing a mask.

"That's not what he told me," Katelyn said. "He said they argue about you all the time."

Daniel stared at her, and she lifted her chin. Standing beside Trick, she wasn't afraid of Daniel and his weirdos.

"This must be why," Daniel murmured. "We chanted for a warrior in this war. We thought it was you, Katelyn McBride. And you've led us to the Hellhound. *He* is our warrior."

Smug, aren't they? I sure as hell wouldn't count you out, Trick said in her mind.

And she managed a smile. He had to be wrong about their being together. They weren't only wolf and Hellhound; they wore human skins most of the time. Even if they had to stay away from each other during their changes, they could build a life together.

"We have given warning to both sides that they must stop this war," Daniel said, his head still bowed.

"You gave warning to neither alpha, but to outcasts," Trick said, his voice colder than she'd ever heard.

Still on his knees, Daniel raised his hand like a kid asking for permission to speak in class. "We gave warning to the two who could *become* alpha, who were most willing and likely to end the fighting."

Trick didn't even glance Katelyn's way, but continued to stare at the Hounds of God. She found herself examining his face, his hands. He had kissed her, held her. Could he really let her go?

"What do you ask of me?" he said.

"We ask for your help in stopping the madness before our secret is exposed to the world," Daniel replied.

"You believe it has come to that?" Trick said, and he didn't seem like her Trick anymore. Not the tortured poet Mike Wright used to bully. Not the douche Cordelia blamed for breaking Haley's heart. Trick wasn't part of the high-school-student equation. It was as if he had come from another world. How had he gotten like this? A bite? A magic spell?

Daniel nodded and all his minions did the same. "The Fenners and the Gaudins have feuded with each other for generations. But now even the death of the Fenner alpha does not give them pause. This war of theirs threatens not only exposure, but more death to both werewolves and humans alike."

"Humans?" Trick asked, his face still unreadable, his tone frigid.

Daniel nodded. "We believe the human casualties in this area were the opening salvos of this war and that if we can end the war we will end the maulings."

Katelyn crossed her arms tightly over her chest. She had nearly been one of those human victims and she had often believed that the same werewolf had to be responsible for all of it.

"Wouldn't it be better to find the werewolf responsible?" she said.

Magus looked at her sharply, eyes wide, as though he had something to say. She met his gaze and he flushed, then gave his full attention to Daniel.

"The werewolf in question might even be dead already," Daniel replied.

And if he's not he will be when I find him, Trick whispered in her head.

She shuddered, wondering if he could also read her thoughts. She hoped not, because if he could he'd know she was feeling uneasy, worried about the fate of her pack even though she had no reason to care about any of them. She was even more worried about Cordelia. If there was a way out of this for all of them, she felt that window was rapidly disappearing.

"And you want my help to do what, exactly?" Trick addressed himself again to Daniel.

Daniel cleared his throat. "We know that the Hellhound won't allow this war to go on. All we ask is that we be allowed to help bring it to an end."

"In exchange for what?" Trick asked.

"For peace. When things are settled here, we'll withdraw to our home and we won't come here again unless it becomes necessary."

"What are you asking of me?" Trick said again.

"To do what the Hellhound *must* do," Daniel replied. "Punish the guilty."

"Kill them, you mean," Trick said.

"Yes."

Silence fell—utterly; no wind blew; no creatures moved in the snow. No fern quivered. It seemed to Katelyn that the entire forest was waiting to hear what Trick would say. He stood, his head cocked slightly to the side as though he were listening to something far away.

The Hounds of God also waited, heads bowed as if they were praying. For herself she couldn't help but stare, wishing she could know his thoughts at that moment, understand what he was deciding and what it would mean for them all.?

They wanted him to kill Fenner and Gaudin werewolves until a truce could be had. She thought of Justin, Jesse, and Cordelia. In Justin's and Cordelia's cases, circumstances had forced them to act as they had. They had been victims of fate.

And where did her grandfather figure into this? Surely if Trick acted, it wouldn't be alone. After all, by his own admission, he was merely the apprentice.

Her heart stuttered as she realized that he might be right: how *could* they be together if he was capable of such things?

"There must be peace," Trick said at last. "We have discussed this and we now agree. We accept the help of the Hounds of God."

We.

Katelyn blinked as she realized that while he'd stood there, seemingly listening, he had been communicating with her grandfather just as he often spoke to her. And her grandfather, being the Hellhound, would have been able to answer Trick. So, whatever was coming, they had decided it together.

Grandpa? she called. Did he know now that she was a werewolf? And that she knew he had killed her father?

"And because of the long-standing rivalries and hatreds between the packs and the need for peace, we have come to a decision. If they do not stop fighting immediately, we will unleash our fury on both Fenners and Gaudins and no willing, active combatant will be spared," Trick said.

Katelyn swayed. Justin would be killed. And even though she hadn't been necessarily willing, Cordelia would probably be slaughtered as well. The "willing" part was probably their way of giving Katelyn an out so they didn't have to kill her. Her thoughts flashed to Lucy and Jesse, who had been safely holed up in that cabin until the war had come to them. What would happen to them? If they fought back to protect themselves, did that make them combatants?

All the Hounds of God were nodding. "A fair judgment," Daniel said.

"No. Wait," she blurted, but Trick silenced her with a look. She burned with resentment. Fine, then; it was going to fall to her to save those she cared about.

Even Lucy.

Daniel and the other Hounds of God rose in unison as though there had been some signal they alone could see or hear. Daniel clasped his hands inside his robes.

"What would *you* have *us* do?" he asked Trick.

Trick crossed his arms over his chest as he considered. Katelyn wanted to speak up again, tell him not to do anything. But something did have to be done. The guilty parties did have to be stopped.

But only the guilty.

"We can't add to the suspicion already brewing thanks to the deaths that have already happened," Trick said matter-of-factly, "so the traditional method is out."

"Would you be able to tear so many apart, Hellhound?" Daniel asked, sounding awed.

"Limb from limb," Trick confirmed. She saw a spot of color rise on his cheek and he steadfastly didn't look at her. Horrified, she told herself he was lying to them. This wasn't what he did, what he *was*. Her mind ran in a dozen directions, spinning alternative stories to explain the mystery that was Trick, but they all made as much sense—or less—than what she was struggling so hard to accept: that he was the death-dealing Hellhound calmly discussing wiping out two packs of werewolves. Cordelia had been right to fear him. To fear *them*.

She slid her glance toward Daniel. Daniel had said he would give Cordelia and her time to stop the war. Was that still the bargain between them?

"So, perhaps a 'natural' disaster of some sort?" Daniel asked. "A fire?"

15

A fire.

Katelyn's mind buzzed on overdrive, leaping from one thought to the next as she listened to them making plans. Would Trick and her grandfather and the Hounds of God force the warring packs to burn in the hills above Wolf Springs? She thought about the tiny winding mountain roads. It would be so easy to block them off, preventing escape. Her thoughts turned to the fire that had started during the earthquake that had killed her mother. They'd investigated it for arson.

No one did that to us, she thought. It just happened.

"When the Fenners moved here and the Gaudins settled in Louisiana, it was a different world," Trick said. "They could hide. They could hunt. There were no humans here. And then they came. And so…we came." He gestured to himself. "When there was nowhere to run, they obeyed the laws or suffered the penalty."

"And we thank God for that, Hellhound," Daniel said, and the Hounds of God lowered their heads…except for Magus, who frowned.

"Now there are cell phones and satellite street views of nearly every square inch on earth. Even up here, it's getting harder and harder to keep our secrets. And they must be kept."

"And when they are not, those who break silence must die," Daniel said.

"No mercy. None," Trick affirmed. His chin was raised, his shoulders thrust back. Power was radiating off him like light. She had walked among werewolves for months, but Trick seemed far more…supernatural, mythic and powerful. The wolf in her was drawn to his air of command…and awed by it.

"And their territory will be destroyed, so no one can claim it. There will be nothing worth fighting over. It'll be a wasteland," Trick said. He looked at each of the Hounds of God in turn. All of them—including Magus—nodded their approval.

"We are with you, Hellhound!" Daniel cried.

"We are with you!" the Hounds of God echoed. They raised their arms skyward and sank to their knees before Trick.

Katelyn swallowed hard. Surely, in the face of their own extinction, both packs could work together to survive.

And if not, they deserve what's coming to them.

She was repulsed by the savage turn of her own thoughts. Waves of hatred at the way they had treated her threw her off balance. And look at how they had treated Cordelia, too. Forcing her to get married at the age of seventeen. It was barbaric. They really were animals.

Like me. I'm one of them.

Daniel and Magus had warned that something like this would happen if she and Cordelia weren't able to stop the packs from fighting. But they hadn't given them any time to do anything.

If I was alpha, she thought, and then she rolled her eyes. Who was she kidding? An hour ago she'd been throwing rocks at shadows.

But I'm immune to silver. I'm the only one. I'm something different. And I'm the only witness to this pact. I could be alpha.

A snatch of a poem she'd had to read for one of her English classes came back to her, something from *Paradise Lost.*

Better to reign in hell, than serve in heaven.

Her eyes drifted to Trick. She studied his profile, the contrast of his skin against the white snow. He had known her own secret all along, and loved her anyway. If a Hellhound could love a werewolf, then rival packs could reconcile. But if a Hellhound had to reject a werewolf just because she was a werewolf…

She was tiptoeing backward before she even realized she'd made up her mind about what to do. She just knew she was going to do *something*. No one glanced over at her. All the Hounds of God were staring at Trick, looks of adoration on their faces. Trick's head was cocked to the side again, communing with her grandfather.

All of them were lost in their own world.

Which was exactly what Katelyn needed so that she could escape back to hers.

A dozen more steps and she was able to put a couple of trees between her and the others.

Just a little farther.

Her nerves were jangling. She was certain that at any moment someone would realize what she was doing and sound the alarm.

No one sounded an alert as she went another dozen steps. Then another.

She was going to make it.

She took to the trees as she had at the mine, at the bayou, doubting that the absence of footprints would slow Trick down if he wanted to come after her. But it was difficult and tiring and finally she dropped back down, running as silently and swiftly as she could, waiting for the sounds of pursuit. But the forest was silent behind her.

Trick might have let her go so she could warn the packs. What if he didn't care if she burned, too? She refused to believe that was true. Trick loved her. She was sure of that. She was as sure as she was that she loved him. But she couldn't let him do this. It was wrong.

The wind whipped by, stinging her face. She heard them cheering again.

She ran as hard and as fast as she could.

Keep going, keep moving, be, came a voice inside her head. Not Trick's voice, hers.

Practically flying, she began to shake from exertion but she had never felt so alive.

So free. She was a werewolf hated and hunted by the pack she'd been forced to join, living in the middle of nowhere with a grandfather and a boyfriend who were Hellhounds.

But despite it all, she felt free for the first time in her life.

After her father had died she'd had to take care of her mother and work at the dance studio. She and Kimi had always acted like they were crazy and carefree but it had never really been so, at least not for Katelyn. Kimi had lived a charmed Los Angeles life with wealthy parents who indulged her and had no significant worries, ever. She'd been the one to believe in Katelyn's dream of making it to Cirque, as she moved in circles where people *did* become movies stars and film directors—where dreams came true every day.

"You just have to make it happen," Kimi used to lecture her. But Kimi had the weapons to make it in L.A.—money, connections. But now, with the lives of dozens of people in her hands, the weight of the world on her shoulders, Katelyn had more power and better weapons than she'd ever had in her entire life.

She even had the power to walk away. Be a lone wolf, even though she'd been told werewolves who weren't part of a pack didn't last. That they went crazy.

But the werewolves of Wolf Springs hadn't lasted, either. How many were dead?

And talk about crazy...Lee Fenner had kept his pack on very short chains, which he yanked whenever he felt like it. He had ruled through fear and oppression.

And he was gone.

Katelyn kept moving, the temperature plummeting. She had no idea where she was going. And then, as if he had been summoning her, she spotted Justin standing in the moonlit snow with his cowboy hat on. He was facing away from her holding a rifle at his side.

She was just about to call out to him when he whirled around with a rifle raised against his shoulder. She screamed and dropped to the ground.

"Shit," he cried.

He grabbed her up and hugged her fiercely. The enormity of everything that had happened, everything that was about to happen, crashed around her and she hugged him back. He kissed her cheek, offering his own, and she kissed it.

"Oh, my God, Katelyn," he said. "I thought you were dead. Lucy said you were at the cabin when they attacked it. And I couldn't find you."

He showered her face with kisses. She broke away and covered her mouth with her hands. Her chest was heaving. She shook her head.

Sea-blue eyes filled her vision. Dark curls framed a face taut with concern. "Katelyn, what's wrong?"

"How are they? Is Jesse okay? Lucy?"

"No one gets past Lucy to anyone she cares about," he said. "She said you came to check on them. That was ... incredible." He gazed at her with joy and longing, and she broke eye contact.

"We kicked their asses at the cabin," he said. "So the rest of the pack has been called in. Ariel, Regan, and I summoned them together. There's no holding back now. The Fenners are going to kill every last one of those Gaudins *tonight*."

"No," she said, but he didn't hear her.

"We've got over a hundred fighters. You, too, What happened down in the bayou? Those Gaudins aren't going to know what hit them."

"Justin, listen…"

"Arial and Regan are still jockeying for position. In a war, you need a leader."

"So nothing's settled yet?"

"Nope," he said, suddenly sounding very tired.

She looked up at him and caught the last remnants of what appeared to be deep regret. He blinked and assumed a more neutral expression, hooking his right thumb in his belt loop, and rolled the sole of his boot back and forth over a pinecone.

"Justin, listen to me. I was just with the Hellhound. And the Hounds of God."

"*What*?" He raised his rifle and swept in a circle, as though expecting them to attack at any moment. "Where?"

"In the woods," she said. "Just past the cabin. I was looking for you and I ran out of gas and I was running, and it found me. It said to end the war with the Gaudins or they would burn the pack out."

Deep down she realized she wasn't ready to out Trick and her grandfather. She cleared her throat. If she could get both sides to see reason quickly then she wouldn't have to.

She saw the hatred simmering in his eyes. "You *talked* to it? What are the Hounds of God doing with it? Why are they on our land at all?"

"They've partnered up," she said. "They're afraid this war is going to reveal your secret—our secret—to the world. They won't allow it. So we have to stop the fighting."

"Who is it?" he demanded, and she wasn't certain he had heard a single word she had spoken. "A shapechanger? Like us?"

"I don't know," she lied, and she didn't know how much she was going to tell him. "It's hideous. Huge, with these big glowing red eyes and fangs. It didn't look like a wolf. Or any kind of hound. I barely got away."

He narrowed his eyes and she could read the skepticism there. "Then how did it talk to you? And why you?"

"It's telepathic," she said. When he frowned at her, she huffed at him. "It *is.* " She walked toward him and pushed his hand down, lowering the gun. "This won't help."

He swore. "Katelyn, it's some kind of Gaudin trick."

"It's not. I have to talk to the pack. This is life or death."

He paced, taking off his hat and running his free hand through his hair. "I'll kill it. And those damned Hounds. Crazy lunatics."

"They say they'll start a massive fire and burn you—us—out."

He snorted. "The ground's covered with snow. There's ice in the trees."

"And we can change into wolves and the Hounds of God say they know about magic. So they can make the forest burn. Justin, you've got to…" She caught herself. He still considered himself her superior. "Please, tell me where the pack is meeting."

He seemed to be making a decision. After a moment, he laced his fingers through hers. Despite the cold, they felt warm. "You're supposed to be there anyway. I'll take you."

"I can find it," she insisted. "I can run fast. You have to wait for the others—"

"No, I don't." He leaned forward and nuzzled her cheek, packmate to packmate.

"They've all arrived. I was just hoping…I was waiting for you." He smiled grimly. "Nothing on my mind but you, and you caught me unawares." He half-lifted the rifle.

"I was downwind," she said. She bit her lip, not sure what else to say. She let several seconds pass, the silence stretching deeper between them. Finally she whispered, "Thank you for believing me,".

He shrugged. "I didn't say that. But I'm not letting you out of my sight until those bastards are put down."

She didn't know who he meant—Gaudins, the Hounds of God, the Hellhound. Maybe all of them.

"We can't take them all on. We will lose."

"We'll see," he said ."

He walked, holding her hand, his rifle unslung. She fell into step beside him. His truck was parked on a slight rise. He opened the door for her and held it as she climbed inside, the whisper of his fingertips against a tendril of her hair. She didn't react, but she did take a steadying breath as he slid

behind the wheel and began to drive down a practically
nonexistent road.

"Tell me how you found them. Tell me every single
detail," he said.

The road was engulfed by trees and shadows, and Justin
had to go very slowly around several hairpin turns to avoid
sliding off into the valley below. Katelyn did the same with her
explanation.

"It was during the attack on the cabin. I was looking for
you. The hunters are out in the woods again. I was worried
about the pack." Her voice quavered.

He raised a brow. "Are you actually showing loyalty
instinct?"

She gave her head a shake. "Okay, *you.* I was worried
about you. And Jesse." Before he could respond, she said,
"Where I come from, we don't let bad things happen to people
we know." She nearly choked when she realized how untrue
that was.

"*This* is where you come from now, Kat," he said.

She let that go. "I was driving and my car ran out of gas. I
just happened to find the cabin—" When he raised his brows,
she nodded emphatically. "I did, Justin. Can you just let me
talk without doubting every single thing I'm saying?"

He pursed his lips. And then he nodded. "Gaudins on our
land, hunters, and now the Hellhound? Things are coming to a
head. I'm a werewolf. I'm not entirely rational on the subject."

"This is really, really bad," she said. "We have to make peace with the Gaudins. Now." She looked through the rear-view mirror, the side mirror, everywhere.

He watched her. Justin watched her. Then he turned a corner, went up an incline, and flashed his lights. A figure standing beside a gate slowly opened it, and Justin drove the truck through.

Justin's family home came into view. Not the Fenner house, but the one Justin and Jesse had left to move in with Cordelia's family after the death of their father. It was a sprawling Victorian building—"mansion" would be putting too fine a point on it—painted in gray and white, and decorated with two beveled turrets. There were dozens of cars, some parked in a bowl-like meadow and others tucked everywhere a vehicle could be put.

The front door opened and a man peered out. Katelyn didn't recognize him. He spotted Justin's truck, raised a hand in greeting, and went back inside.

He turned to her and she said, "Let's go in. I'm ready."

And, surprisingly, she was, too. There had been so much fear and death and now she had a chance to put an end to it all; the last thing she wanted was to delay a minute more.

"It's a firestorm in there," he said. "The pack is completely out of control. You keep that in mind."

She nodded.

Trick? she called. *Ed?*

No answer.

They got out of the truck. He opened the front door and went in first. She came in behind him into a foyer with a cathedral ceiling dominated by a spiral staircase. Justin turned to the right and led her through a door, into a large room lit by candles and camping lanterns. It was crowded with dozens of people. Katelyn wondered where everyone else was.

Heads swiveled toward them and conversation ceased. Arial and her dark-haired, rail-thin sister, Regan, were seated at opposite ends of the room, each with a cadre of people around them. They were like two rival princesses holding court. In a way, that was exactly what they were. Katelyn did a swift head count. It looked like equal numbers of werewolves had pledged themselves to each camp. Given the current state of things she was shocked that there wasn't open civil war raging. The fact that there wasn't might have had something to with the larger group that was clearly trying to be more neutral and sat clustered in the center of the space. Without that group neither one of Lee's daughters could claim his position as alpha.

I can win them to my side, Katelyn thought, the blood coursed through her veins..

"How dare you show your face here?" Regan hissed.

"Traitor!" Arial yelled.

At least the two women seemed to agree on one thing. They both hated Katelyn. Still, only one of them had sent an assassin to kill her. At least, that she knew of.

"She has something to say and we need to hear her out," Justin said, his voice ringing out true and clear.

Unfortunately, that just seemed to be the signal for everyone to start talking at once.

Katelyn blinked at the chaos, the sheer cacophony of noise. She could hear people voicing a myriad of opinions, some of them logical, some of them downright absurd. To listen. To take her throat.

One thing became painfully clear. This was what a pack without an alpha was, pure anarchy. There was no cohesion, no order, no peace.

She blinked rapidly. She hadn't realized just how much stability Lee had provided, even in his compromised mental state. Without a leader soon, the pack would tear itself apart.

"Quiet!" she bellowed at the top of her lungs, a half-human yell, half wolf growl. The sound echoed around the room.

All the talking ceased and everyone stared at her intently, waiting for her to speak.

They really do need someone to tell them what to do, she realized in shock. Werewolves were different.

She licked her lips and then began. "There is a greater threat to the safety of this pack than the Gaudins. The

Hellhound has partnered with the Hounds of God to destroy all of us if we don't end this war now. I've seen him. And I've spoken with Daniel Latgale, the alpha of the Hounds of God. He offered me a place with them, but here I am, trying to save my pack."

She saw a few people begin to nod, clearly appreciating her show of loyalty, just as she'd hoped they would. But she also spotted some rolled eyes–people who didn't believe her.

"We need to put an end to this before they and the Hellhound kill all of us *and* the Gaudins. The existence of werewolves has to remain a secret, and they'll destroy both our packs to keep it that way. The Hounds of God made that very clear to me."

Arial laughed, a terrible, cold sound like cracking ice. "You must think we're idiots. There is no Hellhound and even if there were, why should he partner with the Hounds of God? They're a crazy, reclusive pack on some mission from God to fight demons. They know we're not demons. So they have no reason to come here."

"Well, they don't see it that way," Katelyn shot back. "They're here and they're making plans to move against us."

Katelyn glanced around the room, noting the absence of Lucy and Jesse She saw Steve, who had once hoped to marry Cordelia. Myrna, who had tried to get her daughter married to him instead. They were both listening. She was reaching some of them at least. She just needed to reach more of them.

"You really expect us to believe this?" Regan asked.

Katelyn's gaze rested on Justin's face. He was the nephew of the fallen alpha, pack royalty. It would help her cause if he'd publicly show his support.

He gave her a long, slow nod.

Before Katelyn could answer, the door crashed open and a man Katelyn didn't recognize fell through it, face-first, to the floor.

Everyone stood as though frozen. Katelyn pushed forward, literally having to move a couple of people out of her way. She could scent blood all over the man. He smelled more dead than alive.

She halted and gently turned him over.

He was young. There were deep slash marks across his chest and his throat looked like it had been half torn away. The smell of the blood both sickened and excited her and she swallowed down her revulsion.

"Bobby," Justin murmured, as he moved over next to her. "Who did this to you?"

The young man's eyes were glazing over. He looked up at Katelyn and said, "She knows who."

"The hell?" Justin murmured.

"I *don't* know," Katelyn protested. "Who are you?" she asked the man, but in that instant, the light left his eyes. He was dead.

"He was one of our sentries," Justin said quietly.

Everyone else still seemed paralyzed with horror. Katelyn glanced at Arial and Regan. Both were standing, wearing stupid looks on their faces as they regarded the dead man. Katelyn forced herself to turn back to the body. If this was their sentry then the Gaudins were close.

Either that or...

She glanced down and saw that one of Bobby's hands was curled tightly around a piece of paper. She reached down and pulled it free. She unfolded it, ignoring the bloodstains on it, and scanned the contents.

Shaking, she turned to face the others and held aloft the note for them all to see. Then she read out loud:

"You are hereby commanded to pledge yourselves to peace or seal your own fate. Be warned. If another werewolf sheds so much as a drop of blood, you will all be burned from the earth.

"HH."

So she *did* know.

"It's the Hellhound. He plans to kill us, just like I warned you," she said, shaking the note for emphasis. "*Now* will you listen to me? The only way to save yourselves is to give up this feud with the Gaudins."

"They are savages," Arial said. "Ever since the descendants of the Fenris Wolf settled here in Wolf Springs, they've hunted on our land, murdered our people, and poisoned our streams. They've been looking for our mine for over a hundred years! And I *know* they're the ones who have been butchering humans. And they were doing it to make my father look bad. Did the Hellhound communicate with *them*? I doubt it. It's on their side. You know it is. They would do anything, say anything, to have what we have. They live in a *swamp*, for God's sake!"

"Arial's right," said one of the female werewolves who had cheered Lucy on when she had challenged Katelyn.

Regan, however, was quietly listening.

Katelyn blinked, shocked. Was it possible that after everything that had happened one of Cordelia's crazy sisters could be made to listen to reason? It seemed absurd, but a tiny glimmer of hope flickered inside her. They could make this happen. They could all work out a way to live in peace.

A figure darkened the doorway next to Katelyn, startling her. She nearly jumped, but managed to control her reaction just in time. The newcomer was a woman and she was pale, her eyes fearful.

"Dom and...*she*...have arrived under a white flag," she announced.

Regan lifted a shaking hand and Katelyn held her breath. The next words out of her mouth would be crucial.

Regan let out a little moaning sigh and then she thundered: "Kill them both."

16

"No!" Katelyn protested. "You can't!"

"Are you challenging me?" Regan asked, eyes blazing in her pale face.

Katelyn felt as if the world slowed down and she became hyper aware of every detail of her surroundings. She watched Regan's pupils dilate. She could hear Justin's heartbeat. No, *everyone's* heartbeats. Some were slow and steady, others fast, agitated.

A fly was buzzing around Regan's head and Katelyn wondered how it wasn't driving the woman crazy with its sound. She stared at it and she could see the wings beating.

Everything had been leading to this moment. This decision.

This move.

The Hounds of God had known that the only way to bring peace was if she, Katelyn, took over leadership of the pack. They had believed in her even when pack leadership was the farthest thing from her mind.

That's just crazy, she thought. But was it? Were these selfish, power-hungry women better choices? Was Justin, with all his secrets? She was the most impartial. And she was immune to silver.

So...not crazy. All right then. She swallowed hard, aware that no one else knew she had just made a life-altering choice for all of them.

She couldn't, wouldn't kill Regan. The Hellhounds had commanded that no more blood be spilled. But she didn't have to kill her. She just had to best Regan as she had Wanda Mae, force her to swear allegiance to her and then she, as alpha, could declare that the Fenners wanted peace.

Cordelia might have already achieved her part in all this since she and Dom were coming under a white flag. Which meant it was up to Katelyn to end this.

"If it's the only chance to save all of us, then yes, I challenge you for leadership of this pack," Katelyn said.

Startled gasps rose from some of the onlookers and she saw the merest moment of hesitation on Regan's face. Regan had expected her to back down. Regan didn't understand what was at stake. There was no backing down.

Regan took a step forward and then a roar from the other side of the room drew everyone's eyes. Arial was standing, her body starting the transformation.

Katelyn blinked in surprise. Arial had told her father just a few weeks before that she couldn't change at will yet. Had she been lying? Or was the stress of the moment bringing it out for the first time?

She glanced at Regan, who looked equally surprised, then turned back to Arial.

"If there is to be any challenge for leadership of this pack it has to come to me," Arial said. "*I* am alpha."

More muttering from the onlookers who each took a few steps back, shrinking against the walls.

Making it clear they have no challenges to issue, Katelyn realized. Justin stayed where he was, wary and poised for action. She knew he wouldn't interfere. If she wanted to be the alpha, she had to fight for it alone.

"You are not alpha. You haven't earned the right," Regan said, herself beginning to shift.

Things were going from bad to worse. The two sisters were going to bite and maim each other until one fell. And Katelyn would have been happy to let them do so, but if one of them died it could trigger an attack by the Hellhounds. And even if both of them lived, one would be the winner and presumed alpha and Katelyn would still have to fight her in order to bring peace with the Gaudin pack.

A hand descended on her shoulder, making her jump.

It was Justin, pulling her out of the way. She allowed him to drag her a couple steps toward the wall. He bent down and put his lips against her ear, making the skin tingle.

"Wait and fight the victor, who will be exhausted, easier to take."

She knew he was whispering, but his voice still seemed thunderously loud, ringing in her head. She was shocked no one else seemed to have heard him. All eyes, though, were glued to the two werewolf princesses who were sprouting fur and fangs and beginning to circle each other. They dropped down to all fours as bones cracked and reformed.

Justin's hand tightened around her shoulder, squeezing painfully tight. His heart rate had accelerated dramatically and she realized in a flash that he wasn't afraid; he was excited.

He wants me to be alpha, she realized.

She twisted around, coming face-to-face with him. His lips were a breath away. Out of the corner of her eye she could see Lucy who had arrived at some point, but his girlfriend was staring fixedly at the looming werewolf battle. That was good.

Justin studied her, clearly wondering what she was about to do. She stood on tiptoe and moved her lips toward his ear. Understanding flashed across his face and he tilted his head and lowered it. She placed her lips against his ear and whispered as softly as she could.

"Why don't *you* challenge the winner?" she suggested. Then you could end this war."

It made sense. Justin was older, stronger, more experienced. She had heard he'd been in fights before. And he was a Fenner. Lee had clearly been considering him as a possible successor after Cordelia had been banished.

She pulled away and studied his face. He *had* wanted to be alpha, she knew. He couldn't hide it from her. Something was stopping him, and she didn't know what it was.

He shook his head ever so slightly. "It's you," he mouthed.

He was right. As much as she'd like to pass the responsibility on to someone else, it was hers to take. She alone had to end this and make this pack toe the line for the good of all.

I am my grandfather's legacy, she realized with a start.

And in that split-second, she knew she couldn't risk waiting for one of Cordelia's sisters to best the other.

"No!" she said, and strode out into the middle of the floor.

Both wolves turned to stare at her, saliva dripping from their jaws.

I'm ready for this, she told herself. She had to be.

"I'm immune to silver. I was the chosen of Lee Fenner. He revealed things to me that he hasn't shown to anyone else."

It had been more the other way around, her revealing secrets to him, but none of the others knew that.

SAVAGE

She sneered at the two sisters. "The two of you have had your entire lives to figure out which of you was more fit to be alpha. The answer is neither of you. It was always meant to be Cordelia."

She heard gasps at the fact that she had actually mentioned the banished one's name.

"But even she was weak compared to me," Katelyn said.

That was true. Cordelia had always struggled to placate everyone. Not so with Katelyn.

"We don't have all night for the two of you to battle it out. If you don't already know which of you is the better fighter, not much is going to change except one of you is going to get in a lucky bite at some point."

Katelyn paused and stared around the room, seeking out each pair of eyes. Some met hers, but over half of the onlookers looked at the floor as a show of submission. They were clearly hedging their bets in case she was their new alpha.

"The time for picking out the new alpha based on brute strength is over. We don't need to hunt to survive. And we don't need to tear our enemies apart in battle."

"This is the way it's *done*," a man said. "The alpha has to be the strongest to lead."

Heads nodded, and Katelyn shook her head. "Everything has changed. We're not roaming the fjords. We live in Arkansas, and fighting with other packs for dominance is threatening our existence. We have to change with the times. Do things in a new way."

She saw acute discomfort on most of the faces around the room. "*I'm* new," she said.

"My son is dead because of you," a woman said, practically spitting on the floor. "Quentin Lloyd."

Murmurs of assent vibrated around the room and Katelyn fought not to react. His blood was on her hands, that was true. She had done a terrible thing. But she'd done it to survive.

The two werewolf sisters kept circling each other. Then, sensing her unease, both of them looked in unison at Katelyn as if sizing up how to take her down together.

"Quentin Lloyd got what he deserved," said a sandy-haired man Katelyn didn't know. He was standing beside an unlit fireplace, beneath an oil painting of a man who looked a lot like Justin. "He recruited me months ago to go against our alpha. Said Lee was too crazy—"

The werewolf daughters of Lee Fenner turned and bared their teeth at the man. He clamped his jaw and began to change.

"Enough!" Katelyn shouted. "We don't have time for this!"

"Break your neck!" Jesse cried, and Katelyn looked around, startled. She hadn't realized Jesse was there.

"The Hounds of God are moving against us *right now*," Katelyn said. "The Hellhound has already warned us to make peace."

"You're just a bit-in," Quentin Lloyd's mother said spitefully. "You don't understand our ways."

"I'm not *just* a bit-in, and you know it," Katelyn said. "Everyone in this room knows it. There's nothing magical about learning how to live as a werewolf. There's nothing you can do that I can't learn, but *you* can never become immune to silver. The Hounds of God have communicated with *me*. Not you. Not any of you."

The face of Quentin Lloyd's mother crumpled and she lowered her head. Katelyn realized she was submitting to her, accepting her as alpha.

Katelyn ticked her attention back to Regan and Arial. Fangs glistening, they were both growling, crouching and stalking toward her. More people pushed backwards against the walls. A hush descended.

The wolf eyes of the daughters of Lee Fenner glowed in the light. Katelyn knew that protocol required single combat, but Arial had declared herself the alpha. She might skip over her sister's challenge and go for Katelyn instead, while she was fresh.

"I'll take you on," Katelyn said to the two of them. "You can waste everyone's time and challenge me if you want, but I would advise against it."

It was bold, audacious. And as the two wolves stood there, hesitant, she knew it had been exactly the right move.

She heard the floorboards creak behind her. Justin walked up beside her, turned to face her squarely, and dropped to one knee.

"I am yours to command, my alpha."

More gasps bounced around the room.

"You have my allegiance," Justin continued. "And if you wish it, my heart and body."

He was offering to be her mate.

"No!" Lucy screamed and jumped forward. "You can't have him! He's mine!"

"Not yet, he isn't," Katelyn said. "Pledged isn't married." She was echoing something her grandfather had once said about Justin.

"I'll kill you!" Lucy yelled.

"No, Lucy, no!" Jesse shouted. "Justin will marry Kat! I will marry you!"

"Jesse James, go outside," Lucy snapped.

"Someone take Jesse out of here," Katelyn agreed. She looked at Jesse. "Don't worry, buddy. Everything is going to be okay."

Justin looked around the room. Quentin Lloyd's mother opened her mouth to speak, but Jesse clung to Justin.

"Nobody but you, little brother," he said. "You go with me."

"Jesse, I'm needed here."

"No! Justin!" Jesse shrieked.

Justin swiftly crossed the room and clapped his hand on Jesse's shoulder. "Okay, come on, big brother. I think there's candy in the truck."

Jesse gave Justin a hug. "Lucy is shouting. "I'm scared."

"I've got it under control," Justin said, easing himself out of Jesse's arms. "Just like always."

"It's a secret," Jesse whispered in a stage voice. Then he took Justin's outstretched hand and the two walked out of the room.

"Time to end this, *bitch*," Lucy said as soon as the front door shut.

"Lucy!" Katelyn roared. "Don't be stupid," she said in a softer voice. "Stand down."

She felt for Lucy, she really did. And her head was reeling at the implications of Justin's offer, but now was so not the time to straighten out who was going to be with whom.

"Listen to Miz McBride," an older man urged, taking a few steps forward. "She *is* our alpha."

And he, too, dropped to his knees.

In front of her, the two wolf princesses were no longer staring at her but looking at their packmates, snarling and snapping as they realized that they were dangerously close to losing everything.

"Who am I?" Katelyn demanded, sweeping her eyes around the room.

Most who had refused to meet her eyes a minute before fell to their knees. Several still stood, clearly trying to decide what they were going to do.

Katelyn moved closer to a woman a couple of years older than she, and who had been standing right next to Regan when Katelyn had come in.

"Who am I?" Katelyn asked her, voice ringing.

The woman cleared her throat and dipped her head. "You are my alpha." Then she knelt, and the others who had been standing with Regan followed suit.

Katelyn surveyed the holdouts who had been supporting Arial. "Who am I?" she asked one of the men.

"Our alpha," he said as he and the others knelt as well.

Katelyn moved to her rival. A few tense seconds ticked past; then Lucy capitulated, tears streaming down her face.

That left only Regan and Arial. Katelyn approached both wolves, refusing to show fear even though they were snapping at her.

"Who am I?" Katelyn asked, drawing each word out.

She waited, hoping that the weight of everyone else's acceptance would matter. A moment passed, then another. She dared to hope that she had pulled this off without battle and bloodshed.

Arial's muscles coiled and she leaped, but before Katelyn could react, Regan clamped her jaws on her sister's throat and slammed Arial's head against the floor.

Regan shifted back until she was human again. She was on all fours and rose slowly to her knees.

"You are my alpha," she said.

Pinned, Arial slowly shifted back as well.

"Alpha," Arial gasped as soon as she was able.

Katelyn blinked. She had done it. She had seized control of the pack.

"Swear allegiance to your new alpha!" Justin called, as he came back into the room without Jesse.

A chorus of cheers rose up around her. They changed into howls issued from human throats. A few of the assembled began to shift into werewolf form, then shifted back to human form.

Remaining in human form since she had yet to divulge that she could shift at will, Katelyn nodded her approval. "All right. Now that that's taken care of, let's see what Dom and Cordelia have to say."

She found the messenger. "Tell them to come in."

"Yes, alpha." The woman scrambled to her feet.

"Stand. Rise," Katelyn said, feeling a bit awkward.

Everyone did so and she noticed that now only Justin would meet her eyes. It was a bit unnerving. She realized it was a sign of respect, but it made her feel like she was almost invisible.

"Get dressed," she told Arial and Regan, who both headed through a door in the back.

Justin took her hand, lacing his fingers through it, and led her to the center of the back wall. Someone else dragged over the chair that Regan had been sitting in.

"Sit," Justin said under his breath. "You make others stand."

She sat gratefully. As some of the energy drained out of her body, her legs began to shake. She knew she couldn't lose control. There were still Gaudins and Hellhounds to deal with.

Justin was still holding her hand and he squeezed it. She desperately wanted to talk to him to get her bearings and some breathing space, but there was no time. The others were settling into place around the room. More were entering, acknowledging her, as if word had gone out that it was time to pay homage to the new alpha.

They were trying to figure out what the new ranking was. She wasn't a Fenner, so it put everything into a bit of chaos as they tried to figure out their relationship to her and to each other based on the new power structure. Even the older, stronger werewolves who should have been confident in their positions seemed unsettled.

She was glad that Justin was going to be there to help her. And she would never forget how he had been the first one in the room to pledge loyalty. He had been the tipping point that had allowed others to do the same.

She was still a bit stunned that declaring herself alpha had worked, but looking around the room she began to understand. They needed a direction, someone to take charge and tell them what to do. With the two sisters battling it out interminably they were never going to get that.

"It's going to be okay," Justin whispered.

Katelyn glanced past him to Lucy, huddled in a corner as far from them as she could get. There were still tears on her cheeks and everyone else had moved away from her as if she was an outcast.

Lucy's heart was broken. Katelyn felt for her. But this was no time to deal with her.

Katelyn could hear footfalls walking toward the front door. It opened and the messenger entered.

"Alpha," she said, "may I present Dominic Gaudin, alpha of the Gaudin pack, and his mate."

Dom and Cordelia entered the room. Dom looked calm, collected, but Cordelia was clearly distraught as her gaze flitted around the room.

She's looking for her sisters, Katelyn realized.

"Who's the new alpha?" Cordelia murmured to the messenger.

"I am," Katelyn answered. She felt a thrill of satisfaction at the look of surprise on both Dom and Cordelia's faces.

Dom recovered first. "Alpha, I greet you in the name of the Gaudin pack."

She took a deep breath. "We both know I suck at the formalities, but I greet you in the name of the..." she hesitated, not sure what to call it. Was it still the Fenner pack? Was it the McBride pack now? "...pack that you see here," she finally finished. Definitely something she needed to figure out later. "I hope you've come to talk peace."

"We have. We were sent a message by the Hellhound," he said, holding aloft a similarly blood-stained paper to the one they had received. "He says that if we do not make peace, all of us will be destroyed."

"And I have good cause to believe him," Katelyn said. "The Hounds of God have thrown in with him and they mean to wipe us out to the last wolf if we don't end this war."

It was obvious that the news startled Dom, but he did his best to hide it. Cordelia's eyes went wide and Katelyn could tell she was still wrestling with the new order.

"So, let us talk about how we may end this," Dom said.

"Okay," Katelyn replied. "Agreed."

She paused. This should be simple. Everyone stop fighting. But there would be jockeying for position if there was a ceasefire. Who won, who lost? Did either side concede anything to the other? Long ago, she had overheard Dom accusing Lee Fenner of poisoning Gaudin water with silver. Dom had watched his own sister die of silver poisoning.

Her entire pack was hanging on every word. She couldn't afford to look weak in the slightest or they would turn on her as swiftly as they had turned on Regan and Arial.

She stood abruptly. She had to be free to talk, negotiate, without everyone hanging on her every word.

"Let's go where we can speak more privately. Justin will accompany me."

She headed to the door and the others moved with her. Once outside, Justin touched her arm and nodded to the left. Presumably that meant there were no prying ears in that direction.

When they had walked about half a mile they came to a stop underneath a large pine that towered upward into the darkness.

"Okay, first things first," Katelyn said. She hugged Cordelia hard.

Cordelia hugged her back. "You're alpha?" she said, her voice wondering, admiring.

"Yes, I am."

"Holy shit," Cordelia said, and they both laughed.

Finally they broke apart. Dom was looking amused. Katelyn realized that it probably wasn't alpha behavior, but he should know by now that Katelyn was different.

"And your sisters are both alive and have acknowledged me as alpha," Katelyn said, as much for Dom's benefit as

Cordelia's. It was important that he know she had the entire pack behind her.

"Congratulations, cher," Dom said.

"Thanks, she replied. "*Merci.* Now let's figure out what we're going to do."

"There has been hostility between our packs for so many years, " Dom began.

"But why?" Katelyn asked. "You've both accused each other of the same things: poisoning streams with silver, trespassing."

"We hated each other in the Old World," Dom said, "and our cause to hate each other grew stronger here. When we first claimed our territories, there were so few humans that we could run for days, even weeks, without seeing them. The safe places are being taken by the humans."

"When two packs are squeezed so close together, it's our nature to fight for dominance," Justin added. "That's what wolves do."

Trick had said the same thing. At the thought of him, her heart squeezed hard. She was the alpha of her pack now. She would probably be expected to choose a mate. Probably Justin.

Trick was right that they couldn't be together.

No, she thought fiercely.

"Times have changed. We'll have to change, too," she said, shaking herself out of her reverie. "Here in Wolf Springs, a McBride is in charge and I have no past grudges with you, no slights or insults that I care to dwell on. I have no problem wiping the slate clean and declaring our packs friends, allies."

"Do you think you will be able to get your pack to accept that?" Dom asked, sounding dubious.

"I'm their alpha and they'll accept it if I say so," Katelyn said, chin raised defiantly. Inside, though, she wasn't quite as confident.

"She's the boss," Justin affirmed. "If she declares friendship, we'll live by that so long as the Gaudins do."

"So, I guess the question is whether *you* can convince *your* pack to live by the same?" Katelyn said, aware that she was issuing a challenge.

Dom bared his teeth slightly. "They will do as I say."

"Good. We need to start talking, discuss old wrongs. If your people have been instigating the maulings up here, we need to know. And the guilty need to be punished."

"We haven't!" Dom bristled.

"All right. Good. Let us prove that. And the damage from silver poisonings will have to be addressed. And we have to let the Hellhound know what we're doing."

"I'm afraid that even if we can convince the monster, the Hounds of God will still push for our destruction," Dom said. "In our world, they're terrorists. They've always hated us. Who's to say they won't kill another werewolf and blame it on us just to get rid of us?"

She was also concerned that her grandfather and Trick might have already set their plans in motion and not even she would be able to convince them to spare the two packs. No matter how much she had dreamed of leaving her entire werewolf existence behind, she was in it now, committed.

"We have to force a meeting. Make them see things our way," Katelyn suggested.

"And how to you plan to do that?" Dom asked.

Katelyn was playing a dangerous game and the lives of so many were at stake. She took a deep breath and looked at Cordelia.

Then she said, "I know where the Hellhound's cave is."

17

Snow dripped from the tree branches as the four stood closely together. Cordelia looked so confused that Katelyn had to hide a little smile. Yes, it was risky revealing the location of the silver mine, but it would be riskier trying to withhold it. If everyone knew, the power of that special knowledge would be lost. Wolf Springs had suffered for generations beneath the weight of too many secrets.

She hadn't heard from her grandfather since Trick had revealed himself to be his apprentice. *Grandpa?* she called out again in her head. She mentally rehearsed different ways to greet him, assuming Mordecai McBride would never want anyone to know that he and Trick were Hellhounds. On the other hand, announcing that she was related to the very being who controlled the fates of two and possibly three packs of werewolves would go a long way toward cementing her position as alpha.

She'd have to wait and see, play it by ear.

"How do you know where the Hellhound lives?" Dom asked her bluntly. "I want proof. This could be a trap."

"You need to speak respectfully to me, alpha," Katelyn retorted, and she noted the flush rising up Dom's neck and across his cheeks. He was going to have issues accepting her as his equal.

"You'll get your proof when you reach the entrance of the mine," she said. She narrowed her eyes. "You know the one I mean. The Madre Vena, where all the silver is cached. The one your spies kept crossing into our territory to find."

Dom parted his lips in protest but remained silent. Katelyn and Justin had spared the life of one of them—Babette, the owner—make that *former* owner—of the dress shop where Katelyn and Cordelia used to go clothes-shopping together. Giggling and whispering about boys, or so Katelyn had thought. In reality, Cordelia had been discussing potential werewolf mates.

"Dom, *I* believe her," Cordelia said quietly, and he visibly bristled. Even Katelyn knew that Cordelia was taking liberties. Cordelia had come down in the werewolf world: Lee Fenner had planned to make her his successor, and then she would have been Dom's equal. But since she was only married to an alpha, and not an alpha herself, Dom was her superior.

I'm her superior, too, Katelyn thought, keeping her chin raised and her gaze steely as she continued to press for Dom's acknowledgment of her position. She finally understood why it had been so important to the pack to obey Cordelia's father while he had been alpha, and why Justin had been so shaken even talking about the possibility of challenging the older werewolf for control of the pack. The pride of a pack lay in the strength of its alpha to provide for and protect the group–from predators and enemies, and from disharmony. It seemed a little complex to her, unless she translated it to working in the Cirque du Soleil. A performer could only shine if everyone else–the coach, the choreographer, the riggers and the spotters--all did their jobs. She was the one in the spotlight, but her pack was her team.

It was her job to show strength and leadership by demanding respect from all comers. She even understood that by trying to appear supportive and offering her alpha her opinion, Cordelia was actually diminishing her alpha's stature. Her belief in Katelyn was irrelevant. Dom was in control. And by lessening Dom's status by trying to advise him, Cordelia was indirectly doing the same to Katelyn.

So Katelyn said, "Cordelia, that's nice of you to say, but I'm speaking to Dom."

That got a raised eyebrow from Dom and a barely audible grunt from Justin. Cordelia exhaled, nodded, and crossed her arms over her chest. Katelyn detected a spark of pushback in the other girl's demeanor and wondered if things had been different and Cordelia had become the Fenner alpha, if she would have risen to the task.

"I do know the location of the Hellhound's lair," Katelyn said, "and I give you my word that it's not a trap. I'm the one pushing for peace. Why would I screw it up?"

She jerked her head toward the forest. "We have a more immediate issue. I know you have werewolves on standby waiting for your order to get back to the fighting. My side's the same."

"Alpha, if I may?" Justin asked. When Katelyn acknowledged him, he gestured for her to walk a bit apart so that he could speak to her in private.

Together they walked over icy patches of snow to a stand of trees. Justin reached out a hand to move one of the branches out of her way. As he leaned against a tree trunk, he let out a low whistle and smiled faintly at her.

"First of all, and I mean no disrespect, but *damn*, girl, when did you grow a pair? You're doing great." He gave his head a little shake and took off his cowboy hat. The frosty breeze ruffled his hair and a little tingle settled in the small of her back.

"Thank you," she said. "And thanks for training me."

His mouth quirked up in a half-smile. "I sure didn't teach you any of this. You come by it naturally. This is what I have to say," he continued, getting down to business. "If we're going to tell the Hellhound and the Hounds of God–and may I just say we got an awful lot of hounds around here–anyway, if we're going to swear to them that we're going to stop fighting with the Gaudins, we damn sure better make sure that we have."

"I know," she agreed. "Do you really think we can?,"

"Depends on the strength of our alpha," he replied, flicking snow off his hat, giving the impression to anyone who was watching them that their topic of conversation was more relaxed than it was. "The wolf side of all of us wants to rip out throats today. The throats of all our enemies–Gaudins, Hellhound, Godhounds, anybody. I'm itching for a fight. I'll bet you are too. Itching for all kinds of things." His voice dropped huskily. "I mean what I said, Kat. Lu and me, you–"

So was it the human side of her or the wolf side that felt intense pride that this werewolf prince wanted to be her mate? Which side felt an equal amount of despair about where things stood with Trick?

"I know you've got a yen for that human boy," he went on, and she had to turn away to keep herself from shouting the truth. Trick was not a human boy; he was the very creature they were going off to placate, to *beg* him not to destroy them.

"Hey," Justin said, "alpha."

"Kat," she ground out.

"Kat, then," he echoed. "That's good." He sounded very happy.

Alarm bells went off. Had she just said something she shouldn't have by telling him to call her by her nickname?

"So you're saying we have to make sure none of our fighters attack any of the Gaudins," she said neutrally.

"I'm saying we can't trust the Gaudins farther than we can throw 'em, but we can't strike first. But if the Gaudins take down one of us after you have ordered us not to fight, your next battle might be a challenge to the death for leadership of the pack."

It was very complicated being an alpha.

Trick, Grandpa, can you hear me? I'm the Fenner alpha. We aren't going to fight. We're coming to you. She had no idea if they could hear her. Did her grandfather know about her? She didn't know if she should send out thoughts to him, either. She dug her hands into her pockets and hunched her shoulders, wondering why Trick had let her go...and hadn't contacted her since. Was he testing her?

"What's our best strategy?" Katelyn asked Justin, and pride washed over his features. He liked being asked. Being taken into her confidence.

"We need to get the message out the way wolves always do," he replied. He threw back his head as if to howl. "The easiest way would be for as many of us as possible to call out together. But there's just one problem. The people in Wolf Springs have no idea how many wolves there are around here. If they heard all of us, those hunters would be on us in a heartbeat sure as I'm standing here. And yes, we could take 'em out, and no, we have sworn not to take human life."

"What about making it sound like it's from the Inner Wolf Center?" It was difficult for her to even mention the name. She wondered what her uncle was up to. Why he hadn't followed up his bombshell revelation with some other action; and if he'd told her grandfather that he'd shared his deepest secret with Katelyn.

She caught her breath. *Does Jack even know that Grandpa is the Hellhound?*

Justin considered. "I don't think hill people will mistake those city folks for howling wolves, no matter how drunk and spun up Jack Bronson gets those poor suckers. Best thing would be for you and a few of your most trusted packmates to send out the word."

She didn't reply. She didn't know who her most trusted packmates were.

"To do that, I'd have to be able to shift at will." She could, but she hadn't told anyone except Wanda Mae, who'd seen her.

Once upon a time he would smirk at her for that. Now he was polite, deferential. It was like meeting a different Justin Fenner. He wasn't insincere, or playing a part. It was as if he

WOLF SPRINGS CHRONICLES

completely shifted gears without even noticing it himself. Their positions in the hierarchy had changed, and his behavior along with it.

"I can speak for you," he said.

"No. I'd rather not remind any werewolves that I'm new at all this."

She thought she heard Trick's voice and she visibly jerked. Justin looked at her expectantly.

It had been Trick who had whispered to her in her dreams...scary, almost stalkerlike. She looked at Justin, who was waiting for her to say something, just as she was waiting for Trick.

Some distance away, the Gaudin alpha was frowning, practically tapping his toes in impatience, while Cordelia looked white-faced, worried. Katelyn moved away from Justin and headed for her friend.

Cordelia met her halfway and gave her another hug. Pressing her lips against Katelyn's ear, she whispered, "Dom won't keep the peace. I heard him talking to his highest-ranking warriors just before we came to you. He wants the silver mine for himself, and he'll do anything to get it. He said he would pretend to stop warring against us, but he'll wait until our guard is done, and wipe us out."

"Us," Katelyn said.

"You're my alpha, Kat," Cordelia said quietly.

Then she stopped and let go of Katelyn; her sharp ears had picked up Dom's approach. Katelyn worked hard to hide her suspicions as they turned to face Cordelia's husband. For so long, Cordelia had insisted that Dom wanted peace. He'd even met with Cordelia's father and Justin at the bayou, and told Lee Fenner that if only he would forgive Cordelia, the Gaudin pack would cease hostilities. Mr. Fenner had refused, and Katelyn had assumed it was because he was too angry and unreasonable. But maybe he had known all along that Dom was lying.

"Let's take a couple of hours to inform our people that the fighting's done," Katelyn said. "We need to make sure we really *are* at peace before we go to the Hellhound."

"Is your pack in such disarray?" Dom asked her. "One word from me and my pack stops."

"Then give the word," she snapped.

"I can't allow them to become defenseless against your pack," he said. "If you can't guarantee their safety…"

Katelyn had had enough. She made a mental *push* to begin her transformation. Bone-cracking pain throbbed in her bones and she saw the world in platinum and fire. Brute satisfaction compensated for the agony as Dom registered surprise, maybe even a bit of fear. Good. Let him be afraid. Let them all be afraid.

She pulled herself back from changing and glared at him. "Stop messing with me," she said. "My pack is *fine*. Go deal with yours. We'll meet at my grandfather's cabin in three hours. Then we'll go to the Hellhound's lair."

Justin opened his mouth but she flashed him a look to stay quiet. Seething, Dom studied her long and hard, then turned his back on her and walked away. Cordelia moved to Dom's side and together they disappeared into the forest.

"So now you know," Katelyn muttered.

"Can you shift all the way? Kat, why didn't you tell me?" He looked abashed and tucked down his chin. "I'm *glad* you can shift. But why did you lie to me?"

She didn't have to explain herself. But she still felt awkward that she'd outed herself. Instead, she said, "I don't trust Dom. He's lying to us. But if we strike against him, the Hounds of God and the Hellhound will come down on us."

He was thoughtful. "I agree. I'm not getting the 'peace and love' vibe off that ol' boy. Maybe Lee was right to detest him."

"So we don't want to fight but we also don't want the Gaudins to massacre us," she said, and he nodded. "And if they start a forest fire…"

"Maybe we should send the pack down into Wolf Springs. Not into the town proper, but a sanctuary."

She thought of Trick's vast property. His parents weren't home.

"We'll send them to the Sokolovs' land," she said. "Trick's out with the hunters and his parents are in Europe.

There's lots of space, it's out of the way, and if there's a fire, it won't touch them."

"It feels like retreating," Justin objected. "Letting the Gaudins have the upper hand."

She gave him a look. "Not you, too," she said. "This isn't about fighting or not fighting. This is about surviving. Because the Hellhound *does* have the upper hand. It *will* give the Hounds of God the go-ahead to take us out. And help them do it."

"Something else has happened," he said suspiciously. "Something you're not telling me."

"When you need to know, I'll tell you," she replied.

His face clouded over. "But if you don't trust me—"

"You need to trust *me*," she said. "Now who can *we* trust to make sure they go to Trick's property? Not Arial."

He thought a moment. "Regan, maybe."

Katelyn was startled. "But her husband just died. By Gaudin hands." Luc Gaudin, Dom's younger brother, had loaded the bayou with silver just before the battle. Doug had fallen in and died of silver poisoning.

"Tonight when she and Arial began their challenge, her posturing was only half-hearted. You saw that, right? She would have lost. The fight's gone out of her," Justin said. "But she needs to have some role in the hierarchy. This would be a good job for her."

Katelyn hadn't noticed any of that when the two sisters had confronted each other. But she wasn't about to let Justin know that. Where once he had been her mentor, now he was her follower.

"I'll talk to her," she said.

She and Justin returned to Justin's family's house. She explained to the pack that they needed to get out of the forest. It was the first test of her power as pack leader, and they were unhappy about it, but she stood her ground.

"You put me in charge. You promised to follow my orders," she said. "In return, I'll keep us strong and safe. The best way to defend our territory is to leave it for just a little while." She looked at Regan. "You'll head up the move."

"Sounds like a plan, alpha," Regan said. "Could I speak to you a moment about logistics?"

Katelyn tried to detect animosity in Regan's attitude but could find none. Though Regan had lost her husband, her father, and her chance to become alpha in short order, it was as if she had put her grief and hatred in a box to be opened later. Her alpha—and her pack—needed her.

"All right," Katelyn said. "Justin, start organizing the move."

Justin dipped his head and Katelyn and Regan took the stairs that led to the second story of Justin's home. Katelyn wanted to see the place where he had grown up. They had only moved in with the Fenners that year, but the house seemed as if it had been abandoned longer than that. It felt forlorn, and sad.

As they reached the landing, they turned into a room whose window was filtered by moonlight. The room was heavily padded and there were bars on the window. A twin bed was pushed up against the wall, and leather restraints stretched across the mattress.

"This was Jesse's room," Regan said. "They used to do that to him."

"Oh, my God," Katelyn said. "That's just…"

"…inhuman?" Regan filled in. "A generation ago, they would have killed him. Lucy was the one who suggested they try medication when Justin and Jesse moved into our house."

"Is it working?" Katelyn asked, thinking of the terrible maulings that had occurred, the first one two weeks before she'd arrived in Wolf Springs.

"I think so," Regan muttered. "It's hard to tell. He's so…well, he was an added strain on my daddy, of course. I mean, we're supposed to be a pack, not a special needs daycare center." Her lip curled in distaste.

"Nice," Katelyn drawled.

"Oh, just wait," Regan sneered. "You really think you've pulled something off, don't you?"

Katelyn took a menacing step toward her. Regan took an automatic step backward. The backs of her legs hit the bed and she sat down.

"Okay, I'm sorry," she said childishly. "Things weren't supposed to happen this way. I mean, I knew that someone would challenge Daddy sooner or later if he didn't name one of us."

That he would die, Katelyn translated.

"It's just...*Doug*." Regan studied her hands in her lap. "You tried to save him."

"I did," Katelyn said. "There was an alligator in that swamp. I risked my life to save your husband."

Regan grew quiet. Then she nodded. "Thank you. They were so mean to him. Called him a 'bit-in.' But *my daddy* bit him in." She took a deep breath. "I have to tell you something. Arial's plotting against you. She's got werewolves scattered in the forest who haven't declared allegiance to you, and they're going to try to kill you."

"That was fast," Katelyn said, shaken but trying not to show it.

Regan shrugged. "That was always. You know she's sent others."

Like Wanda Mae.

"She wanted me to join her," Regan said. Then she leaned forward, curling her body in a gesture of submissiveness. "I owe you. And I pledged my loyalty to you in front of the pack. I'm reaffirming my allegiance."

"Good," Katelyn said. "Glad to hear it."

"The situation for our pack has changed," Regan said, as if Katelyn hadn't spoken. "It's not just the Gaudins any more. And I think you know more about what's happening than you're letting on, and that you have a plan." She peered up at Katelyn through her eyelashes. "But if you blow it, I'll take your throat myself."

Katelyn was startled by the depth of her fury. Aggression, pure and simple. She wanted to growl and pull her lips away from her teeth, but she controlled the impulse. It was considered immature to display wolf behaviors while in human form.

"I don't plan to blow it," she retorted, "and you'll never get anywhere near my throat. Meanwhile, don't let anyone know you told me about Arial, and I won't tell, either."

Regan looked monumentally relieved, and Katelyn could feel herself softening toward her. Katelyn reminded herself that the sisters had jockeyed for favor with their father without any regard for anyone else, and both of them had hated and mistreated Cordelia—and Katelyn herself.

"Go deal with the pack," Katelyn said. "I'll be down in a minute."

After Regan left the room, Katelyn walked to the window and looked out at the jumbles of cars, and beyond, the tips of the pines and the jagged shapes of the mountains beneath the moonlight. She knew these woods, knew their smell and the feel of the snowy earth under her paws. The taste of blood in her mouth. She knew how to howl.

This was so crazy. How did she get to be the alpha of a werewolf pack?

"Trick, can you help me out?" she murmured. "I'm trying to stop the war. It just doesn't want to be stopped."

She blew on the glass and wrote *T.S.* Trick Sokolov. Also known as Vladimir Mordecai Sokolov, the Hellhound's apprentice. How had that happened? Had her grandfather bitten him? She wondered if Trick had been his apprentice when he killed her father. Had Trick been there? Watched? He would have been young, like her.

"Oh, my God," she whispered, crashing down after the rocketing speed with which everything had happened. It was like riding with Trick in his Mustang to school; he never slowed down for the curves. But they'd always made it to school in one piece.

Silver girl, came a voice. His voice.

She caught her breath and put her hand on the glass as if he were standing on the other side. "Trick," she whispered. "Can you hear me?"

Silver girl, wolf queen. Come to me.

Come now.

Bring him.

18

Katelyn told Justin she wanted to show him the mine first, and he was so pleased to be taken into her confidence that he didn't ask a lot of questions. They drove in his truck, taking great pains to make sure they weren't followed by going off-road, doubling back, and never moving in a straight line toward the Madre Vena silver mine. It didn't matter too much if they were being followed. The lair of the Hellhound was where they would convene shortly. But Katelyn wanted time alone with Justin.

And with Trick.

Butterflies flickered in her stomach. Trick hadn't contacted her since he had spoken to her at the window. Now that she knew it was Trick, she wondered why he sounded so different when he spoke to her that way—poetic and otherworldly. She supposed he lived in another world now, just as she did. She remembered when he had told her that something was wrong with him. Is that how he saw it? Did he regret it? Maybe it was something passed down from father to son, and it hadn't taken with her father. Maybe he hadn't been a werewolf, but a Hellhound gone wrong.

I'll make Grandpa tell me, she thought. *He owes me at least that much.*

"You're thinking awfully hard over there," Justin said. "Are you okay?"

"As good as can be expected," she replied. Truth was, she was nervous about taking Justin with her. She didn't want to put him in harm's way and if Trick saw him as a rival…but no. Trick had made it pretty clear that there was no triangle here. Trick loved her, but he couldn't be with her..

The thought made her throat raw and tight with pain. If Trick could let her go, make her go… She closed her eyes and chewed her lower lip. All this time, she'd been worried that he'd find out she had become a werewolf. Not only had he known, but he'd kept secrets from her since the day she'd met him. Driving her to school, watching over her—and whispering to her by the dark of the moon.

Furtively, she eyed Justin in the light from the dashboard. He was taking all the changes in his life very well. Too well?

SAVAGE

They sped along in the moonlight forest with its twisted, horror-movie trees coated with ice that sparkled in the light from the high beams. She gripped the armrest nervously, and they bumped along in wordless silence. Every time that she got bars, she tracked their progress on her GPS function. But the directions seemed to be imprinted in her mind—a werewolf skill? She supposed it was. It wasn't just sight and scent that drew werewolves back to their hunting grounds after roaming for miles at night. It was something inside them, a knowing.

"Turn here," she said. "We'll have to walk."

They got out, Justin's fingertips experimentally brushing against the back of her hand. She didn't respond; she was acutely aware that soon she would see Trick with Justin at her side.

Maybe Trick wanted to make sure that someone had her back.

Someone besides him.

"Look," she said, pointing at the waterfall in the distance. The melting ice had made it fuller, and it was easier to detect than when she had first spotted it. "See the waterfall? And the heart-shaped rock?"

Justin cocked his head as they walked closer. The mouth of the Madre Vena came into view, and he froze in his tracks. Then he pushed his cowboy hat off his forehead and swore under his breath.

"All this time it was here? Really?" he said.

"All this time," she said.

"And you've been inside?"

Instead of answering, she took a deep breath and led the way to the entrance, bracing herself to see Mr. Henderson's eviscerated body again. But all traces of him and his camp were gone. They approached the cave and Katelyn strained for sight of Trick or her grandfather. Her nerves were sparking and it took a conscious force of will to keep going.

"Look," he said, pointing.

At the mouth of the cave stood a small pile of some kind of equipment. She and Justin quickened their pace and Justin stood back slightly, giving Katelyn first shot at examining what looked like chunks of modeling clay sealed in thick plastic and two palm-sized rectangular lidded boxes.

"Whoa. This is sophisticated blasting equipment," Justin said. "Looks to be wireless."

"How do you know that?" she asked him.

"My dad and I did some blasting, but we never had stuff this fancy." At her look of surprise, he added, "Breaking new trails up in the hills. Maybe you don't know that Jack Bronson asked me to flatten out some land for him so his Inner Wolf groupies could have a convenient place to jog."

She gaped at him, and he shrugged. "I didn't do it," he said. "But I do know a few things about setting off explosive charges. The Hellhound must be one rich monster."

Trick was rich. Very rich.

He picked up one of the boxes and a piece of paper fluttered to the ground. Katelyn retrieved and opened it. She recognized Trick's handwriting:

To the alpha of the Fenner-McBride pack,

Set it up. There are instructions. If things go south, blow up the mine.

H.H.

"Oh, my God," she said. Stunned, she showed him the paper. He looked from it to her and back again, his blue eyes big and round.

"What the hell?" he said. *"Blow up the mine?"*

She tried to figure out what to say. Trick had told her to bring Justin and then left the note out in plain sight. A note that said, yes, exactly that, to blow up the mine, as if they were in some crazy war movie and they couldn't allow the mine to fall into the hands of the enemy. Which was fairly accurate, except that this was actual real life.

Dubiously she scanned the pages and listened to the echoing silence. It seemed that years passed, and she still didn't know what to say.

"Kat?" he pressed.

"You're supposed to wait for my orders," she retorted defensively as she opened one of the small boxes. "To trust me."

They locked gazes and for one scary moment she thought he was going to challenge her for leadership. That was so very much the last thing they should be worrying about. Then he leaned in as if he were about to kiss her; she could actually feel the heat from his lips as he hovered, waiting. She saw pain in his eyes and then the skin around them crinkled with a smile as he kissed her cheek instead in a gesture of pack solidarity.

"Here's the thing, girl," he said gently. "We're not robots. We're wolves, sure, but we're also people. We don't just mutely obey every order. You know that. You saw that with my uncle. Hell, you were in on Lee's war council. It's okay to talk things over, get some perspective from other members of your pack." He reached out a hand and looped her blond hair around her ear, and her ear lobe tingled. "But it looks to me like you're playing your cards awfully close to the chest."

She wasn't quite sure what that meant, although she had a pretty good idea: she was keeping secrets. Well, wasn't everybody? She looked back down at Trick's note. What if she said no? Refused to "set it up"?

"Do you know how to do this?" she asked him, and to her surprise, he nodded.

"I can figure it out." Justin squatted on his haunches as he retrieved a paper booklet on top of more chunks of clay. As he flipped the pages, she looked over his shoulder, and saw that it consisted of photocopied sections about how to place the explosives and how to set the detonator.

If the mine blew, all the silver bullets and weapons would be buried in the explosion. Maybe Trick and her grandfather wanted them gone because they were too great a temptation, too dangerous. They would lead to more fighting. Maybe Trick and her grandfather had transported them out of there already.

She looked at the note again, wondering if her grandfather had told Trick to write the note. So far Mordecai McBride had steered clear of dealing with her as a werewolf. Her feelings toward him were a jumbled mess and now she had to add stark fear to the mix: he really *was* the werewolf version of the Bogeyman, and he really did kill bad werewolves.

My father must have broken one of the laws. That seemed so insane. He'd been an assistant district attorney, prosecuting criminals with a single-mindedness she had always admired. As she'd grown older, she'd known there'd been threats against his life from felons he'd convicted and members of their gangs or crime families. Katelyn had asked him once if he was afraid of being killed.

"No, baby," he'd told her. "I've got you to live for."

She balled her fists in barely suppressed rage as she watched Justin examining the equipment. Her grandfather had taken her father from her. She didn't care what he'd done. "Kat?" Justin said, as he pulled away the packaging from the clay. It was described as "an advanced material like C4." She didn't know what C4 was. There were small objects that looked like spark plugs. They were the charge caps, which they would set into the clay for the detonator to trigger. Then the clay would explode. "Is everything okay?"

Stirring herself, she nodded. She had to be okay. She was in charge of the pack. She had to protect them.

"I'm really glad we sent the pack to Trick's place," she said slowly. "Because this is bad."

"Bad-*ass*," Justin said grimly. "If Dom tries to ambush us, he's going to get a big surprise."

"Or Arial," she said. "Regan told me she's got some assassins out gunning for me. She wants to kill me first chance she gets."

"Bitch. I wouldn't be sad if she got buried under a ton of rock. Regan, either." He scrutinized the darkness. "I can't smell the silver. You're sure it's still there?"

"No," she confessed. "Let's start placing the charges." She was getting nervous. Soon they'd have to meet the others at the cabin and show them the way here. "We don't have a lot of time."

They both gathered up the supplies and entered the cave. To her relief, her enhanced vision snapped on as if she had pulled a switch. It took her a moment to get her bearings, and then she and Justin were standing before the huge cave painting of the Hellhound. Justin stood quietly for a long time, as if it was finally sinking in that there really was such a creature, and that it lived there.

"I owe Cordelia one huge apology," he said. "I made fun of her for believing in the Hellhound all the time we were growing up."

"Who do you think made this painting?" she asked him.

"There were Native Americans here first, then the Spanish missionaries," he said. "Maybe one of them. Is this what it looks like?"

"Sort of. It's black and it's got fur but it looks put together wrong. It has fangs and its eyes glow like they're on fire. They actually smoke."

"Shit."

"Do you remember when something hit your truck on the way out of the bayou?" she asked him.

He looked expectantly from the painting to her. "I saw the whole thing," she said. "I was there. I was trying to run away, so I lied to you about the truck driver."

"Well, hell." He smiled sadly. "I guess we gave you no cause to stick around." He took a step toward her. "But you have cause now, darlin'."

The heat from his body enticed her. Her bravado was beginning to waver. She'd had a hell of a day and it was far from over. She wanted to be comforted. But she stood her ground.

"The thing that hit your truck was the Hellhound," she said. "It came after me, and then it attacked your truck."

His mouth dropped open and she nodded firmly so that he couldn't deny it. "I saw it happen."

"The Gaudins were the ones," he began, but she shook her head. He glanced back at the painting. "Then what the hell are we doing in here?"

"We're going to convince it not to kill us," she reminded him. "At least that's the plan."

But then she had another thought, one that made her stumble as they both turned from the painting. What if, after he set the charges, Trick and her grandfather killed Justin? What if she was setting the charges that would kill everyone?

Trick? she sent out. *Grandpa? Is this a trap within a trap?*

He stopped walking and looked down at the objects in his arms. She saw his mind working. He was silent for a couple of seconds, and then he nodded as if coming to a decision.

"I'm thinking," he whispered, "that we should set off these charges when we damn well please." At her startled look, he murmured, "This is its lair, right? If it's *here*..."

"No," she blurted, but he frowned intently at her.

"It's killing us," he argued. When she began to speak, he shook his head. "It killed that messenger. Probably killed those other people, too. If we can kill it, we should."

"We don't know how," she said, and he nodded at the detonators in her hands. "If we try and fail, then what will it do in return?"

"So you're just going to roll over for the rest of your life? That's no way to run a pack."

"You all cowered in fear from Lee Fenner. If we live by our laws, the Hellhound will have no reason to bother us."

Justin clamped his mouth together in a tight line. Frustration boiled off him and he averted his face, walking in silence beside her. She started to explain herself, but she realized that the more explaining she did, the weaker she would appear to him. She had made her decision. That should end the discussion.

He hung back slightly, and she moved ahead of him into the dominant position. But she could almost feel his laser-like stare on the back of her neck. For a few seconds all her muscles tensed for fight or flight and images of herself battling Justin in wolf form flashed through her mind like an *anime* movie. When she heard his distant footfalls speeding to keep up with her she realized she was almost running through the twists and turns of the Madre Vena. She had forgotten that they were there to seed the mine with explosive charges, and she stopped and turned around.

She said to him, "Are we good, Justin?"

"Yes," he answered without hesitation. "Gotta admit, this is a little more than I bargained for but no regrets, Kat."

"I'm glad to hear it."

Soon they would reach the silver heart of the mine and Justin would see the arsenal the Hellhound guarded. His reaction would tell the tale of his real loyalty. Seeing all those guns and other weapons, those boxes and boxes of silver bullets, might be too great a temptation for him. Sure, he couldn't hold them *now* but the world had changed since they'd been forged. He could wear special protective gear. They could create weapons out of materials that would shield the shooter from the silver projectiles.

I can't believe how my mind is working, she thought. Mistrust everywhere, even toward the people she claimed to love. But who in her life had been trustworthy?

They hit the tunnel. Her vision revealed rats scuttling out of their way; her wolf brain registered *fresh* and she grimaced but ignored the thought. At the far end, she saw the dangling corpse, and the quick image of it blowing up along with the mine made her grimace again.

"Justin, there's a hanging body at the end of the tunnel," she said. "It's someone who was looking for the mine a long time ago. Just warning you."

"Did the Hellhound do it?" he asked her.

"I don't know," she replied. "I'd think a werewolf or a Hellhound would just rip the person apart. It doesn't matter right now."

"Got it," he said.

They reached the body and as they passed it, Justin gasped. It was a gruesome sight, and it still made her insides twist.

"I smell the silver," he said. "I *feel* it."

She inhaled experimentally, catching maybe a metallic tang, but nothing like what Justin must have been experiencing. He leaned against the rock face, took off his cowboy hat, and wiped his forehead.

"I can't go any farther without a gas mask," he said.

In the bayou, Cordelia had offered Kat her own mask; Katelyn wondered now if her friend had suffered as much discomfort back in the forest. It made her sacrifice all the more precious to Katelyn.

"Well, we're here now," Katelyn said. "Let's go back as far as you need to and I'll learn how to rig the charges and go on into where the silver is."

"Okay." His forehead beaded with sweat as he wrinkled his brow. "Can you take some pictures with your phone so I can at least see it?"

"Yes," she promised.

They doubled back until Justin was no longer quite as bothered, but she could see that inhaling the silver in the air was still affecting him. Together they set a charge at their end of the tunnel. Moving backwards again, she put the next one into place while Justin checked the directions. And then a third even closer to the entrance, all on her own.

"You've got the hang of it," he affirmed. He was wearing a watch; she reached out and looked at the time. They had been in the mine for over an hour. They had less than two more hours before the summit meeting.

"I want you to set a few more back here," she said. "Take pictures with your phone so you can show me where they are.

When you're done, go back to the woods outside my grandfather's cabin to meet up with everyone. I'll go into the silver room and prep it. I'll meet you back here in two hours, okay?"

"Leave you here alone?" he said, sounding massively unhappy. "What if Arial comes for you? Or Dom?"

"If I can't take them down, I'll go to the silver room and wait for you to come back," she said reasonably, although he made an excellent point. She decided that as soon as he left, she was going to make a beeline for the weapons and arm herself to the teeth.

"Before I go, let's make sure you know how to use the detonator," he ventured, and she nodded. Another good suggestion. Justin was smart. She was really glad he was on her team.

Once they were both assured that she knew how to set off the blast, they said their goodbyes near the entrance of the cave, out of sight and hopefully downwind of any newcomers. Justin gazed down at her as if he were memorizing every square inch of her face, and she resisted an urge to cup his cheek. She couldn't read the succession of emotions moving across his features, but when he bent to kiss her, she offered her cheek. He did the same.

And then he was gone.

19

After Justin left, Katelyn's vision shifted back to normal human range and for a moment she panicked. Then she took her phone out of her pocket, flicked it on, and held it up. She could see ahead for only a couple of feet but she couldn't let that stop her. She had a job to do and it was always possible that her wolf-vision would return.

As she shuffled forward, something tickled the back of her neck. She jerked so hard that she nearly dropped the gear in her arms.

"Trick? Grandpa?" she said. Icy sweat broke out all over and made her hands clammy. The light from her phone stuttered against the craggy rock.

No one answered. She whirled around. Her light fell on empty space.

Just her imagination, then.

Still, she was so freaked out that she broke into a trot . After a few minutes she began to worry that she'd taken a wrong turn–surely it hadn't taken this long to get there last time?–and she thought about turning around a second time. But when she checked her phone, she was surprised to see that only ten minutes had elapsed since Justin had left. It seemed like forever.

Doggedly she went forward, everything looking foreign, and just as she was about to completely give up, she turned a corner and saw the shape of a paw on the wall. It was identical to the one she had seen the day she had arrived in Wolf Springs and on some of the trees in the forest. She didn't think it had been there before. She came closer, examining it, and then she saw below it some writing, all of it in glow-in-the-dark paint:

K: YES.

T.

T for Trick. In Trick's handwriting.

"Are you here?" she said aloud. "Trick?" She put her hand over the back of her neck, remembering the sensation of breath on it, and steadied her nerves. He was somewhere close by. Watching her.

No. Looking out for me.

A fleeting smile passed over her mouth and she continued on a bit more confidently. After a minute of walking, she found another paw print on the wall and on impulse turned off her phone.

This print also glowed. He had placed them there to guide her, and had clearly assumed that she might not have a light source and that her enhanced vision might not have kicked in. Even though it frightened her to do it, she left the phone off to save the battery and trailed her hand over the rock to keep herself oriented. The darkness felt heavy and if she listened hard enough, she thought she heard sighing. Breathing. She called out a couple more times, but there was no answer.

Turning another corner, she saw light, and as she drew near, she was dazzled by the reflection of silver against several battery-powered camping lanterns that had been strategically placed for maximum effect. She hurried into the chamber and set down her burden on a wooden crate. Moving from lantern to lantern, she searched hopefully for a note.

She found two. One was from Trick:

Katelyn,

Everything in me says yes to everything in you. I love you. But where it's most important, we have to say no. You know why. It doesn't make it any easier. But I'll be around for my silver wolf queen. And you are forever my love.

Trick

The second was from her grandfather:

Dear Katie,

Forgive me for bringing you here. For not telling you. I didn't know what you already did and didn't know. I figured out quick that you were in the dark.

And I didn't know what happened to you after you got here.

Here is the secret I tried so hard to keep from you: There was another pack, the Blackhydes, from England. They were thugs, more like a biker gang than anything else. They were trying to encroach and I took care of them. The survivors scattered.

One bit your daddy in Tahoe. I don't know how the Blackhydes made the connection between the Hellhound and Sean McBride, but they got their revenge.

Your daddy didn't know anything, but your mama, somehow she knew. I asked her about her family back in France—were they werewolves? She would never tell me. And I guess that secret has died with her.

Your daddy hid what had happened from her for a while. But there were unexplained deaths. A werewolf without a pack can go crazy. There are no boundaries because there are no other werewolves keeping you in check. So you break the laws of werewolves and man, and then of God.

SAVAGE

I tried so hard to save him, Katie. But it was impossible. And so...I put him down. God forgive me, because I doubt you ever can.

Thanks to Trick, I know what you are, darlin', and I know what is happening. And you know about us. We are here for you down the line. But you have to let Vladimir go, honey. I forgot how strong young love can grow, and if I had known that you'd become a werewolf, I would have told you right away that he's not for you. My godson and my granddaughter are paying the price of an old man's blunder, and I am so sorry.

We'll be at your meeting. I'm so proud of you, Alpha of the Wolves of Wolf Springs.

Grandpa

The notes gut-punched her; her knees buckled and she fell to the ground, crumpled the papers in her fist and tried to breathe. Then she smoothed them out and re-read them several times over. The old Katelyn would have broken down. She would have completely lost it. But it was a luxury she couldn't afford. Pushing down her emotions, she got back up and carefully folded the pages, placing them in the pocket of her jeans Then she set to work.

She saw paw prints in strategic spaces around the cavern and quickly understood that that was where she was to place the charges. Then it was done. Stepping back from her handiwork, she took a moment, standing in silence as she worked up the courage to move on. Weariness pressed down on her shoulders; she slipped her fingers into her pocket and touched the edges of the papers there.

After a moment's thought, she placed one of the detonators within easy reach on a wooden lid. Trick had given her two— one for her and one for Justin? But she was going to leave one there for safekeeping.

She wished Trick and her grandfather had been waiting in the silver room themselves. Checking the time on her phone, she saw that there was only an hour left before the meeting.

Only?

As she went back toward the entrance, she occasionally caught sight of the charges she and Justin had set, and then more at the entrance to the cave that he had placed by himself. Had they used too much? Too little?

What are we doing? she thought as she stood at the mouth of the cave and looked out at the forest. The treetops cradled the moon in the deep black sky. She breathed in the piney scent and closed her eyes. The woods smelled like home.

Trick, she thought. *Trick. Always yes.*

Her heart would always know that Trick Sokolov loved her, and in her soul there would be a soft, quiet nighttime where his arms would be around her and her head would be on his shoulder. They would be a world of two, and that world would have no end.

But here, in the outside world, she called out quietly, "Trick?"

The trees to her left rustled as if in answer, and she left the mouth of the cave to investigate. As she approached, she thought she heard...

Chanting?

She hesitated, wondering for a moment if her uncle Jack had brought some of his crazy Inner Wolf Center executives to the party. But he didn't know anything about this meeting. She thought next of Magus and Daniel and the rest of their hooded brethren. In their monk-like robes they looked like the chanting types. They were the wild card in this whole game she was playing.

She knew her grandfather and Trick had her back, but what about the Hounds of God? Would they even care if the other two wolf packs made peace or would they just seize the opportunity to try to exterminate them both and claim their territories for themselves?

She could see it happening so easily. And what would Trick and Grandpa do? Would they stop it or stand back and let it happen, making sure to save her in the end?

She slipped through the trees. A branch cracked under her foot and she silently cursed. The chanting was growing louder and she hoped that it covered any sounds of her approach. She thought about all her lessons in the woods with Justin and she circled around slightly so she'd be approaching downwind, so they couldn't smell her coming. She was getting closer and she did what she could to control her breathing, to keep her pulse steady and slow even though it kept threatening to skitter out of control. Her nerves were fraying. It had been a terrible day of revelations and revolutions and all she needed was a rest, to curl up and go to sleep and recharge so she could face the new challenges coming her way.

But resting wasn't an option.

She'd only been alpha a few short hours but she respected and pitied Lee Fenner more with every passing moment. As alpha, you were responsible for the lives of hundreds, and yet you constantly had to watch your back to make sure someone you were taking care of didn't try to kill you. It was enough to make the sanest person crazy. She couldn't even begin to imagine what it would be like to do this job when you were losing your mind on top of it. What had it driven Lee to do?

Justin had told her that Lee had killed his father, Lee's own brother. Had he done it out of necessity or madness? It had seemed monstrous to her, but her own grandfather also had blood on his hands when it came to family.

And for some reason she believed Justin, that Lee had had to. Buried memories of the weeks leading up to her father's death were slowly coming back...

One night, about a week before he died, he had come home just as Katelyn was getting up in the morning for school. He hadn't looked good; he'd been disheveled, clothes and hair completely rumpled, and he'd smelled of dirt and something more, something unpleasant that had made her wrinkle her nose.

He had cupped her chin in his hand and looked down at her. His eyes were bloodshot. His smile didn't light up his face like it usually did. And with a jolt she remembered what he'd said to her.

"Good morning, sweetie. You look good enough to eat all up."

She'd laughed, she remembered that, but she also remembered being a little frightened of him for the first time in her life.

"But, Dad, I'm a little girl, you can't eat little girls."

"Can't I? I'm the big, bad wolf after all. And you're my little cub."

"Sean!" Her mother's voice had barreled at them like a bowling ball from the end of the hall.

Her father had dropped her chin and turned to stare at her mother. Katelyn had, too. And what she saw frightened her more than her dad's strangeness:

Giselle's face had gone completely white but her eyes blazed. She had been shaking from head to toe, her fists clenched at her side. Dangling from her left fist was a silver necklace her dad had given her mom for their anniversary. Sean McBride had taken a step backward and then laughed low and hard. He didn't sound like himself at all.

Now Katelyn paused, her hand wrapped around a tree. Her mom had clearly thought her father was a threat to her.

Because he was, she realized. *He could have hurt me, even accidentally, or bitten me on purpose to make me like him.*

That must have been when her mom had asked Ed to come out for a visit. And he had come.

He had come.

And he had killed her father.

She gripped the tree so hard the pine needles quivered and a dusting of snow danced in the cold air. She hoped that there would be a chance to tell her grandfather that she understood. She couldn't imagine how hard it had to have been for him to kill his own son.

But the fact that he was willing to love and protect her even though she was a werewolf was further proof that her dad must have given him no other choice.

She allowed herself a brief fantasy as she wondered how things might be different right now if she and her grandfather had been able to be honest with each other earlier.

There was no use in dwelling; what was done was done. The best she could do was promise herself that moving forward she and he would sit down and have a good long talk.

She prodded herself forward until she stood behind a tree and peered into a small clearing ringed by hooded figures. In the center they had built a sort of a stone mound, and on it several dead rabbits lay in a circle. Then in the middle, propped upright, stood the most bizarre animal skull she had ever seen. She'd seen at least two dozen stuffed animal heads on the walls of the cabin, but never anything that would contain a skull like it. As far as she could tell, it was the remains of a large dog, only with horns. Over the gleaming white surface, crosses had been painted in blue.

The Hounds of God, for sure. She strained to make out the words they were chanting, but it was another language. It sounded like it could be Latin. To what purpose, she had no idea. But she didn't like it. Beyond not wanting them there at all, they were way too close to the cave.

Her eyes flitted from figure to figure, seeking Magus or Daniel. All wore their hoods up, but Daniel was so tall she would have been able to tell if he was there. He didn't appear to be. As if by prearranged signal, the hooded figures lifted their hands in unison. The chanting took on a deeper tone, more sinister, and she fought back a shiver.

Her attention was drawn back to the skull. She hadn't noticed before that a burning coal glowed in each eye socket, and tendrils of smoke were rising into the air.

They weren't there before, she realized. *And no one moved to put them there.*

The Hounds of God began flicking their fingers repeatedly, contracting them toward their palms and then thrusting them outward, splayed apart. As one, they dropped their arms to their sides. The chanting swelled, then stopped. In utter silence, they threw their arms skyward.

The coals in the eye sockets of the skull flared.

Around Katelyn the trees took on a blue tinge and she blinked, assuming her vision was beginning to shift. Only the trees appeared to be a different color. There were no splashes of reds or oranges to indicate heat. The ground and the robes of the Hounds of God all looked the same.

The blue danced along the tree limbs, growing steadily brighter. Katelyn stared in fascination, feeling an overwhelming sensation of heat. She shoved up the sleeves of her jacket, sweat popping out all over her body. Water sluiced off the tree she hid behind; and more droplets dribbled on her head.

It's raining.

The patch of snow on a branch above her head shrunk until it was no more. Her lips parted. It wasn't raining. The snow was melting faster, because of the heat.

She stared at the tree limb as it glowed more brightly and began to smoke.

The blue light wasn't just light and heat.

It was *fire*.

The hair on the back of her neck raised. The heat around her increased as if it was singeing her very bones. Panic began to set in.

But then she realized that the blue fire wasn't traveling. It was only destroying the trees immediately around the Hounds of God.

They had summoned it. Could they also control it? Magical fire, a forest. Trick and Daniel had talked about such a "natural disaster." Surely Trick and her grandfather hadn't agreed to this.

The blue flames crackled. Sparks flew into the air like fireflies.

Another ring of trees glowed blue.

Someone was watching her. She dropped to a squat as she whirled around.

A figure materialized out of the dark. She kept herself poised, then relaxed slightly as she recognized Justin. He saw her; she put a hand to her mouth and he nodded, creeping up beside her and peered out at the flaming trees, a look of awe and horror on his face mirroring her own.

She let him look for a few seconds, just so he would clearly understand what was happening. Then she took his wrist and led him back a short ways away.

"What are you doing here?" she whispered. "Where are the others?"

"I marked the trail from the cabin to here as well as I could and I came back to be with you in case anyone showed up early."

"That wasn't what I told you to do," she replied.

He offered his neck. "Then take my throat. But first tell me what the *hell* is going on."

She motioned for him to follow her and they walked on tiptoe back toward the cave. The detonator was in her pocket. If the Hounds of God tried anything, maybe she could lure them into the mine and blow it up.

Could I really do that? Am I a killer?

When they had gotten closer, she picked up her pace. It wouldn't do to be the last to arrive when she needed to be the first. Justin marched beside her without saying anything and she was grateful. She needed the time to think.

Things were going from bad to worse. There were too many variables. You'd have to be some kind of general or chess master to be able to keep them all straight and try to predict outcomes at this point.

Just breathe, she told herself.

"What the hell?" Justin finally muttered.

"Hounds of God. Magic."

"No. No way." He looked back the way they had come. "It's some kind of chemical. They doused those trees. They can't have sprayed the entire forest."

"They did a ritual, and then it happened," she insisted. "And if they can do that, what else can they do?"

As she spoke, a third ring of trees caught fire and blue light shimmered in the sky above them like high-powered lights at a movie premiere.

"The fire is spreading," Justin said. He sounded jumpy, and she assumed it was his animal side responding to the threat. "They're trying to disrupt the meeting."

"Maybe. But that won't work," she said. "The meeting will go as planned."

He took off his cowboy hat and fanned away the encroaching smoke. "If it comes to the cave..."

"We'll go inside," she said simply. She hoped she sounded more confident than she felt.

"And suffocate?" he asked.

"There's a hole in the ceiling. At least one."

"If that's what you want," he said. "You're the alpha."

He was putting her in charge of his survival. It terrified her.

I can handle this. Whatever they throw at me, I'll deal. And I'll win.

"It's like chess," she said aloud. "We just need to keep track of their moves. The fire might drive more players here," she began. "And—"

"Damn, alpha, this isn't a game," Justin cut in.

Out of the darkness, Lucy leaped screaming on top of Justin.

20

As quickly as Lucy had leaped on top of Justin, the two began to transform into wolves and they rolled down the hill in a blur of silvery gray. Katelyn's mind registered a moment of shock. Neither of them were supposed to be able to change.

In human form, Katelyn barreled after the snarling dervish of fur and slid down the embankment. A twig scratched her cheek; then she slowed and bolted upright to take pressure off the detonator. She had crash-landed in a copse of trees. Her vision was normal, human, and she couldn't see Justin and Lucy anywhere. She couldn't see much of anything at all.

A low howl was cut short by a yelp of pain.

Melting ice poured down on top of her head as she pulled herself to her feet. Smoke billowed around her and she looked up. Blue flames wove and danced mere inches above her head and she darted out of reach.

Every tree around her was alight with blue flame. And then, as if someone had flicked a switch, the flames turned orange, yellow, and red–normal everyday fire.

A forest fire, as promised.

The threat of the fire triggered her wrenching, rapid-fire transformation. Agony coursed through her and it happened faster than it ever had before. Her human thoughts began to fade until she forced them to stay with a supreme effort of will. The wolf side was so strong and so much more appealing than her human side. She had a rival to kill, a mate to protect—

A soft, plaintive howl escaped her as she zigzagged out of the trees. The blood scent was nearly overpowering. Justin, where was he? The bitch couldn't have bested him. She had ignobly ambushed him, coward that she was. She would pay, and pay….

Justin, she thought.. Waves of searing, brittle sensation smacked into her and then she was kneeling naked, her sides heaving.

Steam revealed a pool of blood just ahead of her and starlight dotted a human form. She scrabbled toward it.

It was Lucy, lying face down.

Katelyn reached for her and rolled her over. A sigh escaped Lucy's mouth and for a second, Katelyn thought she was still alive. But the sound had only been air escaping from her lungs.

Lucy's eyes were open, sightless. Her mouth was covered with fresh blood. Justin's blood?

"No," Katelyn whispered.

"Kat," said Justin. Barely able to stand, he was holding onto a tree that hadn't yet begun to burn.

She leaped to her feet and ran to him, but he stayed behind the branch and held up a hand. "I'm hurt bad."

"How bad? Let me help you," she said.

"Where's Jesse?" he asked, looking past her, searching the darkness. "He goes everywhere with her."

"We'll find him," she promised. "Let me get help."

"Darlin', you *are* the help." He gave her a hard look. "You have to get to the meeting. And no one can see me like this. Weak. They can't see that we've been fighting."

"Justin, that was *Lucy*. I can't-I can't just move on as if I don't know that."

"You can. You must. Your pack is counting on you. If the Hellhound asks, you tell him that she challenged you. The way I see it, the only fighting they want us to stop is with other packs." He was grim, determined.

She swallowed down her terror for him and gathered up big handfuls of wet snow. She washed her hands.

"Good," he said. "Good, Kat. I always keep spare clothes in the truck. Lucy, too,"

"You changed without the full moon," she said.

"Surprise to me," he replied. "Remember, if he asks, you were protecting yourself against one last challenge. That's normal."

"Normal? Your fiancée is *dead*."

"Don't go there. Don't do it," he said firmly. "Kat, you are my alpha. Don't fall apart on me. "

"It's all going wrong," she said, still shaking.

"Then go make it right. "I'll take care of the body." Not Lucy. Katelyn supposed she wasn't Lucy any more. She couldn't read the emotion in his voice. She didn't know how he was feeling.

"Find my brother. Look out for him," Justin said. "I'll be there as soon as I can. There's nothing I wouldn't do to keep him safe. I'd even take on that son-of-a-bitch Hellhound."

As Katelyn McBride, his words touched her. But as the alpha of the pack, she would have to shut him down if he challenged the Hellhound—both for his own good and the good of the pack.

As the crackling sound of the fire penetrated her thoughts, she stirred, realizing that she was thinking like the alpha. It was like living inside a *Godfather* movie, with everyone looking to her for permission to do just about anything. Not her preference. But now, her duty. She'd taken it on, and she had to see it through.

She made sure she had the detonator and walked back up the embankment. Justin's truck was in sight. She rummaged in the back for the clothes Justin had spoken of. She found a duffel, unzipped it, and found Lucy's things. She put on sweatpants, a T-shirt, a pair of socks, and a hoodie. She placed the detonator in the hoodie's kangaroo pouch. She didn't know what she would do for shoes until she started rummaging in search of the body splash. A giftwrapped box had fallen under the seat, and a pair of worn women's cowboy boots was wedged in beside them. She scented Lucy in the boot leather and checked the size. They would probably be a little big, but she had a meeting to attend.

There was a gift card on the package of body splash: *To Lucy, Love, Justin.* It was vanilla, also a favorite of hers. She used it liberally.

She reached the cave's mouth and turned around, scanning for arrivals. Her mouth dropped open as she saw how vast the fire had become. The sky was boiling with steam and smoke, and flocks of birds were chirping and swirling toward the moon. A wolf howled. Then another. And another.

They're coming, she thought, and she planted herself firmly, chin up, legs in a wide stance to keep her steady and ready for action. She had seen this going differently, with Justin beside her. The last time she had felt this alone was when her mother had crashed through the floor during the earthquake, plunging into the fire on the ground floor of their house.

Katelyn's chest tightened as she placed the hood over her hair, then balled her hands in her pockets.

There was a noise behind her that somehow spoke to her; it told her *danger* and *run*.

And *death*.

"Cher," Dom Gaudin called.

Katelyn tried to act casual as she took a rapid look behind herself and moved toward the alpha of the Gaudin pack.

Dom raised a hand in salute while Cordelia stared wide-eyed at Katelyn, then turned halfway around to take in the encroaching fire. New sections tinged with blue had ignited and older sections blazed orange and red. Katelyn tried to mask her fear and instead locked gazes with Dom.

"I'm not your 'cher,'" she said. "I am the alpha of this pack."

"This...pack?" he said, brows lifting. "We agreed to meet alone." He made a show of looking behind her. "Justin Fenner is here, I assume?"

She didn't answer. A slow smile spread across Dom's mouth.

"He's not. You're all alone."

"The Hellhound might be here," Cordelia said.

Dom's head snapped in Cordelia's direction and he raised his hand just slightly. Cordelia flinched. Katelyn was shocked. Had he been *hitting* Cordelia?

Katelyn studied her friend, whose eyes were cast down. Then Cordelia peered up at her through her lashes and her eyes narrowed. Her lips pulled back from her teeth. Cordelia was in no way loyal to Dom. She was just biding her time until she could turn on him. That could be their answer. If a fatal challenge could be issued from within his own pack, maybe the Hellhounds wouldn't count it as breaking the peace between Fenners and Gaudins.

If I could give her a gun with silver bullets, and she could hold it long enough to shoot him...

She wished now that she'd brought a gun with her.

"It doesn't appear to be here yet. We are a little early," Dom said to Katelyn. "So we have time to work out our treaty based on our own terms."

"Good," she said, wondering what he was up to. Cordelia had already warned her that Dom was not to be trusted.

"Here are the terms, then: Submit to me, now, cher, and I'll overlook your rudeness. We won't simply make peace. We'll merge our packs. I'll allow you to save face in front of the Fenners. You'll serve as my lieutenant, enforcing my orders in any way you wish. But they will be *my* orders."

"Some peace," she scoffed.

He smiled patiently at her as if she was too stupid to understand what he was saying. "But it *is*. And as I understand it, that's all the Hellhound is interested in. Peace. Not *how* we stop fighting, but that we do stop."

That would be peace without harmony. But it would mean survival. Maybe she would have agreed to it if she hadn't seen Cordelia flinch. The rest of the pack might be used to cowering under a tyrant, but she, Katelyn, was not. She had seen firsthand the discontent simmering under the surface, the plotting, and the stress it put on the pack. Like Cordelia, they would bide their time until they could revolt.

She couldn't believe how completely the situation sucked. Justin gone, Trick and her grandfather MIA. More than ever, she wished she'd grabbed at least one gun and enough bullets to reload a few times while she had been setting the charges in the silver cavern.

"There's only one answer you can give me," he said. "Even if we could fight, you'd never beat me."

"When I declared myself alpha, no one challenged me for leadership," she volleyed, working overtime to keep her fear out of her voice. Dom had been a seasoned alpha werewolf for years, and the Gaudins had beaten the Fenners at the bayou. "No one dared."

"That's because we were leaving it to Dom to do our dirty work." Arial drawled.

Dom and Katelyn both tensed as Arial and four members
of the Fenner pack stepped from the trees. They stood in a line
with Arial in front, their clear leader. Alarm bells clanged in
Katelyn's mind…and became Klaxons when Dom simply
raised a finger and eight transformed Gaudin werewolves
trotted snarling from behind the waterfall. They galloped at
full speed toward Arial and her Fenner werewolves.

"You double-crossing bastard!" Arial yelled at Dom.

"Did you honestly believe I would ally myself with *you*?"
he asked her.

"You can't do this!" Cordelia cried. "You can't fight!"

"What does it matter? They've already started the fire, you
idiot!" Arial yelled. She held up a hand and in that instant, she
and her followers changed. They threw back their heads and
howled to the stars. Then they scattered to engage the enemy.
Leader to leader, Arial took on Dom.

Still human, Cordelia darted past Dom and he snarled and
snapped his teeth at her.

"Here!" Katelyn yelled. She was trying hard not to
change. She wanted to show the Hellhounds that she wasn't
fighting.

Arial launched herself at Dom. His jaws snapped at her
throat but she slammed her muzzle against the side of his head.
He crashed onto his back with an infuriated growl.

The werewolf battle was on. Huge jaws—Fenner, Gaudin-
-clamped hard on legs, necks, backs. Arial's outnumbered

fighters were savage, undaunted, harrying Dom's larger group. Dom's warriors began to fall back toward the mine entrance.

As Katelyn ran into the cave, she clutched the detonator in her pocket. If she could get all of them inside, she could depress it and blow up the cave. She could try to run out, or at least get to the most protected spot. If she did that, the rest of the pack would be safe.

"Get out of here," she told Cordelia. "Run away."

"Why? What are you going to do?" Cordelia demanded. Then one of Arial's werewolves was on Cordelia and as Cordelia swerved behind an outcropping of rock, she transformed. Her large jaw clacked as the other werewolf leaped onto the outcropping and then hurled itself down at her. Cordelia moved backwards; then the two clashed on their hind legs, twisted sideways, and rushed each other. Blood spurted. Katelyn didn't know whose it was. It took everything she had not to cut into the fight to defend Cordelia. Then her friend raised her head and howled in triumph as the other wolf collapsed to the ground.

"Get out of here!" Katelyn shouted, and Cordelia-as-wolf seemed to gallop after her. A frisson of fear chilled her insides as she wondered if Cordelia remembered who she was—that she was a friend, and that they shouldn't be fighting.

Katelyn made sure Dom saw her inside the cave. Arial was an enemy, but Dom's real quarry would be the Fenner alpha, and that was Katelyn herself. No matter the state of his wolf mind: werewolves recognized enemies and went after them.

Sure enough, he took the bait. And where the alpha ran, his wolves were sure to follow. Arial and Dom's warriors brought the battle closer to the cave, and then spilled inside.

"Get out of here!" Katelyn yelled again at Cordelia. "Damn it, Cor, go!"

Werewolf-Cordelia cocked her head and danced left and right, zigzagging as other werewolves lunged at her. But she didn't turn tail and retreat, which is what Katelyn wanted her to do.

By then all the werewolves had poured into the cave and Katelyn doubted she would get a better opportunity to take them out. But werewolves from both sides were coming at her. She was an enemy to everyone there.

Everyone except Cordelia.

Cordelia dashed in front of Katelyn and howled. She took the bite of a Gaudin on her forepaw, then bit its muzzle. Blood gushed; two nearby werewolves wheeled like sharks and came at the Gaudin and Cordelia both. Cordelia fenced left, right. She was incredibly fast. Nimble. She growled and rushed both of the werewolves, then darted into the cave, drawing them toward her.

No, Cor, come with me, Katelyn thought, but in a flash, Cordelia appeared and charged two more of the enemy. Just then, a werewolf snapped at Katelyn and she kicked at it, hard.

The tip of Lucy's cowboy boot caught its eye and it shook its head wildly.

Another wolf took its place, lips curled back, fangs drooling as it sized Katelyn up.

This time she ran.

Teeth pierce her calf and she yelled as she pressed the detonator in her pocket. She knew she was going to die. They all were.

Nothing happened.

She pressed it again.

Still nothing.

Six more transformed Gaudin werewolves crested the incline. They harried her back into the cave and the werewolves already inside took on the six. That they hadn't joined forces to attack her was nothing short of miraculous.

She spotted one of Trick's glow-in-the-dark paw prints on the wall and ran toward it, back into the mine. She kept going to the next one, then through the tunnel and past the hanging corpse. Her goal was the silver room. There was a detonator there, too, but an alternate plan was to arm herself with silver bullets and take out Dom, Arial and their fighters herself.. If the warmongers were dead, maybe the Hellhounds would spare the others.

"Cordelia, leave," she pleaded under her breath, with no idea if Cordelia was even still alive.

She had almost reached the silver chamber when she realized she was being followed. Pain spasmed in her joints and tendons. She couldn't change. She mustn't.

Her lungs were nearly bursting; she measured her progress by the numbers of glowing paw prints on the walls, and then she burst into the treasure room. The lanterns Trick had left for her still burned brightly. She ran to the crate on which she had placed the detonator and moved it, prying open the lid and grabbing a gun, planning to arm herself against her stalker.

She hadn't succeeded in putting in even one bullet when Justin stumbled in after her. He had on fresh clothes but they were wet with blood. His terrible injuries hadn't yet fully healed. There were scratches on his cheeks and one eye was swollen shut.

"Kat, no, don't, it's suicide," he said, pushing her out of the way and limping to the spot where she had placed the detonator.

"Justin, stop!" she cried.

He pivoted around, hitting his back against the side of a box, chest rising and falling so fast Katelyn couldn't actually see it moving. She was afraid for him, but she stayed on task.

"I came in here for weapons," she said. "I'll only blow up the cave if there's no other way to stop them."

"Silver," he gasped.

Silver. Earlier when he hadn't been injured he hadn't been able to even get this far into the cave. She turned and surveyed the room quickly and realized that at least three quarters of everything that had been in there earlier was now gone. There was very little left. She blinked, wondering if her grandfather and Trick had removed it. No werewolves would have been able to.

She continued loading the gun.

Justin's florid face was pulled down in fear. "My brother," he said. "Can't find him."

She finished loading the gun and stuffed it in the pocket of the hoodie. She was grabbing another gun when suddenly Justin pushed her behind himself. In that exact instant, her body went rigid with fear:

Warning. Danger. Death.

"Alpha," Trick said.

She closed her eyes at the sound of his voice and let it reverberate through her as powerfully as any bomb. So here they were. Here he was. The Hellhounds who held her fate, her very life, in their hands.

She stepped from behind Justin. Trick faced them, very somber in all black—black boots and trousers, black silk shirt, black cowboy hat—as if he were going to a funeral. His eyes, heavily fringed with ebony lashes, peered from beneath the brim of the hat. Emotions tangled inside her—delirious joy at the sight of him, grief that he had let her go, anger that he threatened her pack.

"Hey, Katelyn," he said softly, and the look on his face told her that he was feeling everything she was feeling, maybe even more so. Justin behind her, Trick before her; she saw his yearning, and his regret.

"What are you doing here?" Justin spat. Then he began to cough uncontrollably. The silver was getting to him.

Trick ignored him. He was looking straight at Katelyn. She saw now that he had come into the chamber by another route. Farther back in the huge room, stalactites and stalagmites had shielded a second entrance, larger than the one she and Justin had just used.

"Lot of fighting going on," Trick said. "*Someone* is on his way."

She knew he meant her grandfather. She held out her hands. They were shaking. "I can make it stop, Trick. Please wait. Don't hurt anyone. The Fenner pack will stand down, but Dom won't. I just need time for Cordelia or me to convince him."

And by convince him, she meant kill him.

"You need time from *him*?" Justin said, laughing through his coughing attack. "How would he *ever*—" He cut off abruptly as understanding that Trick was the Hellhound dawned on his face. "No. No way."

Katelyn said nothing. It was not her place to reveal Trick's secret identity. But Trick's silence told Justin what he wanted to know.

"Someone's coming and someone else is already here," Trick said, moving swiftly across the room toward Katelyn. He was within kissing distance when he reached into the crate of guns and pulled one out. He darted to a box of bullets and quickly loaded the weapon. He handed it to Katelyn.

From the entrance she and Justin had used, the same hooded figures Katelyn and Justin had spied on in the forest burst into the chamber. The Hounds of God. The first two threw back their hoods. One of them was Magus, with his weird tattoos and frightening eyes.

Katelyn thrust the second loaded gun at Justin before she remembered that he would have trouble even holding it. She ticked a glance at him as he pressed a hand to his throat. His skin was gray and he was covered in sweat. The silver was killing him.

Trick remained silent but his gaze traveled expectantly behind the Hounds of God to the entrance. Then howling werewolves burst into the room in a tornado of fur and fangs.

Followed by the Hellhound.

21

"Grandpa, wait! Please!" Katelyn cried.

"*Grandpa?*" Justin grunted.

As her grandfather raised himself to his full height, a panicking werewolf batted her hard, sending her sprawling and her gun skidding across the floor of the chamber. Someone helped her up—she saw blue eyes–and her heart rat-a-tatted like a machinegun as she looked at the battlefield. The werewolves were howling and thrashing, scattering from the Hellhound as behind him, blue flames erupted along the back wall of the cave. Within seconds they leaped to the ceiling, burning bare rock.

Everything was a blur. Katelyn's body was screaming at her to allow the change, to become not just any wolf but an alpha wolf, with claws and fangs to rip and tear. She defied the impulse and felt in the hoodie pocket for her other gun–a weapon far stronger than any ravening werewolf going half-mad with the pain of silver poisoning.

"I can stop them!" she cried. She gripped the gun with a clammy hand as her gaze traveled from wolf to wolf, sighting them down her weapon. Friend or foe?

A limping werewolf slunk over to her, and she knew it was Justin. He snapped his fangs at her. Blood dripped from his mouth.

She shouted, "Justin, it's me! We have to get out of here! Get Cordelia!"

Then time stopped.

Time became a triangle.

At one vertex: in human form, Trick stood ten feet away aiming a gun, possibly the one she had dropped, at Justin.

At the other: Justin, slavering, ready to pounce. No, *not* ready to pounce. He was waiting for her command.

And at the head: she, Katelyn, her gun extended as well.

"Move away, Katelyn!" Trick shouted.

"No, it's Justin!" she yelled.

"I know!" Trick said.

The fire was traveling at an unbelievable speed, engulfing the dry wood crates. She knew the entire chamber was going to blow up.

"Doc!" Trick shouted. "Get her out of here!"

The Hellhound roared and barreled through the battling werewolves as if they weren't even there, throwing them left, right, as he charged. He ignored the fire as he ran straight for her. Hideous, grotesque, fangs and fur and pieces and those glowing eyes—

—and Justin howled and sprang at him—

—and Trick's gun went off.

She screamed and, without thinking, she leaped in front of Justin and took the bullet.

Pain exploded inside her.

With a grunt she fell to her knees. She grabbed her shoulder. Blood spurted through her fingers and she looked at the Hellhound and held up her hand as Trick raced toward her.

"The silver does not kill her! She is touched by God!" Magus shouted. "Look! Look!"

"Stop fighting!" she yelled. "Stop it!"

Around her, the cavern exploded. Rocks and bullets and guns and crates and people shattered and rained down on her like fists. Like waves of the Pacific Ocean. Like the secrets of Wolf Springs.

Something landed hard on top of her.

She passed out.

~

Darkness.

Earth. Silver.

Trick whispered in her ear: "Don't die. Please don't die." His warm breath was on her forehead and when she opened her eyes, she found him cradled protectively around her. His face was coated with dirt and all she could see were his eyes, which crinkled as he realized she was conscious. Behind him, her grandfather, in human form, collapsed down to his knees and grabbed her hand. He brought it to his cheek.

"Katie, oh, God, oh thank God," he said in a rush, kissing her hand, stroking it. "I thought I'd lost you." Tears streaked his cheeks. "My own darlin'."

"Grandpa."

"Take it easy," Trick cautioned, as he unfolded himself and sat slowly up. Dim light bloomed behind him.

Her shoulder ached. The sleeve of her hoodie was caked with blood and mud. She heard voices, and weeping. A howl. Another.

Tremendous piles of rubble surrounded Trick and her, and werewolves wearing gasmasks and heavy work gloves were furiously digging through it.

"The bullet only grazed you," he said. "But the cave exploded."

She looked around in amazement. "*This* is the cave?"

"What's left of it," her grandfather said. "Justin's digging for the survivors. Gaudins brought gasmasks to the party. Maybe Dom had plans to get his paws on all that silver.

Cordelia gave them to us and Justin's got both packs working for him."

"Survivors?" she said.

"So far it's you, me, Cordelia, Justin, and Vladimir," her grandfather told her.

"Where's Cordelia?" she asked.

"Outside with the packs. Dom's dead. We haven't told the Gaudins yet, but Cordelia knows. We need to get you out of here and to your pack, so they can see you. We have to hurry."

"To my pack," she said slowly.

"The ones you were sending away to my place. They weren't all the way down the mountain when everything started happening," Trick said.

"Regan, she was a level-headed woman, I have to give her that. She kept your people together," her grandfather said. "But once she got them here, she died in the fighting."

"I'm sorry," she said, and meant it.

"But it makes things easier," he replied bluntly. "If I know my Wolf Springs volunteer fire department, they're already on their way to make a valiant effort to put out a fire that shouldn't be burning during a snow melt. The explosion will just be frosting on the cake. It's going to take them a while to get up here. I figure we've about forty-five minutes left, tops. We need to conduct our private business quick and disappear back into our human lives."

"What about the Hounds of God?"

"Lots of casualties," Trick said. "A few got out and they look freaked."

Trick took Katelyn's hand. Wearing a gas mask, Justin came up behind him and she watched Trick's face harden, though he made no other gesture to acknowledge Justin's presence. The way he passed her grandfather with a quick nod suggested that he didn't realize that Mordecai McBride was the Hellhound. Justin was completely focused on Katelyn.

Justin took off his mask. There were fresh bruises on his dirt-smeared face.

"*I'll* get her out of here," Justin said.

Trick bristled. His hand tightened around hers Then he let go of it and rose, facing Justin. The two locked gazes; the tension between them was as hard and real as a silver bullet. Though it seemed to cost him dearly in a point of pride, Justin strapped his gasmask back on.

"I'll go out under my own steam," she told all three of them.

Justin's masked face was unreadable; Trick's face was just as inscrutable as Katelyn slowly got to her feet, waving off help. She was an alpha. She had to be strong. The world—such as it was, a complete disaster—spun around her but she stepped through the dizziness. Trick discreetly signaled her to go toward the second entrance, reaching out a steadying hand that she ignored. Justin was next, and her grandfather trailed behind him.

She never wanted to remember what she saw on her way out: bodies in pieces, some studded with silver. Blackened faces. Warring with her self-preservation instinct was her own need to help. When her knees began to buckle, she almost allowed herself to sink to the ground so she could dig for survivors.

Instead, she determinedly walked into the opening, skirting a large pile of rock. Detecting fresh air, she moved faster. It was rough going, but she made it out without passing out. Although the night air revived her, it was still choked with smoke, and as they moved to the right toward the entrance of the cave, she saw that the forest was still burning.

"That's slowed folks from town from getting here to investigate," her grandfather said. "Humans, I mean. But it's just a matter of time before they get through."

Justin took off his mask and dangled it from his fingertips. She wanted to ask him for the names of all their dead. She couldn't be sad that Arial and Dom were on the list, but it was still shocking.

They went out and around to the other entrance and to her surprise, members of both the Fenner and Gaudin packs had assembled in front of the cave, which had not sealed. Katelyn didn't see Jesse. They were wearing their human skins. It took her a moment to figure out that they must have transformed into wolves and run through the forest fire to get there so fast. Their loyalty instincts had kicked in, and another wave of protectiveness surged through her like a tide. Alarmed, she reminded herself what werewolves were: brutal, bloodthirsty *animals*. Supernatural creatures who murdered their own to keep their existence a secret.

My family, came the unbidden thought.

As the four—Katelyn, her grandfather, Trick, and Justin—reached the cave entrance, the assembled werewolves registered their presence and parted, making a path. Unless Justin had told someone that Trick was the Hellhound's apprentice, none of them knew that Katelyn's grandfather was the feared guardian of their laws.

Cordelia was standing just inside the cave, facing the crowd, and her face broke out into a joyful smile when she saw Katelyn. She ran to her and almost threw her arms around her, but her gaze dropped to Katelyn's injured shoulder and she kissed her cheek in greeting instead. Katelyn did the same.

"I greet you in the name of the Gaudin pack," Cordelia said in a loud, bold voice. Unhappy murmurs moved through the crowd. Cordelia's face reddened but she held her head proudly as she waited for Katelyn's response.

"I greet you in the name of the McBride-Fenner pack," Katelyn replied.

"Good job," Justin murmured.

Cordelia and Katelyn stood side-by-side as they walked toward the cave. Justin stood on the other side of Katelyn. Trick took in the two of them, gave Katelyn a long, poignant gaze, and then walked to stand with Mordecai, who stood very sternly as he surveyed the crowd. The two Hellhounds. How many present knew that the two outsiders could transform in an instant and take them all out?

As they all took their places like actors in a play, her grandfather looked at Katelyn with such emotion that it almost made her lose control. She swallowed hard.

I killed your father to protect you, he said inside her head. It was his voice, yet different. Fuller, richer, more majestic. Otherworldly and imposing. *My own son. And I would do it again. It would kill me to do it to you. I couldn't live through it, sweet Katie.*

Be the best alpha that you can be, darlin'. Make them follow the law. Force them. Protect them from their own violent natures.

She nodded at him. *I will*, she thought.

I have to convince these packs to make peace, Katelyn thought. Then, as if Cordelia could read her mind, she turned to Katelyn and slipped her hand in hers. The two squared their shoulders and calmly faced the crowd.

"You first," Cordelia whispered.

"We don't have much time," Katelyn said to the assembly. "The humans will be here soon." Suspicious gazes ticked toward her grandfather and Trick as if to point out that humans were in their midst, but she went on. "This has to be the last of the fighting between us. Or none of us will survive."

"The humans *are* coming," Cordelia echoed. "Dom is dead, and I declare myself alpha. And I say that we're at peace with the Fenners. From now on."

"You're not even one of us!" someone from the crowd shouted at her. Jeers rose, but also a voice that bellowed guttural words in Louisiana Cajun French. The protestors fell silent, sullen.

"I *am* one of you," Cordelia said emphatically. "I'm a werewolf. That's all we are today. Not Gaudins or Fenners or even a McBride." She gestured to the fire, and to the caved-in mine behind her. "Look at what's happened. The Hellhound promised retribution if we fought and it didn't do any of this. We did this to ourselves!"

"No. *We* did it," said a man from among the untouched trees closest to the throng.

Hooded figures appeared. The Hounds of God. And with them came Jack Bronson, in handcuffs. The tremendously tall figure beside Bronson threw back his hood. It was Daniel Latgale, his face cut and swollen, his hands sooty and bloody.

He said, "I offer my deepest apologies to the alphas of the Gaudin and McBride-Fenner packs. Magus, my most trusted lieutenant, set the mine on fire, and that set off the explosion. God struck him down."

Katelyn raised her chin. "You are his alpha. You lost control of him."

"The same may be said of the alpha who led the Fenner pack before you," he replied. "Lee Fenner. I believe we are even."

He had her there.

"Magus might have been acting on his own in the cave, but you set the forest fire." That was a guess. She hadn't seen him in the chanting circle.

"It was our agreement," he replied. "My actions were justified. There *was* fighting. A lot of it."

Katelyn shifted her attention to her uncle. Jack Bronson, John McBride. She should be surprised to see him there, but somehow, she didn't think anything could surprise her.

"Why have you brought *him* here?"

"So that he may confess his crimes before God and those he has wronged. It is written: 'For I would go down to hell itself, and drag out the wicked by their entrails.'"

Katelyn leveled her gaze at Jack Bronson, realizing fleetingly how different their positions were than when they'd last met. He even looked different, wild-eyed, disheveled and crazy, a marked contrast to his previous cool, controlled demeanor.

"What did he do?" she asked.

"It's his fault!" Bronson shrieked, looking over at her grandfather, who stood eyes narrowed, arms folded across his chest. "I waited and waited for my brother to share his power. I wanted to be a Hellhound. I wanted to feel that inner beast. But then he wouldn't. Damn you, Mordecai!"

Katelyn's grandfather betrayed no emotion as his secret was revealed to the entire crowd. Some of them murmured and drew back; others just stared in shock. Justin narrowed his eyes at Trick, and then looked away.

"Hellhound, forgive us," Katelyn said formally, and she sank to her knees. "Spare us."

"Forgive us," Cordelia echoed, and, still holding Katelyn's hand, did the same. Every other werewolf there bent his or her knee except for Daniel, who lowered his head while keeping a firm grip on Jack Bronson

"*I* am the Hellhound," Mordecai said. "I have laws I must follow the same as you. You must never reveal the presence of werewolves to humanity, and I must stop you and punish you if you do. It's not my place to forgive. It's my place to enforce."

They stayed on their knees, and Cordelia's hand trembled in Katelyn's grasp.

"For generations, most of you believed that the Hellhound was a myth. A tall tale like so many here in the Ozarks. Like this lost mine. Now you know that I'm real, and that I'm living among you. As is my apprentice, Vladimir. So, that's different."

"Yes, Hellhound," Cordelia said, and many of the others murmured their agreement.

"And because I'm different, I'll give you this last chance to sort yourselves out and sink back into the forest and the bayou again. All you will ever be to the humans around here is folks like them. Clannish neighbors who mostly keep to themselves, but mix when it makes sense to." He looked at Katelyn. "Who go to school and lead lives."

"What about my life?" Bronson blurted. "What about my destiny?"

"Never featured you having one," Mordecai said coldly.

"Oh? Well, I succeeded in spite of you, didn't I? You didn't want me here but I came, didn't I? "And I prayed to Fenris to make me a werewolf, and he showed me what to do. I made the required sacrifice."

"A human sacrifice," Daniel elaborated grimly. "I was not aware of this until today. But Magus knew. They made a pact to get the silver in the mine."

"Insanity," Justin said, as the werewolves reacted. "That's *not* Fenris's way."

"It used to be. It's how Fenris became a werewolf. You don't know *anything,*" Bronson sneered at Justin, then smirked at everyone in his line of sight. "You've lost the old ways through your generations of inbreeding. You're all pathetic."

"You killed Haley," Trick said, his voice low with deadly menace. The hair on the back of Katelyn's neck rose, and she saw the effect his tone had on the others. Even when he was in his human form, Trick frightened them.

Bronson shook his head. "That wasn't her name. It was…" He thought a moment as if trying to remember. "Becky."

"Becky Johnson. You're the killer," Katelyn said. "All those people. You killed them."

Bronson shook his head again. "No. Just two. Becky was the easy one. Kept sneaking onto my property because she had a thing for one of my seminar students. *She* came to *me*. Then, later, I got rid of *him*, too. So there's my two. That's it. And that was all it took. Magus made contact and—"

"*Magus* made contact," Daniel said firmly, looking at Katelyn's grandfather. "For silver. Like Judas."

Katelyn remembered being told that Becky's body had been moved from the Inner Wolf Center. That was why she and Trick had broken in in the first place. Had Trick known back then that Bronson had killed her?

"You also killed Mike Wright," she accused him. "Say it." She wanted it to be him. Mike had wanted to beat and rape her, and Trick had been thrown in jail as a suspect. Trick said he hadn't done it, but she knew that there was someone else willing to kill anyone who tried to hurt her.

Her grandfather.

She wanted to be reassured that Ed hadn't done it.

"You're as deaf as you are pretty," Bronson said. "I said just the two."

"More than enough," Mordecai growled. "You know the law. Werewolves do not murder humans. And you know the punishment."

"He isn't a Hound of God," Daniel said. "Magus hadn't fulfilled his end of their bargain. He's not a werewolf. I swear it."

"*What?*" Jack Bronson stared at him. "But he said that on the next full moon I would run through the forest!"

"He lied to you. As he lied to me. Clearly he was planning some kind of challenge to me. And after you and he found the mine, he would probably have killed you." He studied each of the Hounds of God in turn, who were still cowering on their knees. "I'll find out who his lieutenants were. And I will punish my own. But you, Bronson, are not one of my own."

"Then he's not ours to punish, either," Trick said.

Bronson gaped at Trick. "*You?* He chose *you?* But I should be the one! It should be family!"

"He is," Mordecai replied. "More than you ever have been." He put his arm around Trick. "This is the Hellhound's apprentice. Lay one finger on him, and feel our combined wrath."

The werewolves kept kneeling. Trick couldn't quite conceal a smirk as he stood beside his godfather.

"Stand," her grandfather said. "There are still questions to be answered. Human deaths to be avenged."

Katelyn wasn't done with her uncle. His actions accounted for the deaths of two people, but not the others.

"If you didn't kill Haley, who did? And how about Mike?" she insisted. Was their killer the wolf that had bitten her? And was that wolf buried in a pile of rubble inside the silver mine?

Jack Bronson knew all kinds of things he shouldn't. Maybe he knew the one thing she wanted most to know.

"Who bit me?"

The air around her electrified; she wasn't the only one waiting to hear his reply. Her life, her destiny came down to this: a single name.

The answer.

Her uncle looked at her coolly. "I don't know who bit you."

There was that same joy in her pain that he'd evinced when he'd told her that her grandfather had killed her father. She saw the bitterness and deep-seated evil of John McBride and she was sorry that she'd asked him even as the fear that she'd never know the answer settled down around her shoulders.

Suddenly, there was a rustling in the trees. Everyone turned just as Jesse stumbled out of them.

"Jesse!" Justin ran toward him. "Oh, my God! Where've you been?"

"I know! I know who bit Kat!" he said excitedly. "I saw."

Justin put his arms around him. "No, buddy, you don't know that." His tone was friendly, but his voice was off. He began to walk away with Jesse in tow.

"But I do," Jesse insisted, stopping. "Mustn't tell. It's a secret. I told Lucy and then she ran away. Bad, bad!" He pounded his forehead.

"Jesse?" Katelyn said.

Justin waved his hand. "You know Jesse. He's just a big kid. He doesn't know anything," he insisted, an edge of fear in his voice.

"Tell me, Jesse. I promise I won't run away," Katelyn said, a sick feeling beginning to coil itself like a serpent in her stomach.

Jesse blinked and looked around, as if he had just noticed that everyone was looking at him. He looked at his brother. Justin was silently pleading with him.

"It's okay," Katelyn said, hearing the edge of fear in her own voice.

Jesse smiled uncertainly at her.

"Justin bit you. He wants to marry you."

"That's not true," Justin said carefully. "You got bit how long ago? I couldn't change back then."

Jesse sucked in his breath and covered his mouth with both hands. He lowered his head and shook it back and forth in terrible distress.

"Could he change back then?" Katelyn's grandfather asked Jesse.

"Lucy!" Jesse screamed. "I want Lucy *now!*"

He pulled away from Justin, turned, and ran back the way he had come. Justin made as if to bolt after him, but Mordecai stepped into Justin's path.

"Think we need to hear a little more from you," he said to Justin.

"I didn't do it," Justin said, but his guilt was written all over his face.

Desperately Katelyn tried to find a good reason. That he had fallen in love with her and had bitten her in a moment of passion without permission from his alpha. That he had had to hide what he'd done for fear of reprisal.

But what he had done to her in the forest had been deliberate, calculating. Passion had been completely absent.

"*You've* been killing people," Cordelia said slowly. "*You*, Justin. You wanted to make my daddy look like a crazy killer. So when you issued a challenge it would look *so* noble and not like the treachery it was."

As Cordelia spoke, Mordecai stood in Justin's path, watching him the way a snake watches a mouse. Katelyn's heart was thundering, wild. She wanted to kill him herself. Justin knew that his life was on the line, but he seemed curiously detached. Distracted.

He was looking past Katelyn's grandfather into the forest.

He was looking for his brother.

"He was talking about getting rid of Jesse," Justin said. "I had to become alpha. I had to protect my brother." He looked at Katelyn with a haunted expression. "After I bit you, and you got away, I realized you went to Cordelia. I knew she was keeping it a secret from her father."

"You fixed it so we were discovered after Katelyn's first change," Cordelia said. "It was *you* who got me banished."

"The alpha's favorite daughter. The one he had picked to succeed him. It worked out great," he said.

Katelyn dug her fingernails into her palms. She wanted to hurt him for ruining her life. But was it ruined?

It was different. In so many ways, it was more magnificent than she could ever have conceived of. She was the alpha of a werewolf pack.

And she had never felt more amazing than when the wolf took her over.

"Katelyn, I did come to care for you. To love you," he said.

"*After* you found out that I'm immune to silver," she said. She looked at the shock on the faces of the other werewolves. That's when you decided to dump Lucy for me."

"No." He shook his head. "Way before then, darlin'. Don't sell yourself short. I wanted you. God, I wanted you."

She dug her fingernails into her palms. There had been so many times when she had felt the desire rise between them, wolfish and savage. She had never given in, and now she was so glad.

"You would do anything to protect your brother. I'll bet you even killed your own father. Lee didn't do it, did he? Did your father threaten Jesse?" Katelyn asked.

"Kat," Justin said, turning his attention toward her. Those blue eyes. She remembered the day he had dropped his motorcycle in front of her grandfather's oncoming truck to save the life of a little girl. He'd had nothing to gain by that. "Darlin', I pledged myself—"

"And Mike?" she asked savagely. "Did you do that so Trick would get blamed? Because everyone knew he and Mike hated each other? You thought you'd throw some doubt into the mix so you could play the big worried hero of the pack *and* get rid of 'that boy'?"

"I killed him because he came after you," Justin said. "I'm from the hills, darlin'. That's what men do."

The branches of the nearest tree moved, and Katelyn moved swiftly toward them. As she passed Cordelia, the other girl stood beside Trick, quivering with rage.

"All this time, you've been manipulating everyone. And *you're* the werewolf that needs to be put down," Cordelia said.

Katelyn parted the branches and found Jesse with his hands over his head. He threw his arms around Katelyn.

"I'm sorry. I'm sorry," he said.

"It's okay," Katelyn said woodenly. It wasn't. It was horribly far from okay.

"Then where's Lucy?" he begged her.

She kept hugging him with no idea what to say. They stood pressed together and he whimpered like a little puppy.

No, like a wolf cub.

"I killed her, buddy," Justin said. "I'm sorry. She came out of the darkness and she scared me. It was an accident."

The werewolves gasped. Heads swiveled toward Katelyn, who had been her rival. Katelyn just held Jesse, waiting for him to lose control the way he had when Lee Fenner had died. But to her surprise, his face went slack and ashen and he shut his eyes. He began to shake, and she was afraid he was going into shock.

"Jesse, I'm sorry," Justin said. "Oh, God. I tried to keep him quiet. I told him I wanted to make a mate for him. That it was a special secret." He covered his face with his hands, then dropped his arms to his side. His swollen eye was nearly normal-sized again. His injuries were healing.

He would soon be at fighting trim.

"Alpha, what are you going to do?" one of the werewolves asked Katelyn.

"It's not the alpha's problem," Trick growled, stepping forward. "It's mine."

Justin and Trick locked gazes; both shifted fast as lightning. Justin, a large gray blue-eyed wolf. She would have gone to her grave swearing he had not been the werewolf that had bitten her. Trick, huge and night-black and monstrous. The werewolves screamed and scattered as he bore down on Justin. He swiped his claws at him, and Justin howled with rage and pain as bloody paths striped his flank.

Justin defiantly snapped at the Hellhound's throat, fangs missing by the barest margin. Trick's claws slashed again and in a matter of seconds, Justin was on the ground, morphing back into his human form horribly wounded, panting. Trick stood over him, one massive paw pinning him down with supreme ease.

"Vladimir," Mordecai said, stepping forward, "it's time."

Trick—she had to think of him that way—waggled his ugly head. Smoke poured from his eyes. Saliva roped from his fangs as he looked back down at his victim. From a safe distance, everyone stood in horrified silence, holding their breath.

Justin was bleeding in a dozen different places. Katelyn thought back to the first time he came to the cabin and she rode into the forest on his motorcycle. How he had trained her to survive, and helped her, and did love her.

He did love her, in spite of everything.

Slowly Trick began shifting back, massive head beginning to shrink, smoking, blazing eyes to smolder. Claws and fangs started to retract.

"Doc," Trick said quietly. He spoke the name like a question.

A request.

"No," Katelyn's grandfather said. "It's got to be done. You're my apprentice, and you took an oath before I made you what you are."

"Just do it," Justin muttered. "Get it over with."

Trick's never killed anyone before, Katelyn realized with a thrill.

Trick loomed over Justin. He was distraught.

Yet determined.

A shape hurtled forward and then stopped directly in front of Trick. It was Jesse. Fear and awe mingled on his face, but he stood his ground. Slowly, Trick began to shift back to his Hellhound form, and Katelyn shouted, "Jesse, get back!"

Jesse seemed dazed as he looked down at his brother. Tears streamed down his face and dripped from his chin.

"Softly, softly," Jesse muttered, sliding to the ground. He cradled Justin's head in his lap and stroked his hair like the fur of a pet. Like LaRue, the cat he longed to own but couldn't because he might pet it too hard and break its neck.

Katelyn realized what was coming and leaped toward him, but it was too late. He grabbed Justin's head and twisted hard.

Katelyn heard the pop above the gasps and screams and Jesse's wails as Trick morphed back to human form and reached his arms out to Jesse. Cordelia flew to Jesse and rocked him as he let out a low, mournful howl.

No pack member answered him.

Until Katelyn did. She let out the same howl she had heard the first day she had arrived in Wolf Springs. Maybe it was wrong to salute Justin's passing with the gift of grief, but she did it anyway.

Then the howling died away, and Jesse kept sobbing in Cordelia's arms.

Time ticked by dangerously fast. The fire crept closer. Her ears picked up the whine of a fire engine far below…but on its way.

Katelyn finally found her voice and said, "This is what happens when old customs collide with reality. We *have* to live differently."

"But how?" someone asked fearfully.

"Leave Wolf Springs?" another voice fretted.

"I don't know," Katelyn said. "Yet."

She looked over at her grandfather. His stern expression softened and he grabbed Trick's hand, marched him over, and placed it in Katelyn's. Her skin tingled where it touched his, and she sucked in her breath.

Mordecai McBride surveyed the werewolves and lifted his chin. "I approve of this," he announced.

"Hellhound?" Trick said cautiously. "What are you doing, sir?"

Her grandfather shrugged as if it were obvious. "We're immune to silver," he said. "They aren't. But she is." He brushed his fingertips against her cheek, not quite, but almost, a pack greeting. He looked like her father, and the complicated love that seemed to pass down in each generation of her family wove itself into her careful joy.

"She is immune, and she's right. The old ways need to die," he said.

"I didn't say *that*," she blurted.

"More or less." Trick squeezed her hand. "I'm with Doc on this one." He was blazing with happiness. "If you are."

She cleared her throat. "This is a private conversation we need to have." Then she faced the werewolves, who were agog.

Cordelia stepped forward. "This is *our* alpha. We've lost so many pack members today. Dominic and Luc Gaudin are both gone. My sisters are both dead. There aren't very many of us left. I say it makes more sense to band together than to fight."

Cordelia knelt. After only a moment's hesitation Daniel Latgale pushed Jack Bronson down and followed suit, and Katelyn knew it must have cost him dearly. Maybe he could do it because he considered her silver immunity to be a sign of holy favor.

The rest of the Fenner clan and the Hounds of God fell to their knees as well. The Gaudins remained standing. Then an older Gaudin male gestured to Trick and said, "Even if she's not our alpha, she is a Hellhound's mate." He knelt.

Then one by one, the others hit their knees, until Katelyn, Trick, and Mordecai were left standing.

And awestruck by what had just happened.

The war was over.

And Katelyn had won it.

22

Three hours later, Katelyn, Cordelia, Daniel, and two high-ranking Gaudin and Fenner werewolves entered the McBride cabin for their first summit meeting. The orange glow of the dying fire tinged the night sky. The little fire department and police force of Wolf Springs had finally managed to arrive, but by then the fire had all but died. It had been started and fueled by magic, and Daniel Latgale and the Hounds of God killed it with magic as well.

The police did not know about Jack Bronson's guilt. He would never return to the Inner Wolf Center; he would never return to human company. Katelyn hadn't countenanced his death, and the Hellhounds had no jurisdiction over him. The Hounds of God had agreed to take charge of him, and she thought he was delighted with his outcome. She resented his happiness. He didn't deserve it.

Trick and her grandfather stayed out of the proceedings as she parlayed with the other werewolves. They remained in the woods, prowling in Hellhound form to make sure that Katelyn and her people were safe as they worked to form a merged pack. The negotiations went better than Katelyn could have hoped. Having a Hellhound as a boyfriend was proving to be very convenient.

Dawn was coming, metaphorically and in reality, and the meeting broke up. Then Trick and Mordecai returned and her grandfather made coffee. It was so weird to see him bustling in the kitchen; Katelyn caught Trick staring at her and he chuckled.

"I know, right?" he said.

Katelyn started laughing, and laughed until she cried. Later she would probably do some real crying, too, mourn for those who had been lost.

Justin.

Not now, she told herself. *Not now*. She didn't have the capacity to deal with that now. But she would.

Cordelia laughed, too. It was the most relaxed Katelyn had ever seen her. Out from under both her father and Dom, Cordelia looked free for the first time.

When they finally stopped laughing, Cordelia reached over and hugged Katelyn.

"I can't believe it's all over," she said.

"I know," Katelyn said, although in reality, things were just beginning. But Cordelia was right about the nightmare being done.

"And I still can't quite believe everything that's happened," Cordelia added.

"Join the club," Trick drawled.

Cordelia gave him an eye sweep. "And you, Hellhound Junior."

"And you, Werewolf Princess."

"No wonder we couldn't stand each other," Cordelia said. Before Trick could answer, she said, "That seems so long ago." Then she sighed and smiled at the two of them. "It's right, you two becoming mates."

Katelyn fell silent as her grandfather brought over steaming mugs of coffee. He said, "I'm not pleased with the lingo. 'Mates'. But is it what my Katie wants?"

For a fleeing moment she thought of the look on Kimi's face when she got an invitation to their wedding. That was all too soon. She was seventeen years old. And they had yet to make sure that things would work out.

And there were other questions to be answered first.

"If Justin was a regular werewolf, and he was the one who bit me, how come I'm immune to silver?"

"You were attacked," Trick said slowly, as if going over that horrible night. "And you told us it was a dog that bit you."

"I did," she agreed. "And then the stitches came out by themselves—"

Cordelia nodded. "So, antibiotics? The rabies shots? You have to be bit in, then get some kind of medical treatment?"

"I have a theory," her grandfather said.

He and Trick traded significant looks. Trick put his hands around his coffee cup and studied the steam while his grandfather set down his own mug and leaned forward slightly. He looked left and right as if ensuring they were the only ones in the room.

"New hellhounds aren't made like werewolves," he began. "It's not a bite." He hesitated. "It's nothing physical."

"So, it's by magic then?" Cordelia asked excitedly. "Like the Hounds of God say they're created?"

"We have our own secrets," Mordecai said.

"In other words, we can't say," Trick finished for him.

Katelyn's grandfather cocked his head at her. "You might not remember, but when you were real little I was out visiting and you took a tumble on your roller skates. You had a head wound and you were bleeding so much you needed a small transfusion. I was so scared for you I volunteered because we were the same blood type. Since being a Hellhound isn't transmitted through blood or saliva I didn't think much of it. But I guess you must have gotten something from me, namely the silver immunity."

Like Trick, she watched the ripples in her cup as she swirled the hot beverage. "That sounds logical. I know my father wasn't immune."

There. She'd said it.

Her grandfather looked stricken and the pain on his face was so great that she couldn't stand it. She set down her coffee and covered one of his gnarled old hands with both of hers.

"I understand and I forgive you," she whispered.

He put down his own cup and wrapped his arms around her, squeezing so tightly she was afraid her ribs would crack. She didn't complain, though. Her bones would heal by themselves but the relationship with her grandfather wouldn't.

When he finally let her go, he stood up. "I'll do one last patrol before bed," he said gruffly.

As soon as he was out the door, Cordelia stood as well. "I should return to the Gaudins, to reinforce the fact that we are of one pack. Then in a couple of days, I'll go home."

Katelyn caught the confused look on Cordelia's face. Father and sisters dead, cousin dead. Where was home?

"To Jesse," Katelyn said softly, and Cordelia nodded as if to herself.

Katelyn walked Cordelia to the door. Cordelia lingered there in the early light.

"I would never have wished this on you, Katelyn, but you'll never know how grateful I am that he bit you."

Katelyn nodded, not trusting herself to speak, and gave her a final hug before Cordelia slipped outside. Katelyn closed the door and turned around.

Trick was standing right there, eyes practically glowing.

"Um, so hi," Katelyn said, suddenly very shy.

"You never answered your grandfather's question," he said.

She reached up and grabbed his face, pulling it down to hers. As his lips met hers, she knew that there were no more secrets keeping them apart. Nothing was keeping them apart. Nothing ever could anymore.

She thought about the family she'd been born into, the family she'd been bit into, and the family she might have one day with Trick. It was all so crazy, but one thing had become crystal clear to her:

It was all about the family you choose.

Silver wolf queen, he said in her head.

To her heart.

And to her very existence.

You are mine.

"I have marked you, Hellhound," she replied, gazing lovingly into his eyes. Claiming him. "Run with me."

THE END

ACKNOWLEDGEMENTS

Thank you so much to Becky Stradwick, the most amazing and gracious editor ever, and our entire team at Random House UK: Sue Cook, Sophie Nelson and Kirsten Armstrong from editorial (proofreaders, copyeditors par excellence) and our designer, the lovely Dominica Clements. Many thanks as well to the fantastic Ruth Tinham in sales. Thank you to our wonderful agents, Howard Morhaim and Caspian Dennis, and to Team Morhaim: Kate McKean and Beth Phelan. Thanks as always to Belle and the fam.

Nancy

Thank you to our fantastic editor, Becky Stradwick. You are a dream to work with! Thank you also to our brilliant agent, Howard Morhaim. I also want to thank Natalie Cleary, Stacey Bennett, Vivian Mah, Kris McCormick, Marissa Cahill, Kylie Marie Bates and Lisa Graziano for their endless support and encouragement. You are all true Superfans.

Debbie

CPSIA information can be obtained at www.ICGtesting.com
Printed in the USA
LVOW04s2242290715

448121LV00010B/206/P